"I hope your ⟨…⟩ **⟨…⟩rily."**

Even as he sai⟨…⟩ ⟨…⟩anessa would confide in ⟨…⟩

"I am working on it," she replied, ambiguously. "But I do thank you for asking."

He was disappointed, even though he did not expect her to pour out her troubles to him. "If there is anything I can do to help, I hope you know I will be happy to assist in any way I can."

"You are too kind, but I'm afraid nothing more can be done." She rose and moved to the window, staring down at the small back garden and mews behind.

He joined her, startling her as his shoulder brushed hers.

"Perhaps your tread is not as heavy as I thought."

"Are you saying I could be a successful thief, after all?"

"I would need more than this one instance to determine your ability for the life of a successful burglar."

He was encouraged that she was not so down-pinned that she could not respond to his bantering. He turned to her and she looked up, meeting his gaze. Her eyes were golden in the light coming through the window and he was mesmerized by them. All thought of what might be disappeared from his mind and he found himself nearly whispering to her.

"I feel that something is gravely wrong and I don't want you to suffer." He leaned toward her and she closed her eyes. He pressed his lips against her temple. "Tell me what is bothering you," he murmured, nuzzling the wisps of hair that curled around her face. He traced a line with his lips to the delicate shell of her ear, where he allowed himself a small taste of her. He knew then he must kiss her. . . .

A SPIRITED ROMANCE

Alana Clayton

ZEBRA BOOKS
Kensington Publishing Corp.
http://www.kensingtonbooks.com

ZEBRA BOOKS are published by

Kensington Publishing Corp.
850 Third Avenue
New York, NY 10022

All Kensington titles, imprints, and distributed lines are available at special quantity discounts for bulk purchases for sales promotion, premiums, fund-raising, educational or institutional use.

Special book excerpts or customized printings can also be created to fit specific needs. For details, write or phone the office of the Kensington Special Sales Manager: Kensington Publishing Corp., 850 Third Avenue, New York, NY 10022. Attn. Special Sales Department. Phone: 1-800-221-2647.

Zebra and the Z logo Reg. U.S. Pat. & TM Off.

First Printing: July 2002
10 9 8 7 6 5 4 3 2 1

Printed in the United States of America

*For my good friend
Lynne Forney,
with great appreciation for
her discerning eye.*

One

"Are they here?" whispered Lady Atterly, peering about the room before returning her gaze to the young woman sitting across from her.

Holding back a sigh of exasperation, Vanessa Grayson opened her eyes and forced a smile to her lips. "Not yet, my lady."

"But surely they should be here," insisted the duchess. "After all, you claim you have spoken to them on several occasions."

"And I have, but spirits are not always predictable, my lady. They do not appear upon demand," explained Vanessa. "Remember, they are not entirely of this world, therefore, our rules do not apply to them."

"Well, it is quite rude of them to keep us waiting." Lady Atterly sniffed, touching the tip of her aristocratic nose with her embroidered handkerchief. "I also find it extremely embarrassing. I promised my guests they would meet my ghosts this evening."

"I warned you before you sent out your invitations that the spirits in your house might not choose to appear. Sometimes the very presence of a number of people gathered together will keep them away."

Lady Atterly thought herself imposing in a black bombazine gown and black lace cap, which were worn for a husband who had passed away some dozen years before.

She drew herself up and straightened her shoulders. "Tell them to show themselves at once," she ordered. "Or I shall make it extremely uncomfortable for them in the future."

Vanessa held back a smile, wondering how her ladyship could discomfort a pair of spirits who had been dead for well over a hundred years.

"They do not respond well to threats, my lady, but if you will give me a few more moments I will attempt to contact them again."

"Then do it quickly, girl, or I shall be the laughingstock of the *ton* by morning! The *on-dit* will be that I have gone dotty in my old age."

"I will do my best," murmured Vanessa, once again closing her eyes and forcing herself to concentrate despite the rising noise of voices in the room.

At first, Vanessa was distracted and merely allowed her thoughts to flow without direction. She did not enjoy putting either herself or her conversations with the spirits on public display; however, she had learned that it was necessary if she wished to make a living. People paid her a great deal to search their homes for spirits that lingered there and it would not do to refuse to attempt to call them forth at their request. There were times when the spirits turned stubborn and no matter what she did they remained silent. It was those times she felt particularly pleased that she insisted on receiving her payment in advance.

Vanessa frowned, thinking it might prove to Lady Atterly that she was doing her best. She was grateful that pursuing family ghosts had become the latest thing with the *ton*, for she was the sole support for herself and her sister Melanie. While she had to be away from home a great deal of the time, she was able to earn enough to keep them in comfort and remain in the house in which they had grown up.

Suddenly, she heard a sigh which was not Lady Atterly's and a voice murmured softly in her ear. *Was there nothing you could do about this?* it asked.

Vanessa kept her eyes closed. It wasn't necessary that she do so but she found it impressed people far more than sitting wide-eyed while speaking to someone no one else could see.

"Nothing whatsoever," she replied.

"Oh, my dear!" gasped Lady Atterly. "Do you hear them? Are they here?" Her black-gloved hands were pressed tightly to her chest and she had paled significantly.

The room became deathly quiet when Vanessa replied, "They are here."

There was a rustle among the observers as they shifted uneasily and stared about the room, attempting to see something.

"What are they saying?" whispered Lady Atterly.

"You need not speak so softly," said Vanessa. "They will not be frightened away unless they wish to go."

Lady Cornelia Burnett held her fan before her lips and spoke to Ellery Lawford, the Earl of Trent, in an undertone. "Isn't this exciting?" she murmured.

"If you enjoy this sort of thing," replied Lord Trent in a bored tone.

"You mean you don't believe there are actually spirits in this room?" she asked, moving closer to Ellery and taking his arm.

"Not unless I can see them or talk to them myself," he said. "Miss Grayson is clever; I will give her that. She has the entire Town convinced of her ability and I assume she is making a tidy sum from it."

Ellery was not so high in the instep as to look down on anyone who worked to make a living; however, he did not believe in hoodwinking people in order to do so. As he watched Miss Grayson close her eyes and tilt her head as if listening to someone speak, he could not think highly of her choice of professions. Surely being a governess or a companion was better than hoaxing people into thinking that she could commune with some long-dead soul.

"Well, I believe it," contended Lady Cornelia.

Ellery glanced sideways at her and smiled. "I somehow thought that you would."

Cornelia looked around to see if anyone was listening in on their conversation, but all eyes were riveted on Miss Grayson.

"And just what does that mean?" she demanded in an undertone.

Ellery realized he must make amends. "Just that you are extremely sensitive to this sort of thing."

Lady Cornelia seemed appeased by his answer. "I'm glad that you recognize the delicacy of my perceptiveness and it is that very thing that tells me Miss Grayson is all she claims to be."

"I bow to your judgment, my lady. I cannot argue with you and the other ladies of London as to Miss Grayson's credibility."

But Lady Cornelia's attention had strayed from him. "Look. She is speaking again."

Ellery obediently turned toward the center of the room to watch Miss Grayson's performance.

Well, go ahead, if we must take part in this, said the voice in Vanessa's ear. *I think you are a fine young lady which is far more than I can say for some gathered in this room.*

That's true, agreed a second masculine voice. *We realize you do this only to keep a roof over your sister's head and we do admire you for that.*

"Thank you," said Vanessa.

"What is it?" asked Lady Atterly, leaning forward until she nearly slipped from her chair.

"There are two spirits in the room," replied Vanessa.

A buzz of conversation followed her announcement, with everyone drawing closer together and again looking nervously around the room as if they could see the two spirits Vanessa mentioned.

"They are Lord and Lady Granville. I believe the history of the house will show that they lived here in the early 1700s."

"Oh, my!" said Lady Atterly, sinking back into her chair and rapidly fanning herself with a silk-painted, ivory-ribbed fan.

"There is no need to be alarmed," Vanessa reassured her. "They are extremely amiable and well disposed to sharing the house with you. They say you were very kind to them when you first discovered they were here. You did not shriek or throw things or run from the house."

"No, I did not," confirmed Lady Atterly, encouraged by Vanessa's comments. "In fact, I was afraid I would disturb them and tiptoed about for days before contacting you."

"They say you must not feel ill at ease merely because they are here. You are, after all, the current resident and they are quite happy that it is you, rather than a skeptic, who lives here."

"Will they speak to me?" asked Lady Atterly.

"It is not that they do not speak to you, my lady, but you cannot hear them. It is nothing out of the ordinary," she went on. "There are few who can speak with the spirits."

"But how will I know what they want?"

"Their wants are few," said Vanessa. "If they desire to contact you they will do it in other ways. Perhaps they will move something or leave a message for you. If all else fails you can summon me and I will be your intermediary."

"And collect another fee for doing so, I'll wager," muttered Ellery.

"Shush," said Cornelia, tapping his arm.

A cynical smile twisted his lips, but he kept further criticism to himself.

"Can you tell me where they are?" asked Lady Atterly.

"Lady Granville is sitting here next to me," replied Vanessa, indicating the empty space beside her on the settee. "And Lord Granville is standing behind her."

"Oh, my," said Lady Atterly, peering intently at the two places Vanessa had pointed out.

"Lady Granville has just remarked that you are a very attractive lady. She says that time enough has passed since the loss of your husband and you should do away with your black mourning clothes and wear some other color even if it is only lavender or gray."

"Oh, I could not," replied Lady Atterly, a bit shocked at the suggestion.

"Lady Granville was a leader of fashion in her day," revealed Vanessa, "and would not advise you to your detriment. You have shown respect to your husband for the past twelve years. It is time for you to continue with a full life. She has seen the gowns you stored away when Lord Atterly died and knows that you had a great fondness for color and fashion. She begs you to enjoy that fondness again."

"Well, I suppose I could wear something other than black since it has been so long. I will consider it, but please thank Lady Granville for her interest."

"Rubbish!"

Vanessa heard the remark as clearly as everyone else in the room. It had fallen into one of those lulls that occasionally occurs in conversations. She turned her head slightly toward the side of the room from which the remark came and saw a blond-haired woman use her fan to place a disapproving rap on the arm of a tall gentleman by her side. He appeared annoyed, but not particularly embarrassed about being overheard.

Vanessa had been faced with scores of people who doubted what she did and they no longer made her uncomfortable. She chose not to waste a frown on the man, but turned back to Lady Atterly, who seemed extremely discomfited that Vanessa was being belittled. The remainder of the people in the room looked on eagerly, hoping to view the latest scandal to be passed about and embroidered upon in the telling.

"I'm so sorry, my dear," murmured Lady Atterly.

"You have no reason for apology, my lady. It was not your rude remark that was heard."

A small collective murmur arose from the onlookers. Set-downs were not unheard of in the *ton*, but no one of Vanessa Grayson's standing had dared to direct such a remark toward Lord Trent. The ladies could not wait until the sun rose the next morning and they could begin their rounds repeating what had happened here this evening. Those gentlemen who were envious of Lord Trent held back their smiles and silently thought that he was finally getting a little of what he deserved.

"Both Lord and Lady Granville would like to congratulate you on the fine needlework you are doing."

"But that is in my private sitting room. How could you know?"

"I did not, but Lord and Lady Granville spend time watching you embroider," said Vanessa, hoping this revelation would end any skepticism that the earlier remark had created.

"You could have seen the embroidery before we arrived," said one gentleman, evidently emboldened by Lord Trent's comment.

"She has never been in my suite of rooms," protested Lady Atterly.

Vanessa sighed and realized she must do something to draw the people back into believing or both she and Lady Atterly would indeed be laughingstocks the next

morning. She had become fond of the woman and felt
a responsibility not to allow that to happen.

"It is Lord Granville, my lady. He wishes me to tell
you how much he admires the locket you wear around
your neck. The design of a heart with interlocking hands
is unique he believes. He is guessing it was a gift from
your late husband since you never take it off. But you
should wear it outside your gown sometimes so that others may enjoy it. He wishes he had given something of
its kind to his own wife.

"Lady Granville has commented that he gave her
many glorious gifts and she could want nothing more
than to be with him. They are a very loving couple,"
added Vanessa.

"I'm certain they are," said Lady Atterly. "And Lord
Granville is correct. My husband had the locket especially created and presented it to me when we married."
She reached up and pulled a locket from its hiding place
beneath the severe black gown she wore. "I am never
without it."

Another murmur swept around the room; however,
this was one of approval. At last, Vanessa allowed herself
to relax. She had won them over, she thought with a
sense of triumph. That is, with the exception of the dark-
haired gentleman who had declared her work to be rubbish. She glanced again in his direction, but while the
blond woman was still there talking to another man, he
was gone.

Later, when people were moving around the room,
conversing and partaking of the abundant refreshments
Lady Atterly had provided, Vanessa stood and moved to
the window alcove: a small, quiet oasis in the midst of
the room. However, her serenity was soon to be broken
by the very man she had no desire to see. She watched
him approach in the reflection of the window and
turned as he reached her.

"Miss Grayson, I am Lord Trent and I have come to apologize."

"There is no need," said Vanessa. "I have heard far worse."

"Still, there was no reason for me to make such a remark for everyone to hear. I have made my apologies to Lady Atterly and, in order to clear my conscience, am here to beg your forgiveness."

"If it is important, then you have it," she replied with little grace.

"I shall sleep better this evening," he said and seemed to mean it.

"If you will excuse me, my lord, I find I am fatigued."

"Of course. I assume it's tiring to call forth spirits."

"Are you ridiculing me again, Lord Trent?" asked Vanessa, impatient with the disbelief she faced on nearly every occasion that she revealed her ability in public.

"It can't be new for you to meet nonbelievers, Miss Grayson. While I don't want to insult you, you cannot think that everyone you meet will embrace what you do without question."

Vanessa studied him for a moment. He was a tall, well-built gentleman, who evidently had an excellent valet, for he was immaculate in dress. His blue coat bore not one speck of lint and his cravat was intricately tied with a blue sapphire in the center of the pristine white linen. He was not handsome in the classical Greek sense of the word, but his face had an arresting quality which no doubt left ladies dreaming of him long after he was gone.

At the moment, the expression on his face was puzzlement and Vanessa realized she had gone too long without speaking.

"I expect people to believe what they choose," she replied evenly. "No one who has used my services has had reason to complain."

"All believers, I suppose," he said.

"Why would anyone who does not believe engage me?" she asked.

"Then perhaps I should attend more of your . . . er . . . gatherings," he suggested. "With time, you might win me over."

"The gatherings are not mine, my lord. If it were up to me, I would use my talent with no other audience save the person who hired me. Unfortunately, many of my clients do not share that outlook and I end up here," she said, indicating the room with a wave of her hand. "As for winning you over, I feel each of us has more important things to do."

"You speak bluntly, Miss Grayson. If I did not have such thick skin, I believe I would be offended."

"You should not be offended, my lord. It meant nothing more than your remark earlier this evening," she replied. "Now, if you will excuse me, it is time I left and allowed Lady Atterly's guests to discuss me without restraint."

Ellery could not but admire her sharp tongue even though he had been on the wrong end of it. Single women who were not of the upper ten thousand did not fare well in society. Their choice of employment was limited to positions of low pay and little respect. Miss Grayson had found a niche into which she fit and evidently did not intend for anyone to threaten her into leaving it.

"I hope to see you again, Miss Grayson," was all he said in return.

"If you travel in these circles, you certainly will. I have agreed to search for spirits in the homes of many who are in attendance tonight. I suppose you have noticed that what one does, the other must do better."

Lord Trent laughed out loud. "I certainly have. I have lived with it my entire life and it never ceases to amuse me."

"And I hope it never does or I might be forced into a far less desirable way to earn my living."

With that she slipped out of the room, leaving him looking after her with a smile lingering on his face.

"Did you make amends with Lady Atterly?" asked Lady Cornelia once he had made his way back to her side.

"Of course. I merely explained that you had whispered an outrageous story in my ear about her and I couldn't help myself but react," he explained gravely.

"You . . . you didn't!" replied Lady Cornelia, gasping in disbelief.

A devilish smile curved Ellery's lips. "I did not," he assured her.

"Oh," she said in a huff, not at all amused by his teasing. "It would serve you well if I found another way home this evening." She turned a shoulder to him, waiting for him to beg her to stay.

"Should I wait to make certain you will be safe?" he asked, the remains of the smile still lingering on his face.

Cornelia should have known that her ruse would not work. She had heard that Ellery had never had to beg for a lady's company in his life and she couldn't expect him to begin now. Many of his friends were surprised that he had committed as much time to her as he had since previously he had made certain not to favor one lady over another. Rumor was that Lord Trent had finally been snared and she would do nothing to jeopardize her standing until it was too late for him to escape.

She turned and gave him a smile that would have stopped most men in their tracks. "It would not be courteous of me to desert you so abruptly," she said, moving closer.

"It would not," he agreed, allowing her to withdraw

her threat without embarrassment. "Only think how empty my coach would be without you."

Cornelia preened at his flattery. She must be more careful in the future if she wished to keep his interest. "You should invite Miss Grayson to search your houses for spirits," she suggested, turning the attention from her untimely threat to leave without him.

This time he laughed out loud. "I cannot picture myself and Miss Grayson gathered cozily around the tea table speaking to ghosts."

"But everyone is doing it," said Lady Cornelia.

"Exactly," responded Ellery.

"Aren't you at all curious?" she asked.

"If I haven't been bothered by spirits by now, then I never shall," he said.

"They could be there, merely not allowing you to see them," argued Cornelia.

"If they do not want me to see them, then why should I intrude?" contended Ellery. "You should be complimenting me on giving them their privacy."

"You are teasing me again," charged Cornelia, pouting a bit.

"Not at all," he insisted. "I am absolutely serious about not engaging Miss Grayson to talk to my ghosts. If I have any, they have been remarkably happy and silent. I see no reason to disturb them at this time. Think what would happen if I found I was giving shelter to a quarrelsome couple, or a woman who complained incessantly. Why, my peaceful life would be turned on end and I would be driven from my home by insubstantial wraiths."

"I do not care how much nonsense you speak. I am convinced you should have Miss Grayson visit your homes. I would never seriously consider a gentleman unless he did so."

Ellery did not answer Cornelia. He had not yet offered

for her, although he had to admit that the thought had crossed his mind more than once. And even though she might become the mistress of his homes, he would not allow her to persuade him to engage Miss Grayson. In fact, he vowed to stay away from the spirit lady, for her sharp tongue amused him a little too much for his comfort.

The next morning, Vanessa waited in the hall of Lady Atterly's home for the coach to arrive at the front door.

"I suppose there is nothing I can say to encourage you to stay a few days more," said Lady Atterly.

"Thank you, but I'm anxious to get home and see my sister," explained Vanessa, her face lighting up.

"I can see you have missed her."

"She is my only family and we are very close. I've been away longer than usual this time and I have only a few days until my next engagement."

"Then I will wish you a pleasant journey," said Lady Atterly. "If you should ever have time for a visit, I would welcome your company. Here is a little something I want you to have." She handed Vanessa a velvet box.

Vanessa could tell by the richness of the box that whatever was in it was something she could never afford on her own. She began to raise the lid.

"No, don't open it until you are well on your way," instructed Lady Atterly. "I don't want you attempting to return it. I have no children of my own and you have become very dear to me during your stay. If you cannot accept it as a gift, then consider it a bonus for a job well done."

"But . . ." began Vanessa.

"The coach is here," said Lady Atterly, giving her hand a squeeze. "I'm certain I shall see you again during the remainder of the Season."

"I will make certain you do," said Vanessa, her eyes suddenly blurring with tears. Lady Atterly reminded her of all that she had missed since her mother had died. Vanessa rarely allowed her emotions to break through the wall she had built to hide her weakness. However, her confrontation with Lord Trent the evening before had left her feeling far more vulnerable than usual.

She held the box in her hands as the coach made its way through the crowded streets and thought about what had brought her to this point.

Vanessa Grayson had been six years and twenty-eight days old when she first spoke with a spirit. The events leading up to it began when her father came to the nursery, which was unusual enough in itself; he seldom climbed the stairs to see his children, instead waiting for them to be brought to him.

He sat and lifted Vanessa onto his knee. She could see that his eyes and nose were red and that he held a large crumpled handkerchief in one hand. He spoke in a halting voice, interrupted by several unsuccessful efforts to hold back tears, endeavoring to explain that her mother had gone to a place called heaven. He held her too tightly, all the while repeating that although Vanessa's mother would not be with her any longer, she would be watching over her every moment of the day.

For three days after Vanessa had accompanied her father to the cemetery, where she watched a box being lowered into the ground, she continued to miss her mother and struggled to make some sense of her father's words. Vanessa knew her mother would not leave her alone, yet her questions as to when her mother would return brought only more bouts of tears from the people around her.

One evening the longing to see her mother was too intense for Vanessa to remain still. She threw back the covers, climbed out of bed, and took her place on the floor, where she usually sat when her mother told her stories.

She closed her eyes and thought of her mother in the chair before her, holding her little sister, Melanie, and rocking back and forth while she wove tales of fairy princesses. Vanessa heard a creak, and then another. She opened her eyes and discovered the chair rocking back and forth just as it always had when her mother had occupied it.

Vanessa sat a long time watching the chair and listening to her mother's voice. The fear that had filled her during the past days slipped away and she felt safe again. She understood what her mother told her far better than her father's muddled explanation. And while she was not wholly satisfied with the idea of her mother not physically being in her life, she was cheered by the knowledge that she had not deserted her completely.

"What are you doing, child?"

Vanessa glanced around to see Annie, a young maid, standing in the door.

"I'm talking to Mama," she answered, turning to look at the chair again.

Annie's gaze followed hers and her eyes widened when she observed the chair rocking back and forth. "You mustn't say such things," she scolded, her voice quivering. "It would upset your father if he heard you utter such nonsense. It's just a breeze that set that chair to rockin'." She glanced at the window, which was tightly closed, and took a step backward.

Vanessa tilted her head sideways and listened for a moment. "I'm sorry, Annie. I won't say it again," she promised.

Annie hesitated, then crossed the floor and took her by the hand. She led Vanessa back to the bed, lifting her into it and tucking her in. "That's a good girl," she said, her hand smoothing the child's hair. "Now close your eyes; you should be fast asleep by now." Annie hurried from the room as if she couldn't get away fast enough.

In the dim light of the candle that had been left burning, Vanessa smiled and wiggled her fingers good-bye as the chair ceased its rocking.

Vanessa came back to the present, still stroking the soft velvet, which was comforting to her. London was already disappearing behind her when she decided to open the box. She gave a small gasp when she glimpsed the contents. Inside were a topaz necklace and matching earrings. While they were modest compared to the *ton's* standards, they were nevertheless of excellent quality.

Vanessa ran a fingertip over the glittering stones and tears once again came to her eyes as she thought of the woman who had given them to her. Perhaps some might say she should return them; that she was taking advantage of Lady Atterly. However, from their brief acquaintance Vanessa knew that to do so would hurt the woman who had given them in friendship. She would keep them and hope that Lady Atterly would see her when she wore them. It would be a testimony to the bond that had grown between them. She would write a note as soon as she reached home.

Home. It had been a fortnight since she had seen her sister Melanie and Annie. She disliked being separated from them for so long. However, the Season was her busiest time of the year and she took the opportunity to earn as much as she could while it was possible. The fickleness of the *ton* changed from one day to the next and if she fell out of favor, her ability to earn a living would drop dramatically.

But she had an entire week at her disposal to visit her home and she meant to enjoy every minute of it. Still clasping the velvet box, she watched the countryside pass as the coach continued its way toward home.

Two

Vanessa caught a glimpse of herself in the mirror as she paced across her room in Lord and Lady Pomeroy's home. As befitting her status, while her suite was not the best in the house, it was very fine indeed. The walls were covered in watered silk and the furniture was of an elegant French design, delicately made and brushed with gilt which glimmered when the candlelight touched it. The carpet was deep and covered the entire floor except for a narrow space around the edge which revealed a highly waxed oak surface.

Vanessa paused in front of the tall cheval mirror and studied her reflection in the glass. Her brown hair was pulled back loosely and formed a mass of smooth curls at the back of her head. The golden highlights were not apparent in the dim light of her room, but would come to life beneath the chandeliers that were sure to be in use that evening. Her face was a pale oval in the mirror, with delicate brows arching over hazel eyes which appeared more golden than green, and lips that were surprisingly full with no need of artificial color. The blue gown she wore was respectable, but plain, and she knew it would pale into complete insignificance beside the gowns worn at this evening's soiree.

She would rather stay in her rooms and enjoy a quiet evening reading Miss Austen's latest novel or work on her embroidery, but it was not to be. Lady Pomeroy had particularly requested that she attend the soiree this evening. Vanessa knew it was not kindness that prompted Lady Pomeroy's request, but a desire to show those present that she now had the Spirit Lady in her home, which would increase her consequence a step above the rest for the moment.

Vanessa looked at herself once again and shrugged. She could not afford to squander her money on evening gowns. If Lady Pomeroy insisted she go about with her, she must accept her as she was. Vanessa collected her paisley shawl and reticule and prepared herself for a prolonged evening of forced smiles and endless questions.

"Look who is here," said Viscount Huntly to Lord Trent.

"Where?" inquired Ellery, glancing about the room.

"Over by the door. Lord and Lady Pomeroy have just arrived and I believe that is Miss Grayson accompanying them."

"It is," agreed Ellery, "but I see no reason why their arrival should mean more than any other to me."

"Come, now, Ellery. Admit that you were intrigued the last time you met the Spirit Lady."

"I will do no such thing," snapped Ellery. "She is merely a woman who has everyone convinced she can do the impossible. I predict she will be all but forgotten before the Season is over."

"Don't be too confident," replied Max. "Some who know her seem sincerely fond of her."

"That will also fade," judged Ellery. "I have no interest in either Miss Grayson or the spirits that presumedly gather round her wherever she goes."

"Perhaps you should reconsider that," suggested Max.

"The reason being?"

"Look who's approaching her," observed Max, directing Ellery's attention across the room once again.

"Rudolph Montgomery, Lord Corbin," murmured Ellery. "I wonder what he wants."

The soiree was as much of a crush as Vanessa feared it would be. There were many people there with whom she was acquainted, but none she could call a true friend until she finally spied a familiar face in the crowd.

Vanessa had known Rudolph Montgomery, Lord Corbin, for many years. They had grown up in the same part of the country and while they had not seen one another as often as they grew older and he had taken his place as a peer of the realm, they remained friends.

In truth, it was Lord Corbin who had introduced her to the *ton* and convinced them to believe in her gift. Vanessa felt she owed her popularity and her ability to earn a substantial living to him.

"Lord Corbin, how good it is to see you," said Vanessa, flashing him a smile.

"Good Lord, Vanessa. Why do you insist upon such formality. When I pulled you out of the trout stream when you were ten, you certainly didn't call me Lord Corbin."

"That was a long time ago and you were not a lord at that time," she pointed out. "We are grown and in society. Imagine the scandal if I began addressing you as Rudy."

"I would prefer Rudolph at this point in my life."

"Even so." She sighed.

"The devil take scandal and all the old cats who spread it if that is what keeps you so straitlaced when we are together."

"You know it is different for women. You would be forgiven an impropriety, but I would be completely ruined at the slightest appearance of an indiscretion. I can't afford to lose my standing because then I could not use my talent to earn my way. I must think of Melanie and Annie. They depend upon me for their livelihood."

"I know. I know," grumbled Rudy. "But it does not seem at all fair."

"It isn't," acknowledged Vanessa, "however, it is the way things are and I don't expect them to change anytime soon. At least not until we are too old and gray to care what we call one another."

Rudy smiled at her weak jest. He realized her predicament better than anyone else. "All right, Miss Grayson, you have made your point. But promise me when we are private we will return to being Vanessa and Rudy."

"If we are completely correct, we should never be private," she replied with a devilish smile.

"You are mocking me now," he accused her. "Remember, I am a lord and am deserving of respect."

A giggle escaped from between Vanessa's lips, just as he had hoped. "I don't believe I can fully give you the respect you deserve since I remember seeing you thrown from your horse and coming up covered in mud." She giggled again and Rudy attempted to form a severe expression on his face. He failed and they both laughed out loud.

"It certainly appears they know one another well," remarked Ellery, watching the smiling couple across the room.

"Evidently they were acquainted before Miss Grayson's arrival in Town. I understand it was Corbin who encouraged Lady Mountjoy to engage Miss Grayson. Lady Mountjoy was thrilled to be the first to meet the spirits in her home. After that, Miss Grayson has rarely needed Corbin's help, but nevertheless he continues to introduce her to the right people and to recommend them to employ her."

"Are you still of the opinion that Corbin is involved with this resurgence of the Hell-Fire Club?"

Max took a moment before answering. "I have learned nothing to dissuade me of the idea," he said. "He is often in the company of the ones we believe are members and seems to be on good terms with them."

Ellery's gaze had not left the couple who were still engaged in conversation, unaware that their every movement and expression were being observed.

"Does it follow that Miss Grayson is also involved?" he asked.

The question brought Max's attention back to Ellery. "I have no reason to believe so," he remarked. "I have seen her with none of the others except for Corbin and she does not appear to be Hell-Fire Club material."

"Sometimes it can be extraordinarily simple for a woman to convince a man that she is an innocent, particularly when she is skilled in the art of deception. After all, we are taught to believe it from the cradle on."

"I don't believe she has duped me," said Max. "I'm fully aware that women were involved in the old Hell-Fire Clubs, but Miss Grayson does not at all seem to be one of their ilk."

"Before this is all over, we shall know exactly where Miss Grayson stands. In the meantime, I intend to keep a close eye on her."

"You've heard nothing from Phillip?" asked Max.

"Not a word," confirmed Ellery.

Phillip was Ellery's younger brother, who was at the age where he felt the need to be involved in something of importance and intrigue. Unfortunately, he had chosen to attempt to unveil the people involved in the revival of the Hell-Fire Club.

Ellery couldn't lay the fault completely at Phillip's feet.

A group—secretly backed by the Home Office—had enticed him to join them in wiping out the club's members. In the past, the club was not only known for its lewd ceremonies, but also for its attempts to influence politics by insinuating itself with the King.

Even today, certain government figures feared the club would direct its attention to drawing the Prince Regent into their web. They had formed a group which swore to do everything possible to disband the Hell-Fire Club and destroy its ability to control the Prince Regent once he became King.

Ellery assumed the scheme appealed to Phillip's sense of the dramatic because he had had an air of secrecy about him for weeks. He would not divulge the reason to Ellery, only intimating that it was of the highest confidentiality and that the fate of England could depend upon his actions.

Ellery paid him little heed until Max revealed what he knew of the group, which had dreams of working its way into the good graces of the Prince Regent and gaining enough influence to use him politically once he ascended to the throne.

What had previously seemed to be mere acting on the part of a group of highly excitable young men now held sinister implications for everyone involved. Ellery had attempted to talk with Phillip about his activities, but his brother kept his tongue between his teeth and would not reveal any part of the plans that were in place.

Phillip would disappear for days at a time and Ellery had no idea where he was or what he was doing. It troubled him, for he had promised his father he would look after his younger brother and he felt he was not living up to his word. He also worried that Phillip had finally gotten himself into a situation that was potentially dangerous and could threaten his life.

Ellery decided to do some investigating on his own.

He had a friend at the Home Office who was able to pass along the identities of some of the people who were under suspicion of being affiliated with the Hell-Fire Club. He intended to keep a close watch on them and to discover whether Phillip was keeping company with them.

Rudolph Montgomery, Lord Corbin, was one of those names on his list and it did not bode well for Miss Grayson that they seemed to be on particularly good terms. Their friendship was forcing him to disregard his decision to ignore her in order to discover more about Corbin.

"Phillip will most likely show up tomorrow," said Max.

"And without a word of explanation," added Ellery. "He is so careful about what he says around me it is near impossible to discuss even the simplest of subjects."

"At all events, he will grow out of it," forecast Max.

"But will it be soon enough to keep him out of serious trouble?"questioned Ellery. "He is driven to follow in our father's and grandfather's footsteps. If you remember, both of them were involved in putting the Hell-Fire Club out of business in their day. Phillip considers it a family duty to save the monarchy from the club."

"Even though Phillip is young and untried, you must trust that he will use his good sense," said Max.

"Phillip has no experience in the world, particularly not with confronting men who are involved in this game. If he would only confide in me, perhaps I could help."

"I thought you wanted nothing to do with anything of this sort," said Max.

"That was before Phillip's involvement drew me into it. I cannot sit back and allow him to become embroiled in such a potentially dangerous conspiracy."

"Might be little you can do about it since you're not a part of Phillip's group," commented Max.

"I want no part of those fools," snapped Ellery. "They

are mostly dilettantes and are completely unaware of the danger they're in. I'll take my chances alone. If I could only talk some sense into Phillip; but he's convinced that the fate of England rests in his hands and he will not be dissuaded from that belief. I can only ferret out whatever information I can and attempt to keep my eye on him."

"You know I'll do what I can to help," said Max.

"I know, my friend," replied Ellery, placing his hand on Max's shoulder, "I've always been able to rely on you. Perhaps you can help me observe Miss Grayson's activities."

"You still consider she's part of the conspiracy?"

"I don't know, but I am not going to ignore her in case she is."

"Just what do you expect to do?" asked Max.

"I suppose I must ingratiate myself with her," replied Ellery with a grimace.

"She's attractive enough that it shouldn't be such a chore," commented Max. "If you should need help, I'll be the first to volunteer."

"No need," Ellery said shortly. "I'll handle this myself and I believe I'll begin immediately." He turned and began making his way around the dance floor toward the spot where Miss Grayson and Lord Corbin were still involved in a spirited conversation.

"I hope I'm not interrupting," he said, once he had arrived at Vanessa's side. She gave a start at hearing his voice so close.

"Of course not, my lord."

If there had been a bell which rang whenever Miss Grayson did not tell the truth, it would be pealing wildly at this moment, Ellery observed silently. Her conversation with Lord Corbin had ceased immediately and he was studying Ellery with a sharp eye.

"Have you met Lord Corbin?" inquired Vanessa of Ellery.

"I know of him, but I have never had the pleasure."
He gave a small bow in the other man's direction. "Corbin."

Corbin returned the bow and spoke his name.

Ellery returned his attention to Vanessa. "Are you going to speak to the spirits tonight, Miss Grayson?"

"No, I have merely accompanied Lady Pomeroy at her request. I don't understand why she felt the need for my company, but she insisted I come along."

"You sound as if you do not enjoy these entertainments."

"I do not belong here, my lord, as you well know. I am not a member of the *ton* and have no close friends with whom I can converse."

"I object to that," said Corbin.

"Besides you," she replied, bestowing a warm smile upon him. "But I cannot always count on your presence."

"Then I hope you will consider me as a substitute when Lord Corbin is not around," said Ellery.

Vanessa stared at him as if he had spoken in an incomprehensible foreign language. The silence lengthened until Ellery felt the need to break it.

"I know, of course, that we are not well acquainted as yet, but I should like to know you better."

"For what earthly reason?" replied Vanessa so bluntly that it brought a smile to Corbin's face. "We have nothing in common."

"You are friends with Corbin," Ellery pointed out.

"We have known one another since we were children. If we had not, I can assure you that I would not be such friends with an earl."

"My dear Miss Grayson, you wound me," said Corbin, placing his hand over his heart. "I would offer my friendship if you were but a milkmaid."

Vanessa laughed out loud at his foolishness, tapping

his arm smartly with her fan. "You know that isn't true. In the normal course of events, you would not waste a glance on me," she teased.

Ellery felt like the outsider he was and did not enjoy the sensation. He silently swore to himself that she would soon be as much at ease with him as she was with Corbin.

"In any event, I hope you will not avoid me in the future," said Ellery.

"I have never avoided you, Lord Trent. I have just never known you before and would not be forward enough to speak before we were introduced. You may rest assured that if and when we meet in the future, I will give you my full attention. However, I doubt that it will occur that often."

"Do not be so sure, Miss Grayson. I find myself taking a keen interest in your ability to communicate with the spirits. I hope to attend any future demonstrations you may hold."

"I have told you that it is my clients who insist upon making a spectacle of the event," she replied sharply, a frown on her face.

"Even so, I find it a subject I would like to pursue. I have even been encouraged to arrange to have you visit my houses."

"There is no need," she replied promptly, "for surely spirits would not dare to linger there."

Corbin smiled and met her glance. Ellery felt the link between the two again.

Vanessa looked across the room. "I'm afraid I must go. I see Lady Pomeroy summoning me and she is not a patient woman."

"I don't like you being at everyone's beck and call," growled Corbin.

"That is part of what I do," she said gently. "It does not bother me; don't allow it to annoy you. I shall talk to you later." She glanced at Ellery and nodded before walking away.

"You know her well," stated Ellery.

"Well enough," replied Corbin, studying him. "I would not like anything unpleasant to happen to her."

Ellery understood his unspoken message.

Vanessa stood beside a massive display of flowers, hoping that she could gain some semblance of privacy for a few minutes. Over the past hour, she had been dragged from group to group by Lady Pomeroy, displayed like a rare prize and expected to smile and say all the right things. She had finally made her escape and wanted nothing more than a short time without the incessant questions which were aimed at her. It was not to be.

"My dear Miss Grayson, how fortunate it is that you chose this particular spot in which to make yourself scarce."

Vanessa looked to her left and saw a woman sitting in one of the chairs that had been placed along the wall. She was not young, but her face showed little sign of aging. Her dark hair had only a small silver streak near her right temple and was arranged in an intricate design, including two purple plumes which swayed gracefully with each dip of her head.

Her gown was a shade darker than the plumes in her hair and was of the latest style. A heavy amethyst necklace hung about her neck with matching earrings dangling from her lobes. Amethyst rings also adorned nearly every finger. Altogether, she was an imposing sight and Vanessa was left with nothing to say.

"Come, come, my girl. Don't attempt to convince me that you are too overwhelmed by my mere presence to speak." She smiled at her own jest, eyes sparkling as bright as her jewels.

"No, ma'am. I am wondering whether we have met. I do not think I would forget you, but I have been introduced to so many people over the past weeks that I fear I cannot recollect all of them."

The woman laughed out loud. "Not many people forget once they have met me and you are certainly not one of those few. I've seen you before but we have never spoken. This seemed like an opportune moment. I hope you don't mind."

"Of course, I don't," said Vanessa.

"Of course, you do," echoed the woman. "I have watched you this evening and know that you hoped to find a measure of peace by hiding yourself here." She held up her hand when Vanessa attempted to speak. "There's no need to deny it. You have my sympathy. I have been forced to do the same thing at times. By the way, I am Lady Venable. I hope that before long you will feel comfortable enough to call me Charity."

Uncertain as to how to respond, Vanessa said only, "Thank you, my lady."

"Don't tell me I've frightened you. Anyone who can summon spirits cannot be missish."

Vanessa fought down her irritation at Lady Venable. Thus far, she had spent a tiring evening and she did not need to be bullied by this overbearing woman. "You do not frighten me at all," she stated unequivocally, her chin tilted at a stubborn angle. "And I do not summon spirits."

"Then what do you do with them?"

"I like to think that I simply give them an outlet to speak; to connect with our world should they desire."

"And you make a great deal of money doing it, I am told."

"I charge for my services, ma'am. I did not inherit money, nor did I marry into it. I have responsibilities and this is the way I have chosen to support them."

"No need to get on your high ropes, my dear. I admire what you are doing. Far better than being a governess or a companion, I'd wager," said Lady Venable.

Vanessa relaxed a bit at Lady Venable's remarks. "Far better," she agreed.

"I have no desire to meet any spirits if they indeed inhabit my residence or I would certainly have you do the job," revealed Lady Venable. "And I hope you will not take offense at anything I say. I mean no harm. I merely have an insatiable curiosity about people. Some call it nosiness, others say I am a meddlesome old woman, yet all of them come to me first to learn the latest *on-dits.*" A contented smile spread across her face at the thought.

"And am I to be one of your bits of gossip?" asked Vanessa.

"No, indeed. You are one of the truly interesting people to arrive in Town this Season and I hope that we will come to know one another better."

"Thank you, my lady, but when I am in Town I have little time for socializing."

"Pshaw! I can't believe you don't have a single moment to call your own. Surely you could take tea with me one day."

"Thank you for the invitation, but I doubt that I will be able to do so. I am scheduled to go directly from one house to another for the rest of the Season and, as you mentioned, my clients pay a good sum to have me in their homes. I do not want it to appear that I am here to enjoy myself at their expense."

"How sad to live with strangers the majority of the time. Do you not have a family who misses you?"

Vanessa could not make herself object to Lady Venable's personal questions. From the lady's manner, she felt sure that the woman inquired into everyone's business without regard to standing.

In truth, she found herself nearly smiling. Lady Venable was more entertaining than the other people she had met this evening.

"I have a younger sister," Vanessa willingly divulged. "She is at home with our maid Annie, who has been with our family since before we were born. I return whenever I have a few days between engagements. It is difficult for me to leave them, but I must insure that we will be able to afford to live comfortably."

"Did your parents not leave you sufficient funds to live on?"

"We have our home with some property and a small trust to see us through. What I earn I put aside in case anything untoward should occur." Vanessa could not understand why she was speaking so freely with Lady Venable. She usually kept information concerning her family to herself. However, the woman seemed to command confidences without the least bit of effort.

"I admire you greatly, my dear," said Lady Venable. "And I am convinced that we will become great friends before the Season is over.

"Perhaps we will," replied Vanessa, surprised at her agreement. "But I have been hiding away too long. I am certain Lady Pomeroy is looking for me."

"There is no harm in Eleanor," said Lady Venable speaking of Lady Pomeroy. "She does not have a mean bone in her body, but she is tight with her money. Don't let her convince you to do more than you bargained to do. If you are not alert, she will have you helping out in the kitchen before you know it."

"I think she would find that I'm better at talking to her spirits," remarked Vanessa.

"Then she does have some?"

"I will only answer that question to Lady Pomeroy. Then, she may tell whomever she wishes," said Vanessa.

"Oh, you are too honorable," complained Lady

Venable. "I see that I will not get one word of gossip from you."

"Other than Lady Pomeroy's spirits, I fear I have not one anecdote of interest worth repeating."

"I'm certain you will improve as the Season goes along," observed Lady Venable. "And I will expect you to pass along every scandal broth which comes your way." Lady Venable's sharp brown eyes studied her another moment. "I've heard some call you the Spirit Lady."

Vanessa nodded. "Some do, but I do not encourage it."

"Well, I am known as the Listener. People talk to me about things they would not ordinarily mention to anyone. I am the recipient of so many confidences I am unable to count them."

"Then you will not miss my contribution."

Lady Venable ignored her remark. "People trust my discretion. That includes knowing when to pass on certain information and when to hold it back. That is why I know a great deal about what is going on in our society. If there is anything you wish to confide at any time, rest assured that I will keep it private."

"I have no idea what I would ever be privy to that would be important enough to divulge. I do not come from a titled family and am in Town to work. I cannot understand why you would be interested in anything I might know."

"I find you to be an interesting young lady. You have enlivened my evening."

"Then I am glad to have been some use to you, ma'am. Now I must return to Lady Pomeroy." Vanessa dropped a small curtsy and escaped from the flower arrangement. She saw Lady Pomeroy motioning for her to join her once again. As she made her way through the crush, Vanessa thought of the two people who had offered her friendship that evening—Lord Trent and Lady Venable. She was suspicious, for she could think of no reason that either of them should seek a closer relationship with her. Why were they attempting to curry her favor?

On the ride home, Lady Pomeroy spoke incessantly of whom she had seen that evening and what had been said, leaving Vanessa only the need to make a sound of agreement on occasion.

Vanessa considered her meetings with Lord Trent and Lady Venable again. She shook her head, still unable to discern what interest they had in her. Weary of attempting to understand the ways of the members of the *ton*, she turned her thoughts to her last trip home.

Her sister Melanie had seemed unusually languid during her visit. When Vanessa had asked if she was well, Melanie blamed her listlessness on the summer heat. Even Annie had seemed a bit fidgety, but she had also insisted that nothing was wrong.

Vanessa did not feel comfortable about leaving the two of them, but she was set to begin her next engagement and had been forced to depart the next morning. She worried about the two women and vowed to finish with Lady Pomeroy's household as quickly as possible so that she could return home for a longer length of time.

The coach pulled to a stop in front of Lady Pomeroy's town house, where they stepped down onto the cobblestones, ascended the shallow steps, and passed through the door into the hall. Lady Pomeroy's chatter did not cease until Vanessa closed her door behind her with a sigh of relief.

"You didn't tell me last night how you and Miss Grayson got along," said Maxwell to Ellery as they rode along a path in Hyde Park.

The day was bright and clear with few people yet in the park to ruin their ride. Ellery would have much rather discussed something more pleasant than the irritating Miss Grayson.

"From her actions, I don't believe Miss Grayson is at all impressed with me."

"Do you want her to be?" asked Max.

"Only so she will connect me to Corbin and possibly lead me to information about the Hell-Fire Club and Phillip's part in it, if he has one."

"Phillip's too smart to allow himself to be involved with the club."

"Not if he's attempting to destroy it. It would be just like him to attempt to infiltrate it and then expose the members to all of England."

"Have you heard from him yet?"

"Not for a month or more and I'm becoming extremely worried. It isn't like him to remain away from home for such a length of time without contacting me."

"And the fair Lady Cornelia? Is she still pursuing you?"

"I've avoided her for the past few days and will, no doubt, pay dearly for it."

Max smiled and nodded. "I saw her last night after you left. She asked all manner of questions about where you had been and what you had been doing. I told her I had no idea and escaped as quickly as possible. Do you still intend to offer for her?"

"I never said I was going to," said Ellery.

"You nearly did," argued Max.

"The longer I am around her, the more I am persuaded she might not be for me."

"Then you should let her know and not lead her on. She still has time to find someone suitable before the Season is over."

"I am not keeping her from anyone. She is free to

see whomever she wishes without any complaint from me," said Ellery.

"But she won't, unless she knows for certain that you are unavailable. It's no secret that there isn't a single woman in the *ton* who wouldn't like to catch you in the parson's mousetrap and Lady Cornelia is no exception. She has assumed that you intend to offer and you have said nothing to dissuade her. If you do not act soon, you will be forced into marriage whether or not that is your intent."

"I know. I know," grumbled Ellery. "It isn't fair. I haven't made up my mind yet."

"Should do it soon," advised Max.

"As soon as I find Phillip and he is off my mind. I will begin my search this morning. Will you come along?"

"Of course. I have nothing planned for today."

"How convenient," commented Ellery. "Isn't that Fitzhugh up ahead?"

"I believe so," replied Max.

"He is a friend of Phillip's and should know his whereabouts if anyone does."

The two men spurred their horses forward and took a place on either side of Lord Fitzhugh, peppering him with questions about Phillip.

Vanessa was on her way home again. The summer day was hot and from the look of the sky it would be another dry one. Clouds of dust billowed up from the coach wheels that carried her out of Town, causing Vanessa to dab at her face with a wrinkled handkerchief. She had discarded her bonnet and gloves as soon as they had reached the outskirts of London, but that had done little to reduce the heat. She wondered what the coachman would say if she climbed up to sit with him, where the air had to be clearer and cooler and the breeze stronger.

Vanessa sighed and waved her fan in front of her face.
The joy she usually felt when going home had been replaced by a sense of dread. She kept telling herself that
the feeling was merely brought about by too much time
spent in the city. As soon as she was at home with Melanie
and Annie, she would be her old self. She looked forward to the day when she would have enough money
invested so that she could discontinue hiring herself out
and return to living a normal life.

But it was Melanie who weighed heavily on her mind
at the moment. The last time she was at home her sister
did not act at all like herself. She stayed abed far later
and retired far earlier than usual. When she did arise,
she spent most of her day sitting in the house instead
of being out and about.When Vanessa asked if she was
feeling well Melanie had replied that it was simply too
hot to be running about like a child.

Questioning Annie yielded little more information.
The maid agreed that the heat had been stifling and
that everyone had been staying in out of the blistering
rays of the sun.

Their assurances did not completely satisfy Vanessa.
There was something they were not telling her and she
meant to find out what they were hiding before she left
for Town again.

Three

That evening Vanessa was wishing she was anywhere but home. She and Melanie were in the sitting room and Melanie had uttered three words that Vanessa never thought to hear.

"You are what?" she gasped out, unable to believe her own ears.

"I am increasing," Melanie calmly repeated.

"But how can that be?" she asked, grappling with disbelief.

"Do I need to explain it?" inquired Melanie with a smile.

"This is no time for joking," said Vanessa, breathing deeply and attempting to calm the pounding of her heart. Now she understood why Melanie had been so listless during her last visit. Then there were the gowns that were cut so full that Melanie explained were much cooler for the summer. How easily she had been fooled, thought Vanessa. How trusting she had been.

"I'm sorry, Vanessa. I just didn't know how to tell you. And don't be angry at Annie. I made her promise not to say anything."

"It wasn't her place to tell me; it was yours," she replied accusingly.

"I know, but I knew what your reaction would be and I didn't want to spoil my happiness."

"Happiness! Don't you realize that you are ruined beyond all redemption? What is the name of the blackguard who is responsible?"

A stubborn expression appeared on Melanie's face. "I will not tell you. You will only spoil everything."

Vanessa was speechless, wondering how she could convince her sister that her life was already destroyed. "Melanie, tell me who it is. If he is respectable, perhaps it isn't too late to save you from scandal. We could arrange a quiet wedding and the two of you could live elsewhere until the child is born. When enough time has passed you could come home explaining the baby had arrived early. There might be questions, but nothing could be proven."

"I will not sneak about like a thief," spat out Melanie. "My baby's father is from a respectable family and we have plans to wed."

"Then where is he?" demanded Vanessa.

"He—he—I don't know," admitted Melanie, dropping her head, her lip quivering. "I haven't seen him for some time. He did not meet me as we last planned and I have not received even a note from him since." Tears formed in her eyes and spilled over her cheeks. She brushed them away and sat up straight. "But he will be back. He promised that he would," she said, her gaze begging for Vanessa's assurance.

"I don't believe that we can assume that he will return," remarked Vanessa, speaking as plainly as she could. "If I had not left you alone so much you would not be in such a bumblebroth."

"You could not have stopped us," declared Melanie proudly. "We love one another and are going to be wed."

"I ask you again—then where is he? If he truly loved you, he would have married you as soon as he knew you were increasing," she argued. "He does know, doesn't he?"

"Yes!" Melanie flung the word at her with a vengeance. "We planned to wed the next time he returned, which he expected to be but a fortnight. He said we could go to Gretna Green for the wedding and then he would take me to meet his family. But that was the last time I saw him. Now, I don't know where he is and I am worried that something terrible has happened to him."

"He should be called to book for this. Do you know how to get in touch with him?" Vanessa asked.

Melanie looked down at her hands clasped tightly in her lap. "He couldn't tell me. He confided that he was working on a secret mission and said knowing him in any way could put me in danger. He vowed that as soon as his task was completed we could be public about our acquaintance."

"I think you have more than an acquaintance," Vanessa remarked dryly.

A blush rose to color Melanie's face. "We are in love," she insisted doggedly.

"And where has it gotten you?" cried out Vanessa in frustration. "You are but a green girl and are increasing, without a trace of a husband to lend you a smidgen of self-respect. There will not be a respectable home in all of England that will receive you. You will be whispered about and shunned for the rest of your life. And your child's life will be even worse."

Melanie burst into tears and buried her face in her hands. "He told me he loved me and that he would be back," she sobbed. "I can't imagine what has happened. Do you think he could be de—dead?" The last word ended in such a dreadful wail of anguish that even Vanessa could not resist feeling pity for her sister.

"I'm certain he's fine as fivepence," she said, patting Melanie's shoulder. "He's probably like many other men. He's gotten caught up in something and assumes you will be waiting for him when he is good and ready to return."

"But he's always been a perfect gentleman and honored his word. I know something hideous has happened to him. That is the only thing that could have kept him away."

"Forget him for the moment. It's more important that we decide what to do." Melanie glared at her. "In case he doesn't return," she added. "I don't suppose anyone suspects that you are increasing yet so we can arrange for you to take a trip. We'll tell everyone that you're coming to London with me, but I will find a private place for you to have the child. You can return home alone, then I'll bring the baby along later and claim that it belongs to our cousin who died in childbirth."

"What are you saying? This is my child and I intend to raise it with or without its father."

"And you shall," agreed Vanessa. "You will simply raise it as our cousin's child. That way both of you will be welcomed into society."

"I will not deny my own child."

"If you do not do as I say, neither one of you will have a life worth living."

"You are exaggerating," charged Melanie.

"You know that I am not."

Melanie's shoulders sagged and she looked far older than her age. "I know you are right," she admitted. "But I cannot give up hope that he will come back."

"He?"

"I will not tell you his name," Melanie repeated, her voice sounding frail. "Can we put off this decision until later. I will do as you say if only you will allow me to stay home until the last possible moment."

Waiting in vain for the father, Vanessa supposed, but Melanie looked so miserable that she could not ignore her plea. "I can see no harm in it as long as you continue as you have been. I must return to London, but I will be back as soon as I am finished at Lord and Lady Summerfield's home. We shall make plans then but, in the meantime, don't fret. We shall find our way through this one way or another."

"I'm so sorry to cause you such trouble," said Melanie, sniffling.

"Now don't become a watering pot again," teased Vanessa. "The time to cry is long past. We must put our minds to solving the problem. Go to bed now." She hugged her sister and watched as she made her way out of the sitting room and up the stairs before she allowed her own shoulders to droop under the weight of what she had just learned.

Vanessa had just begun to feel confident that their futures were secure even if neither of them married. They had their home and a small income from their parents. Her earnings were being invested and promised to bring them enough to live more than comfortably.

Now she had a child to provide for because she was certain that the father would never show his face again. Although their family was a reputable one, her father had not had a title and they had not grown up in the upper ten thousand. Perhaps after his and Melanie's last meeting, this mysterious man had decided a wife of inferior birth and a child were not to his liking, and he had deserted Melanie, leaving her to bear the burden of their illicit love.

Vanessa's heart broke for her sister and for all the things she had given up for a man who was not worth the worry that she lavished on him.

The candle in Vanessa's room burned until dawn and the bruises under her eyes the next morning attested to her sleepless night. After a silent breakfast, she bade her sister and Annie good-bye and climbed into the coach to return to London. She removed her bonnet and leaned her head back against the squabs, hoping to get some rest during the journey so that she could begin a job for which she had no enthusiasm.

"Just why are we here?" asked Max, looking around Lady Russell's drawing room. "Thought you didn't believe in this kind of thing."

"Miss Grayson is here," Ellery pointed out. "Since we were unable to get any information from Phillip's friends as to his whereabouts, I must return to the Spirit Lady in hopes that she and Corbin might lead me to him."

"Haven't seen Corbin yet, but Miss Grayson is over by the fireplace. Looks a little pale this evening," observed Max.

"Too many devil-worshiping ceremonies, I'll wager," quipped Ellery.

"Don't tell me you have condemned the lady without proof."

"I don't care about proof. She and Corbin can spend the rest of their lives wearing masks and cavorting among church ruins, I merely want to get Phillip back in one piece."

"Have you once again deserted Lady Cornelia?" asked Max.

"She told me she would be here this evening, but I don't see her yet. I've no doubt she'll turn up soon. She seems enthralled with Miss Grayson's ability and is still urging me to use her to discover any spirits that might be in my houses."

"She will need to arrive soon for it looks as if the show is about to begin," said Max, watching as Lady Russell indicated to Miss Grayson that she should join her on the raised hearth of the empty fireplace, giving them a small platform on which to stand.

"I wonder what yarns she'll spin tonight," replied Ellery, turning toward the two women.

"Miss Grayson has told me that she has discovered spirits are inhabiting this house," announced Lady Russell.

There was a buzz of conversation in the room, and, as before, people looked about as if expecting to see ghosts walking among them. Some ladies moved closer to gentlemen, but the reaction was milder than Ellery expected.

"I suppose everyone is becoming accustomed to sharing rooms with spirits," whispered Ellery to Max.

"Evidently we do it all the time," murmured Max. "We just did not know it until Miss Grayson came to Town."

"Lady Russell has three spirits who are in residence," announced Vanessa. "One is a couple who owned the house before Lord Russell's father acquired it. They were very fashionable in their day, but left no heirs to carry on the line. Perhaps some of you know of Lord and Lady Hastings who were close friends of George II."

"I believe I heard my grandfather speak of them," said one young man standing near Vanessa.

"And who was that?" she asked.

"Lord Maybury."

Vanessa tilted her head a moment. "They remember him well," she said. "Lady Hastings said he was a wonderful man except for the foul-smelling cigars he smoked."

The crowd laughed and the young man's mouth opened in amazement. "That is so," he said. "No one could bear to be around him when he blew a cloud and my grandmother sent him out of the house every time."

Most of the people applauded, but others shook their heads in disbelief.

"Who is the other spirit?" asked someone in the crowd.

"A man called Jack," replied Vanessa. "There is no need for alarm, but Jack was a highwayman."

"Watch your jewels," said Lord Rumford.

The spectators uttered a nervous laugh, but many of the women nonetheless touched their necklaces or the bracelets glittering on their wrists.

"Surely Jack didn't live in my home," said Lady Russell.

"No. Jack was plying his trade long before the Hastings built this house." Vanessa paused a moment, again listening. "He wants us to know that he was quite successful and had a dozen men working with him. He says it was a woman who brought him down."

"Isn't it always," remarked one of the guests, eliciting further amusement from the crowd.

"What happened?" asked the young man whose grandfather had known the Hastings.

"It seems that Jack had just completed a successful robbery. There was a tavern of sorts on this site and Jack was enamored of one of the barmaids. He stopped on his way out of town to see the woman. Jack drank a little too much in celebration and bragged to the woman about his successful robbery. He even showed her a few items of jewelry he had stolen. Unbeknownst to Jack, another of the woman's admirers was in the tavern and she passed along what Jack had related. The two made plans for her to lure Jack into a room at the tavern where the other man waited. Jack was struck over the head and relieved of the booty he had recently acquired.

"While Jack was seriously injured, he would probably have survived except for the woman's fear he would seek revenge on her. The man was ready to flee, but she took a cloth, placed it over his nose and mouth, and held it there until he expired."

The ladies were especially shocked at her revelation; such things were just not spoken of in public. But Lady

Russell was paying Vanessa well and she meant to give the woman everything she could for her money. She was certain Lady Russell's gathering would be talked about for days and that, after all, was what tonight was all about.

"Do you mean we could be standing on the exact spot where he died?" asked one fragile looking, blond-haired woman.

"I don't know where the deed was done," said Vanessa. "Oh, wait." There was complete silence while Vanessa evidently listened to someone. "Jack says it was more at the back of the house."

"Why didn't Jack come back and do in the people who robbed and killed him?" asked Ellery, interested despite his insistence that this was all a ghostly farce.

Again Vanessa listened. "He said the man murdered the woman so that he would not need to share what they had stolen from him. By then, the man had a . . . a disease which was slowly driving him insane and would eventually kill him. Jack thought it more appropriate to let the disease have its way with him. It was a slower death which insured the man would suffer far more than what Jack could do."

"How do Jack and Lord and Lady Hastings get along?" came another question from the crowd.

"They are from far different times and seldom interact with one another. He says they are proper genteel people. Lord Hastings describes Jack as having the makings of a leader of men and Lady Hastings says he could charm any woman he met."

"They admire one another then?" asked Ellery with the proper amount of disbelief in his voice.

"I believe they do," said Vanessa. "Class does not seem to count as much in the spirit world."

"Are they here?" asked Lord Rumford.

"Yes, they are, but you will not be able to see them."

"Could they do something to prove they are present?" he asked.

"They say they are not performing animals," said Vanessa.

"I did not mean that at all," objected Lord Rumford. "I meant no offense."

"Lady Hastings says since you apologized so sincerely and since her husband has no objection. . . ."

"By George!" exclaimed Lord Rumford, putting his hand to his cheek.

". . . she will give you a small kiss to prove she is here," finished Vanessa.

Vanessa knew when to quit and stepped down from the raised hearth to a smattering of applause.

Lady Russell appeared extremely pleased with the evening and did not object. Instead, she also stepped to the floor and began mingling with her guests, accepting their congratulations on having such interesting spirits, while guiding them to the refreshment tables.

Vanessa escaped from one group only to run directly into Lord Trent.

He looked down at her, noticing not for the first time that she was an attractive woman. It was unfortunate her character was in question or he might have found a dalliance with her interesting. But enough. He must put his mind to finding Phillip. "You gave an excellent performance tonight."

"Thank you, my lord. It seems I am becoming more adept at appearing in front of a group of people. Perhaps I shall be on stage before long."

"Then you admit your spirits are all of your making," he said.

"Absolutely not. I merely said I was gaining confidence in explaining about the spirits I contact. They are real," she insisted. "I have never made them up and will not no matter how much is paid me."

"The more I see you, the more I believe I should have you search my homes for ghosts."

"Since you do not believe in what I do, it would be a waste of both our time and your money."

"They are both mine to waste," he said with a wry smile. "I find little enough to entertain me. Perhaps a few spirits flitting around would enliven my life."

"I am not here for your amusement, my lord." Her voice was cool and so was her gaze, which did not falter as it held his.

"I did not mean to make light of either you or the spirits. If you found any, I would take their presence seriously."

Vanessa gave a sigh. "I doubt that you could or would, my lord. Somehow I cannot see you sitting across the tea table from Lady Russell discussing the souls who inhabit your home."

"Perhaps I would not go that far," he replied, venturing a small smile and hoping it would not offend her. "But I would respect what you say."

"I have very little time that is not already promised and I need to visit my home on occasion," she replied, attempting to politely refuse him.

Ellery was equally as determined to wring a commitment from her that she would visit his homes. "Surely, Miss Grayson, you can squeeze me in somewhere."

Vanessa thought of Melanie and the child that was on the way. She was convinced that they would never see the father again and that would mean they would be the sole support of the baby. Everything that she could earn would be needed to get them through. She couldn't count on being popular with the *ton* forever and once this source of income dried up, she did not know what she would do to earn more. To be sure, her investments were doing well, but that might not be enough to see the child was well established in the world.

"Let me review my obligations, my lord. Perhaps I can find a few days free."

"So little? I hope you will be able to do better than that, Miss Grayson."

"I will do the best that I can," she promised.

"In case you are worried about propriety, my aunt is in residence at the town house and will be happy to serve as chaperone while you are there. She has been at several of these gatherings and is impressed with your ability."

Vanessa seriously doubted that any aunt of his could admire her. "I would not move into your house, my lord. If we can reach an agreement, I will take a room in Town while I investigate your premises."

Ellery was disappointed. He had hoped to get her beneath his roof so he would have ample time to find out what she knew about the Hell-Fire Club and the disappearance of Phillip.

"Once you meet my aunt, you will find that your reputation will be unsullied should you decide to stay at the town house. She is a pattern card of respectability and admired by everyone who knows her. And I would think that you would need to be there night and day in order to fully explore whether there are spirits."

"It is a little too soon to be discussing where I will stay, Lord Trent. First I must determine if there is time available to visit your home."

"I have faith that you will be able to accommodate me," he replied, then thought of one last plea. "Surely you will not refuse to help a desperate man. Lady Cornelia—a particular friend—has said she will not venture into my homes until you have ascertained that they are spirit-free."

Vanessa felt an unexpected flash of disappointment when he mentioned his lady friend. She immediately wanted to refuse him, but would not allow herself to react in such a fashion.

"And if they are not?" she asked, curious to hear his answer.

"Perhaps you can drive them away."

"That is not part of what I do," she replied seriously.

"I suppose that Lady Cornelia will need to be satisfied to seeing my homes from the outside only."

Vanessa was surprised at his answer. He sounded as if he did not care one way or another as to whether Lady Cornelia ever set foot in his house.

"I would not want to be the cause of Lady Cornelia being kept from your home," she said.

"Yes, it would be a shame to deprive her of that honor."

She could not tell whether he was joking. "You make it difficult to decline."

"I was hoping to make it impossible," said Ellery, with a smile designed to melt away her last bit of resistance.

"I shall contact you within a day or two and advise you of my findings," she said, beginning to turn away.

He reached out, touching her arm to stay her departure. "In the meantime, will you ride in Hyde Park with me tomorrow?"

It was Vanessa's turn to smile. "What? And cause a scandal, my lord? It would be entirely inappropriate for me to ride with you and you full well know it."

"I certainly don't. I see no harm at all in a carriage ride."

"The rumors would abound before we cleared the confines of the park," said Vanessa. "While I am treated well, I am not a guest in these homes. I am being paid to perform a service and that is all. It would not be acceptable for me to socialize with anyone, particularly such an eligible peer of the realm as yourself."

"I cannot agree, but I will not argue with you at this point."

"Then you will excuse me, my lord. It has been a long day and I believe that I shall retire." With that, she turned and made her way across the room.

Ellery watched her every step, noting how gracefully she moved. She did not look back as many women would do and he wondered whether he had made any impression at all on her.

Max appeared at his side. "Any success?" he asked.

"I don't know," admitted Ellery. "Miss Grayson is evasive, to say the least. She has agreed to see whether she has any time free to visit my homes; however, I cannot count on that being any more than lip service in order to escape from me easier. I would not be the least surprised if I received a message in the morning advising me she is unable to accommodate me."

"Not an easy lady to charm," commented Max. "Perhaps you're losing your touch."

Ellery grimaced. "Her reaction certainly puts in doubt any pretension I might have about being able to flatter the ladies," he agreed.

"It had to happen one day. In the meantime, take heart in knowing that there are dozens of others who will simper at your every glance."

Ellery thought that he much preferred Miss Grayson's treatment to those misses who agreed with his every word. He was remembering how her eyes seemed to take on a dark golden color when Max spoke again.

"Where to now?" he asked.

"Since Cornelia has chosen not to appear, it will give us an evening to pay a visit to some of the gambling hells. Perhaps we can hear something about Phillip or the club there."

The two men made their way through the crush of people to seek the dark, smoke-filled rooms that occu-

pied houses in some of the most dangerous streets in
London.

Vanessa closed her door behind her with a heartfelt
sigh. She leaned back against the cool oak wood and
closed her eyes. The evening had seemed endless and
she wondered whether she could complete her commit-
ments with so much weighing heavily on her mind. Then
she reminded herself that she had no choice in the matter.

Pulling herself up straight, she walked across the room
and flung herself into a chair by the empty fireplace.
Why was Lord Trent pursuing her so relentlessly? She
knew he was no believer in what she did, even though
he professed an interest in it. He could, however, be
sincere in his desire to have her seek out spirits in his
homes to put Lady Cornelia's fears to rest.

Vanessa heard the two spoken about quite often as if
they were a couple. It had meant nothing to her until
she had actually met Lord Trent and now she wondered
at the unease she felt whenever she thought of Lady
Cornelia actually marrying the earl.

She shook her head, as if that would clear away the
unwelcome pictures that had filled it. There was something about Lady Cornelia that Vanessa could not like,
but it was no concern of hers if Lord Trent decided to
spend the rest of his life with the woman.

Vanessa leaned her head against the back of the
Queen Anne chair and closed her eyes. She immediately
saw Melanie as she had appeared the last time she had
visited home. There was a sense of unrest in her sister's
image that caused Vanessa to leap to her feet and begin
pacing the floor. Something was wrong; she was certain
of it. She would return home before beginning her next
engagement, she decided.

Shrugging off the weariness that had enveloped her, she began pulling clothes from the armoire. She would be packed and ready to leave in the morning. She hoped she arrived in time to help her sister.

Four

"Why didn't you let me know?" Vanessa whispered to Annie.

"It only happened last night," protested the maid in a low voice. "Even if I had found time to write the message would not have gotten to you before you arrived."

"I'm sorry, Annie. I know you're right. It is just that I've been so worried about Melanie and then last night I felt she needed me and I was so far away . . ." Her voice trailed off.

"I know, Miss Vanessa. No need to apologize. I'm happy you're here now. Miss Melanie called out for you all night."

"How I hate to be away from home," said Vanessa.

"Maybe you won't need to be much longer," said Annie, attempting to console her.

Vanessa gave a wry smile. "I would say this event means that I will need to work as long as I can."

Vanessa had arrived home around noon. Lady Russell had professed disappointment at her hasty departure, asking her to stay on a few days as a guest. Vanessa had refused, with thanks, with the excuse she must visit her home. She paid the coachman to make better time than usual and she was vastly relieved once the house came into view.

It had taken her only a moment to climb down from

the coach and hurry into her home. It was then she heard the baby's cry and knew she was now an aunt.

Vanessa leaned over the crib, which had first been hers and then Melanie's. She studied the small wrinkled face, topped with wisps of blond hair. She could see no family resemblance in an infant so small but, then, perhaps the child looked more like its father than the Graysons. She felt a flash of anger that the father was not here to support Melanie when she needed him. Vanessa did not have the faith in this nameless man that her sister did.

"What is this?" she asked, touching a mark on the baby's forearm as the small fingers curled into a fist.

"A birthmark, I'd say," replied Annie. "It looks like a clover."

"And a four-leaf one at that," added Vanessa. "Well, he will need all the luck he can get."

"Vanessa?"

Vanessa moved quickly to Melanie's bedside. "I'm here," she said.

"How did you know?"

"Last night I felt you needed me, so I came as quickly as I could."

"I'm so glad you're here," said Melanie, reaching out for her hand. "Can you stay long?"

"Long enough to be certain that you and the baby are all right."

Even though Melanie's face was pale and her hair lay in disheveled strands about her head, she smiled at the mention of her baby. "We can't simply call him baby. He must have a name."

"Have you thought of what you want to call him?" asked Vanessa.

"I want one of his names to be Jonathan after our father," Melanie answered. "I suppose. . . . She faltered for a moment. "I suppose his father will want a hand in naming him too."

It was no time to argue, so Vanessa merely said, "I suppose he will." Although reluctant to bring any unpleasantness into their conversation, she felt compelled to ask the question that hung over them. "Have you heard from him?"

"No," murmured Melanie, allowing her eyes to drift shut. "But he will be here as soon as he is able," she announced, her eyes opening, daring Vanessa to disagree with her.

"In the meantime, I suppose we will make do with one name and I believe little Jonathan is awake," she said, raising her voice to be heard above the baby's cry.

Vanessa left Melanie cradling Jonathan and went into the drawing room. Annie sat near the window, sewing in the bright afternoon light.

"He'll grow out of these faster than I can make them," she said, holding up the small garment for Vanessa's inspection.

"I suppose you made those same gowns for us," said Vanessa.

"With your mother's help," Annie agreed. "She did fine work with the needle. Always embroidered flowers and added a bit of lace to make them special. I'm afraid these will be plain."

"Don't let it bother you," said Vanessa. "I don't believe little Jonathan will object."

"Jonathan, is it?" asked Annie, looking up from her sewing. "After your father."

"That will be one of his names," explained Vanessa. "Melanie says she will wait and let the father add another name."

The maid nodded and went back to her stitching.

"Annie, do you know who he is?" asked Vanessa. "I'm not asking you to betray a confidence. I would merely feel better if someone knew the man and could vouch for his appearance being one of a gentleman."

"I wish I could, Miss Vanessa," said Annie, allowing her hands to rest on top of the gown in her lap. "It would ease my mind, too, but I didn't know what was happening until it was too late. Miss Melanie never allowed him to come to the house. She always met him on one of her walks and there was no way I could follow her without being seen."

"I wouldn't expect it of you," Vanessa assured her. "If you're worrying about this being your fault, do not let it weigh on you. I doubt whether anyone could have stopped Melanie once she made up her mind. We will need to decide what to tell anyone who calls and discovers that we now have a baby in the house."

"The heat has been keeping everyone indoors lately," said Annie.

"Nevertheless, someone will call sooner or later. I doubt whether Melanie will agree to disown her child so we will stick to the truth as closely as possible. We will say that Melanie was married quietly and that the wedding was performed in London so that I could be witness. Her husband is working with the Home Office and left soon after the wedding. We have no idea when he will finish his task and be able to return home. Does that sound believable?" asked Vanessa, noting the skeptical expression on Annie's face.

"Reckon it will do as good as anything else. Though the only thing that will save Melanie is for that man of hers to show up."

"You're right," acknowledged Vanessa. "But I don't think Melanie believed me when I told her the reaction to her and the baby if she had no husband. She's never been mistreated in all her life and it's difficult for her to even consider that people will shun her or not accept her in their homes."

"I pray he'll decide to return before any of that happens," said Annie, picking up her sewing again.

"So do I," said Vanessa. "So do I."

It was four o'clock in the afternoon and the cloudless sky allowed the sun uncontested access to Hyde Park.

Ellery and Max walked their horses beneath the trees to take advantage of the shade. It had been dry for a fortnight and traffic in the park was light due to the heat that engulfed the city. Even the Cyprians who delighted in appearing in the park to shock the ladies had stayed inside today.

"Heard from Miss Grayson yet?" asked Max.

The frown that now seemed to be an almost permanent expression on Ellery's face recently appeared again. "Not a word and I don't know where she's staying or even whether she is in Town. I talked to Lady Russell last night and she said Miss Grayson was making a quick trip home before taking on her next engagement. Since I haven't been able to locate her, I must assume she hasn't returned yet."

"Heard her say she has a sister. I suppose she misses her. Must be difficult to move from house to house, looking for people long dead, then facing a roomful of disbelieving individuals if she finds them."

"Never say you're feeling sorry for her," said Ellery.

"She seems to be a respectable woman," Max replied. "I have never heard an unkind word said against her and her manners are impeccable."

"And she fleeces people of their money with tales of spirits that only she can see or hear," snapped Ellery.

"But who is to say she isn't telling the truth?" questioned Max.

"Only another charlatan like herself," retorted Ellery, his tone biting.

"That is harsh speaking," said Max, surprised by the vehemence of his tone.

"I am galled to the quick by this whole situation. Phillip gets some bacon-brained idea to single-handedly save the monarchy and disappears without leaving a trace. Then I am forced to practically beg a . . . a spirit lady to enter my homes on the pretense of finding some of my long-departed ancestors and disturbing their peace. All in hopes that she knows something about my rapscallion brother. And if she doesn't, it means that I have spent all of this time and most of my patience for naught."

Ellery's chestnut stallion shook its head and sidestepped nervously at the irritation in his master's voice. He soothed the animal with a few soft words and a pat on neck.

"Not much else to go on," said Max. "We've talked to everyone who might know something about Phillip's whereabouts. If any of his friends are involved or know something about him, they aren't talking. Friendships are particularly sacred at that age and they'll hold their tongues even though it isn't the wisest thing to do."

"Damn puppies! If I find out they've been holding back, I'll make them wish they never heard my name."

"I think they wished that while you were questioning them," joked Max. "They looked as if they would rather be facing the devil himself than you."

"And well they should. I'm worried, Max," said Ellery, a rare admission for him. "Phillip has never been gone this long without getting in touch."

"Have you thought about engaging the Bow Street Runners?"

"Yes, but since the Home Office is involved, I don't think it's a good idea. I want to keep the search as quiet as possible. Did you find out anything more about Corbin?"

"Asked around, but couldn't pin down anything specific. I've learned he's well liked by the people who know him. He's never had a serious argument with anyone, always has plenty of blunt and is generous with it. There is one thing though: lately he has been disappearing for anywhere from a day or two to a sennight without any explanation. Of course, he owes no one an accounting of his time; however, it's fairly usual for a person to mention where he's been or what he's been doing to his friends. Corbin never offers an explanation; simply disappears and reappears on a somewhat regular basis."

"Do you think he could be attending a Hell-Fire Club meeting?" inquired Ellery.

"Your thoughts on his activities are as good as mine. I received absolutely no indication from the people with whom I spoke."

"He and his good friend Miss Grayson are the only remaining leads I have in finding Phillip. I must do something to get her into my house where we can become better acquainted. In the meantime, we will continue asking questions of as many people as we can. We will go back to Phillip's friends and hope they become so irritated with our interrogations that they will tell us something helpful."

The men were nearly out of the park when Ellery was hailed by his aunt. She was an impressive woman and Ellery held her in high regard.

After greeting Max and inquiring about his family, she turned to Ellery. "I have a bit of gossip for you," she said.

Ellery urged his mount closer to the carriage. "Tell me it's pertinent to my search," he said. His aunt knew all about Phillip's disappearance. She had been Ellery's staunchest ally on many occasions and he kept nothing from her.

"Indirectly." She vigorously plied her fan in front of her face. "I don't know why I'm out here in this heat," she grumbled. "There is nothing to be gained by it for no one of any interest is here."

Ellery grinned good-naturedly. "You are here because you would not take the slightest risk of missing anything of note. Now, what is it that you have to tell me?"

"I have learned that Miss Grayson is back in Town," she announced proudly.

"What! How long has she been here? Do you know where she is?"

"Patience. I can answer only one question at a time."

Ellery knew his aunt liked to draw out her information, so he gritted his teeth and sat his horse silently.

"From what I understand, she returned late yesterday. She is at Lord and Lady Halburton's home where she has been engaged to practice her art. Lady Halburton has been waiting all Season to have Miss Grayson and is anxious for her to get started scaring up all manner of her aristocratic ancestors' spirits. Lady Halburton is so high in the instep that I'm certain she'll make up something to outdo anyone else even if Miss Grayson finds nothing."

"I must see her," muttered Ellery, barely listening to his aunt rattling on about Lady Halburton. He returned his full attention to his aunt. "Do you think I could call on her?"

"Miss Grayson? Indeed not," remarked his aunt. "It wouldn't be acceptable."

"To the devil with propriety," he growled. "I must see her."

"Then it seems you must rely on me," said his aunt, nearly preening at his close attention.

"What do you mean?"

"Lady Halburton, or Susan as I call her, and I have known each other our entire lives—which, I hate to admit, is a long time indeed. I have been berating myself for not having called on her all Season."

"And . . ." prompted Ellery.

"And I thought I would visit her tomorrow, that is, if you could spare the time to escort me."

A wicked grin appeared on Ellery's face. "My lady, have I praised your cunning lately?"

"Never enough," she replied, peering over the top of her fan and batting her eyes in a preposterous parody of a shameless hussy.

Vanessa's eyelids drooped from lack of sleep and it took an effort to put one foot in front of the other. She had been in the upper regions of Lady Halburton's town house, attempting to attract any spirits which might inhabit the home, when a maid approached. She had been sent by Lady Halburton to ask Vanessa to come downstairs to the drawing room.

Vanessa had traveled up to London just the day before, then had spent nearly the entire night worrying about Melanie and the baby. Annie would take good care of them, but Vanessa still wished she could have stayed at home longer.

She had dragged herself from bed this morning and had begun investigating the house even though she was tired to the bone. She hoped Lady Halburton had not invited a roomful of ladies to take tea, expecting her to entertain them with ghost stories.

Vanessa sighed and began descending the stairs. This was only a part of what she accepted to be paid the fees she charged. Normally it would not annoy her at all, but her fatigue caused her to feel put upon.

She arrived at the drawing room door and paused

before she entered. Lady Halburton and another lady sat facing one another across the tea table.

"Come in, Miss Grayson," invited Lady Halburton. "I have a friend of long-standing I wish you to meet."

Vanessa entered the room and moved across the pale green carpet to where the two women were seated. She had seen the light lavender and purple-striped gown from the hall and was not at all surprised to be facing Lady Venable.

"I wanted you to meet one of my very best friends," said Lady Halburton to Vanessa.

"We have already met, my lady," replied Vanessa.

"It's true," confirmed Lady Venable. "I don't remember where it was exactly, but we introduced ourselves and had a nice chat."

"Botheration!" exclaimed Lady Halburton. "I had hoped to be one up on you this time. I should have known you would have already met."

"Don't be vexed, Susan. There is precious little that gets past me before the rest of the *ton* learns of it." Lady Venable turned her attention to Vanessa. "I hope you are well, Miss Grayson."

"Tolerable, my lady."

"That does not sound at all convincing," replied Lady Venable. "Don't tell me that Susan is mistreating you." She smiled to ensure Lady Halburton did not take offense.

"Not at all," replied Vanessa. "Lady Halburton has been all that is amiable. I am still a little tired from the travel yesterday. A good night's rest will put me in fine feathers in a trice."

"After tea, you must relax for the rest of the day," instructed Lady Halburton. "The spirits—if there are any—have been here long enough that another day will not harm anyone before they are discovered."

"Thank you," said Vanessa.

"There is one favor you can do, though," added Lady Halburton.

Vanessa kept her face expressionless, wondering what she was expected to do in return for an afternoon off. "And what is that, my lady?"

"You can keep my nephew company," answered Lady Venable with a scowl. "He insisted on driving me, but I will not allow him to listen in on my private conversation with Susan."

Vanessa did not look forward to spending time attempting to converse with a fledgling barely out of leading strings. He probably had no conversation other than to either turn red and remain mute or to compliment her on her eyes or nose or whatever other attribute which caught his eye.

Young men should be forced to attend a school to learn the niceties of sociable conversation without resorting to preposterous praise of a woman's beauty, thought Vanessa. It should not be assumed that every male was born with a silver tongue. Perhaps she should not condemn Lady Venable's nephew before she met him. He could take after his aunt and be an entertaining conversationalist.

"I should be happy to spend time with your nephew," said Vanessa.

"Ha! It is probably the last thing you want to do," replied Lady Venable candidly. "But he is not all that bad. At least, I do not find him so."

"Not bad? Is that how you think of me, Aunt?"

The voice came from behind Vanessa, but she thought she recognized it nonetheless. Could fate be so unkind as to burden her with the very man she hoped to avoid? She turned and saw Lord Trent standing near the window.

"You are Lady Venable's nephew?" she asked, still unable to believe the obvious.

"The very same," he replied affably, coming forward to greet her.

"I did not know."

"There was no reason you should," he said, taking her hand and lifting it to his lips.

A shiver ran up her arm and caused her heart to beat more rapidly when his lips brushed the back of her fingers. She had been greeted numerous times in the same manner, but had never found another man's touch as exhilarating as his.

Vanessa controlled her impulse to clasp her fingers around his in order to prolong the warmth of his touch. He seemed just as reluctant to release her, but eventually their hands parted and she was aware of Lady Venable's gaze fastened on them.

Lord Trent glanced toward the tea table. "Ladies, you may gossip all you like. I am certain that Miss Grayson will be able to keep me amused. If you think it proper, we will step outside where I can blow a cloud without sullying your room."

"Of course, it's proper," said Lady Halburton, with a small laugh.

No doubt thinking that Lord Trent would never be drawn to such a nonentity as herself, thought Vanessa, gritting her teeth with irritation. If Lady Halburton thought that she was at all attractive to the earl, she would never have called Vanessa to the drawing room. She was certain that she could lay that at Lady Venable's doorstep, but why would the woman want to throw her nephew into Vanessa's company?

"Go along," said Lady Venable, waving her hand in a shooing motion. "You know I cannot abide those cigars you smoke."

Lord Trent opened the French door leading onto the small terrace and followed her through it. "I hope it is not too cool for you," he said, as they walked toward the parapet.

"The weather has been hot and dry for weeks or hadn't you noticed?" she snapped, irritated with the thought that she had somehow been maneuvered into finding herself alone with him.

"I have, but some ladies still find the outdoors unfriendly without their shawl."

"I am not one of them," she replied shortly. "I grew up in the country and am not a frail blossom." She did not mean to sound sarcastic, but realized that she probably did. Her reaction was not, however, directed toward the women who were fortunate enough to have wealth at their disposal. It was meant for Lord Trent, who knew full well that she was not one of the *ton*, yet insisted upon treating her so.

Then, the irony of their situation reared its head, for she would have been insulted beyond all reasoning if he had not treated her with such respect.

He was due an apology even though she was loath to give it. "Forgive my shortness," she said, unable to say more. "As you heard, I have had little sleep and am not at my best at the moment."

"Lady Halburton should have allowed you to rest today," he commented, his dark eyes examining her face.

"She is not paying me to rest," retorted Vanessa. "I have an obligation to perform my services as quickly as possible."

"And if you do it swiftly, you will have saved enough time to visit my house."

So that was the reason behind this tête-à-tête. "It will certainly depend upon how long I am here," she agreed, relieved now that his motive was out in the open. "Is Lady Cornelia still apprehensive about the spirits in your house?"

"She reminds me each time we speak," he replied,

amusement lurking in the depths of his eyes. If it took dangling Cornelia's fears before the Spirit Lady in order to convince her to visit his home, then he would persist in recounting it until she gave in to his request. "I am hoping to have a house party at my country estate and she will not even contemplate attending."

"I did not know that you meant you wanted me to visit your country home," she said. "That would take far more time than I have."

"My house party is not planned for some time yet. My first priority is to free Cornelia's mind about my town house. Perhaps if that is successful, there will be no need for concern about my country estate."

"I am sympathetic to your dilemma, my lord, but at this time I do not have a spare moment."

Ellery could not believe he was failing in his endeavor. He could not remember the last time a woman had refused any request of his. They were usually willing to do whatever it took to give him his way. Now this slip of a girl was dismissing him with barely a hint of apology.

"Miss Grayson, I don't believe that you understand the importance behind what I am asking of you."

"Trust me, Lord Trent, I do. You are a gentleman who likes his way; that much is obvious. What is also true is that I value my word and I have committed to being at different homes at particular times with an allowance for unforeseen difficulties. I intend to honor my word, my lord, no matter how much you play on my sympathy."

"Are you certain you cannot slip me in before your next engagement?"

"I cannot," she answered firmly.

"You are a hard woman, Miss Grayson."

"Merely an honest one, my lord."

He studied her for a moment. "There is nothing I can say or do to sway your mind?"

"Nothing at all."

"I would be willing to double your fee," he said.

Just for a moment his offer was tempting when she thought of Jonathan. "I cannot do it, my lord, but even if I accepted, think of what would happen. The news that I had put someone aside for you would get out and sooner or later everyone would turn against me. I would not be able to earn a living if I accommodated you, Lord Trent, and I know you do not want that to happen."

Damn it! thought Ellery. He had begun this to gain her sympathy and use it to his advantage, but she had very nicely turned the tables on him. He had to give her that even though he had not gained his objective.

"No, Miss Grayson; I would not like to take anyone's livelihood from them, but I must admit I am sorely disappointed."

"If I could assist you I would, but I'm certain that Lady Cornelia will come around and feel welcome in your homes," said Vanessa, ignoring the twinge of guilt that accompanied the words.

"We shall see," replied Lord Trent. "In the meantime, I suppose I will continue residing with whatever unknown spirits are beneath my roof."

"If they have not harmed you thus far, they are unlikely to cause any problems," she assured him.

"And you do not even know them," he murmured.

She smiled at his jest. She was feeling more comfortable since he had ceased his appeals to her. They were far more disarming than she cared to admit.

"We have been out here for some time," she observed. "I would think your aunt and Lady Halburton have had ample time to exchange gossip."

"There is never a long-enough opportunity to listen to *on-dits,*" replied Ellery, good-naturedly, as they crossed the terrace to the French doors.

Whey they entered the room, Lady Venable gave Ellery a questioning look. He shook his head slightly, indicating he had not accomplished his objective. His aunt was surprised, since in the past Ellery had seldom failed to change a woman's mind after a few minutes alone with her. She had given him his chance. It was time she took the matter in her own hands.

"Miss Grayson, it was so good to see you again," she said, rising to leave.

"Thank you, my lady."

"I was just asking Susan where your next stop would be. I don't want to miss any of your revelations."

"I will be at Lord and Lady Roundhill's home once I leave Lady Halburton," she revealed.

"Which I hope will not be for some time yet," said Lady Halburton. "We have not even had time to get to know one another yet."

"It is your spirits with whom you are going to become acquainted," said Lady Venable.

"Do not tease me so, Charity. I am feeling some trepidation already."

"There is no need," Vanessa assured her. "For the most parts spirits are benign. They have nothing to gain by causing problems. So if you do have spirits, I don't believe there is anything to fear from them."

"There, you have nothing to worry about," said Lady Venable, patting her friend's arm. "Now, I am due at my mantua maker to be fitted for a new gown."

"Should I guess the color?" remarked Ellery, while offering his arm to his aunt.

"Do not become smart with me, young man," she said with a chuckle. "Susan, you must call so we can finish our conversation. Miss Grayson, I look forward to seeing you again."

Ellery bowed to Lady Halburton and Vanessa before escorting his aunt from the room.

"I had no idea Lady Venable was Lord Trent's aunt,"

remarked Vanessa once the two had departed. "She did not mention it when we spoke the other evening."

"She probably forgot that you are new in Town," said Lady Halburton. "Charity is a wonderful person. We have known each other since we were children and have never exchanged a harsh word."

"She seems to be quite amiable," agreed Vanessa.

"And Ellery is one of the most eligible men in all of England," gushed Lady Halburton.

Vanessa recalled the touch of his lips on her hand and felt a vulnerability that was unprecedented in her experience. Her intuition told her that Lord Trent was not through with her yet.

Five

The two figures made their way along the stone passageway until they came to a door which gave way to a small room, perhaps a cell for one of the monks who had made this their home in the last century. There they donned black robes, then hoods which allowed only small holes for their eyes and noses. To finish covering their bodies completely, they pulled on black gloves which disappeared into the sleeves of their robes. When they had finished, they left the room and continued down the hall.

"Did you encounter any problems?" asked the taller of the two.

"None whatsoever. It was nearly laughable the way he willingly jumped into our net. He was so concerned with toadying up to us we had to do nothing but lead him into the cell. We told him we were holding a ceremony there and he followed right along."

"He's a young cub attempting to prove himself and it made him vulnerable."

"I'll wager he won't make that mistake again," said the short, stocky person.

"I'll wager he won't have the chance," the other replied, eliciting a nasty chuckle from beneath the other black hood. They had stopped in front of a door with a grill set into it.

"Who is it?" came a voice from within.

"Your fellow Hell-Fire Club members," said the tall one, evidently the leader of the two.

"Why am I locked up in here? Is this a joke or part of the initiation?"

"Neither," the black-robed figure answered shortly. "We know about your plan to infiltrate our group and reveal our names to the government."

"I don't know what you are talking about."

"It's far too late to deny it. We are holding you here until our next meeting when you will be the guest of honor at our ceremony." Both of the figures laughed again—a sound not of merriment, but one that could only forebode a night of terror.

"When will that be?"

"It will not happen for some time yet. We want to allow you enough time to think about your sins. There are also others who will join you in the ritual and it may take longer to bring them into our fold. In the meantime, you will be our guest. We will give you the best of food and lodgings until then, although I must apologize for the lack of entertainment." They were still laughing and joking as they returned to disrobe and join the outside world.

Even though Phillip Lawford had pressed his face against the opening grate in the door, he had been unable to recognize either of the people hidden underneath the layers of black cloth. Nor could he identify the voices since they were muffled by the hoods.

Even if he had been able to determine who they were, he did not know what good it would do him. He was locked in all right and tight and there was no way of escaping this hell unless he could overcome the guards who brought his food. But there were always two of them and the pistol that was trained on him for the short time the door was open did not invite escape.

He had thought himself so clever to locate members of the Hell-Fire Club and to work his way into their good graces so quickly. He had appealed to them time and again to attend one of the meetings, but they had told him that first he must be initiated.

Two nights before, they had told him the time was at hand and he had willingly ridden with them to the old abbey and followed them through the cool, dark passageways into the cell where he now found himself imprisoned.

It was all too clear to him now that it was too late. They had known all along what he was up to and had led him a merry chase, allowing him to finally catch them and convince them he should be one of them. He was chagrined when he considered how they had most likely laughed at him behind his back, but that was a small thing compared to the fix he was in now.

He did not know who was to join him in the upcoming ceremony, but he was convinced that they would never live to tell anyone of the Hell-Fire Club.

He would give up his life attempting to escape rather than go meekly to his death, but he would wait until the last minute. Phillip thought of his brother. Ellery would rescue him if it were at all possible and he had no doubt that he was searching high and low for him at this very minute. However, it would take a miracle for Ellery to discover this hiding place.

Phillip fought off the surge of despair that nearly overwhelmed him and closed his eyes, praying that Ellery would provide the miracle he required.

Lady Venable sat in the drawing room of Ellery's town house, where she resided when in Town. She had invited both Lady Halburton and Miss Grayson to take tea with her and was anxious for them to arrive. She prided herself on aiding her family in any way possible and if Ellery thought this young woman might help him locate Phillip, then she would do all she could to bring it about.

Ellery looked through the door and saw his aunt sitting in the drawing room. "Do you think they are coming?" he asked.

"Yes. And I don't want you anywhere to be seen when they get here," she scolded, waving him away. "Just do as we discussed previously and be sure to enter at the right time."

A few minutes later Lady Halburton and Vanessa arrived. After the usual greetings, they were soon seated and served a cup of well-brewed Bohea tea, along with plum cake and fruit tarts which were placed on the table between them.

"I do not want to talk about the weather," announced Lady Venable. "That was the subject of nearly every conversation I heard last night and it is dull as dishwater. I have been praying it would rain simply to dispose of the topic."

"Since you are so vexed, you must choose an issue to discuss," said Lady Halburton, smiling at her friend's impatience.

Lady Venable caught Vanessa glancing about the richly appointed room. "You expected it to be all purple, didn't you?" she quizzed.

Vanessa did not know how to reply. She did not want to insult Lady Venable, but she was surprised not to see even a hint of purple in the room other than Lady Venable's clothing. Her gown today was a medium shade of lavender with dark purple violets sprinkled over it. It was decorated with three bands of purple ribbon around the hem and also at the neckline.

"I know you did," continued Lady Venable without waiting for her to answer. "But this is Ellery's house. I only stay here during the Season, so I don't impose my

eccentric whims on him. I will tell you something else."
She leaned toward Vanessa and lowered her voice as if
it were a great secret. "I do not use purple in decorating
my own home."

"Yet you wear only purple," observed Vanessa.

"I didn't plan to do so. It came about on its own. After
I came out of first mourning for my husband and put
away my black gloves, I decided to continue with half
mourning and settled on wearing lavender instead of
white or gray," explained Lady Venable. "The color became me and I found it was far easier to continue with
it rather than be forever deciding on what suited me.
Since then it has become my own distinctive peculiarity
which sets me apart from everyone else."

"Do you ever tire of it?" Vanessa asked.

"I endeavor to never allow myself to think about it. I
consider it permanent and, therefore, unchangeable.
However, on occasion, a stray thought escapes and I wonder how I might look in blue or yellow or even crimson."

"And what do you think?"

A wicked grin spread across Lady Venable's face.
"That the world is not ready to see me dressed in crim-
son." She began to laugh uproariously and Vanessa and
Lady Halburton felt safe enough to join in.

"Have you discovered any spirits in your house," Lady
Venable asked once the laughter had died down.

"I don't know whether to be disappointed, but Miss
Grayson has found no indications that any are there."

"I think I would be grateful," Lady Venable replied.
"Think of how awkward it could be knowing you had
spirits. Could you dress or bathe or do any other thing
without wondering whether they were staring at you—or
worse yet laughing? I think not."

"I suppose you're right, but think of the others who
will feel superior because they have spirits and I do not."

"Why not have Miss Grayson come back next year. Perhaps you will acquire some by then."

Lady Halburton's face brightened as she looked at Vanessa. "Do you think it possible?" she asked.

Vanessa did not like to give anyone false hope, but she could not completely extinguish Lady Halburton's dream. "There might be a slim chance," she equivocated.

"Then we shall do it," she said firmly.

"How often does it happen that you find no spirits in the homes you visit?" asked Lady Venable.

"I usually find spirits more often than not since most of the people who call on me have seen or heard something that causes them to believe they are there," answered Vanessa. "But I also find them in homes where the owner has no idea whatsoever he is sharing his house with old souls."

"So you are finished with Susan's house now?" asked Lady Venable.

"Yes. It's off to Lord and Lady Roundhill tomorrow," Vanessa replied.

"I've asked her to stay and visit with me for a few days more. She is such pleasant company, I shall miss her." Lady Halburton cast a fond gaze on Vanessa.

"I wish that I could, but I have very little time compared to the list of homes I have yet to visit."

"Oh, that reminds me," said Lady Venable. "I met Lord Roundhill yesterday evening and he asked if I knew how to reach you. I told him you were with Susan and that I expected you at tea today. He gave me this note to pass on to you." Lady Venable lifted a square of heavy cream-colored paper from the table beside her and handed it to Vanessa. "Lord Roundhill said to apologize for getting it to you in this roundabout way."

"Thank you, my lady," said Vanessa, staring down at the envelope.

"Well, go ahead, girl. No need to stand on ceremony with either of us. I know you are bursting to find out the contents."

"If you are certain you don't mind," said Vanessa, breaking the seal, and unfolding the paper. She perused the note a second time before folding it again and putting it in her reticule.

"Not bad news, I hope," said Lady Venable.

"It is nothing secret," said Vanessa. "Lady Roundhill is suffering from a summer cold and asks whether I can come at a later date."

"Then you can stay longer," remarked a delighted Lady Halburton.

"I believe I shall see if I can go on to my next engagement. If not, I will make a short visit home."

"Or you could come here since you now have the time." Ellery stood in the door, staring directly at Vanessa. "I was passing by and couldn't help but overhear," he said, stepping into the room. "I believe that time was the only reason you gave for not being able to visit my home."

He did not know what magic his aunt had worked to convince Lady Roundhill to feign a cold, but he hoped he could find some way to thank her. Perhaps a new set of amethyst jewelry.

"That's true, my lord," agreed Vanessa. "But if I could go on to others . . ."

"They are not expecting you until later, so you will not be inconveniencing them. Nor will you be cheating them," he added.

"My dear, we would appreciate it so much if you could do us this favor," pleaded Lady Venable. "There is so much that rests on what you may find."

"Lord Trent has explained to me about Lady Cornelia," revealed Vanessa.

"Then do it for him," she pleaded. "Or do it for me

for I would do anything to see Ellery happy. I know that is what every aunt wants for her nephew, but there is a special bond between us and I want to see him settled before I am gone."

"Lady Venable! Do not even think such a thing," exclaimed Vanessa. "You are far from . . . from . . . departing."

"Yes, Aunt, we will have many years together yet," said Ellery, standing in back of her chair and placing his hands on her shoulders. You may even order some purple hyacinths for the drawing room if you will stop speaking such nonsense."

Lady Venable dabbed at her eyes. "You are such a comfort to an old woman." She sniffed, reaching up to place her hand over his.

Vanessa was quite impressed with the closeness of Lord Trent and his aunt. She thought of all she had missed without having a mother for most of her life and decided she could not refuse both the earl and his aunt.

"Very well, I shall place your house next on my list."

"Oh, thank you, Miss Grayson," said Lady Venable. "I knew you would not let me down. If it isn't too sudden, we will expect you tomorrow."

"Not at all. I will call after breakfast and depart just before dinner. That should give me ample time to find out if there are spirits here."

"But you should stay here in order to be certain one way or the other, shouldn't you?"

"It's always best, but I will hire some rooms until I am finished here."

"If you are worrying about propriety, you may put that to rest for I reside here with Ellery. No one would dare hint at any indiscretion while I am present."

"I can't see anything wrong with it," added Lady Halburton.

"Say I may send my coach for you in the morning," entreated Ellery.

Vanessa could not stand up against all of them. "All right, I will stay here if it means that much to you."

Ellery relaxed, pleased that he had finally gotten his way. Miss Grayson would be under his roof by the next day and he could begin getting to know her better. Eventually, he might determine where Corbin went and what he did when he disappeared so quickly. He wondered whether her trips home coincided with Corbin's vanishing acts. He would ask Max to help him out in that area.

"Now that everything is settled, let me call for some fresh tea and cakes. You may go along, Ellery, and do whatever it is you do at this time. I have days of gossip I have saved for this very occasion," revealed Lady Venable.

Ellery bid the ladies good day and went on his way. He was anxious, but he would wait until tomorrow to begin his scrutiny of Miss Grayson.

Vanessa said an affectionate good-bye to Lady Halburton and stepped out into the morning's heat. It was yet another cloudless day and she found herself wishing for a dark, brooding day filled with rain which would wash away the dust and soot that had settled onto every surface of London. She hoped that it was cooler in the country so that little Jonathan and Melanie would not suffer too much discomfort.

Lord Trent's large black town coach with the family crest awaited her. She swallowed nervously as she climbed into it and made herself comfortable on the thick, soft squabs. A small vase attached near the window of the carriage held a single white lily which spread a sweet fragrance inside the coach. Vanessa could visualize

Lord Trent's strong hands plucking the fragile flower and tucking it into the vase.

She smiled, shaking her head in amusement. The earl would hardly take the time to do such a thing himself when the coach was carrying someone as unimportant as herself. It was probably a standing order that a flower was put in the vase each time it was taken out. Lady Venable would be just the person to make such arrangement. She must compliment her on it when she arrived.

The streets were clogged with all manner of conveyances and it took longer than usual for the large coach to make the short trip from Lady Halburton's to Lord Trent's town house. As soon as they stopped in front of the house, the door opened and Lord Trent came down the stairs to greet her.

Vanessa's tongue felt like cotton as she stared down at the handsome man waiting to hand her down from the coach.

"Surely you do not intend to sit in there all day," he teased, his lips curving into the smile that made her stare all the more.

Vanessa cleared her throat and adjusted her gaze toward the ground, hoping to break the spell he had cast over her. She accepted his outstretched hand, her own tingling where he touched it. She was puzzled at her reaction to him and decided it was merely his reputation as one of the most eligible men in all of England that had caused such feelings.

"I hope I am not arriving too early and upsetting the household," she remarked to break the silence.

"My people are trained not to allow anything to overset them, so your arrival will cause no one any inconvenience. My aunt has been waiting impatiently since breakfast. I think she finds the house empty since I am in and out so often."

"The lily . . ." she began.

"Did you like it?" he asked before she could finish. "Its fragrance somehow reminded me of you—light, yet so sweet." He had stopped outside the door of the town house and faced her, still holding her hand. His gaze seemed to reach into her very soul, searching for an answer to questions she had never been asked.

"It was beautiful" was all she could manage to murmur.

"I'm glad you enjoyed it," he said, finally releasing her from his spell and leading her into the house. A tall, thin woman of middle age waited in the marble-floored foyer. "This is Mrs. Johnson, our housekeeper. She will show you to your room so that you can get settled in. Aunt Charity will be in the drawing room when you have made yourself at home. I have an appointment, but she can show you around the house as well as I can. In the meantime, if you need anything at all, you need only ask."

"Thank you, my lord, but you need not take any special steps to ensure my comfort."

"Of course I do," he responded. "It has taken me long enough to get you here and I don't want you to regret your decision. He glanced at his pocket watch. "I'm afraid I must go or I'll be late. I will see you at dinner."

He turned toward the door, while Vanessa followed Mrs. Johnson across the foyer to the stairs that led to the upper floor. When he reached the outside door, Ellery paused and looked over his shoulder, watching her gracefully lift her skirts as she ascended the stairs. A flash of a delicately turned ankle and a slipper tied with ribbon caught his attention. He berated himself for staring like a young cub who had never known a woman. Accepting his hat and gloves from his butler, Thomas, he departed without another backward glance.

* * *

Vanessa returned to her room late that afternoon and relaxed with a sigh on the small settee that was situated in front of the fireplace. Immediately after luncheon, Lady Venable had shown her through the house and then had left her alone to begin her work. The house was beautifully decorated, the rooms perfect in every respect in Vanessa's eyes.

She had wandered through the house on her own, stopping here and there, sitting and closing her eyes, relaxing and listening for any sign that the house was occupied by anyone but those of flesh and blood. She had found nothing.

Lady Venable had found her in an upstairs bedroom just a short time earlier and had insisted that she had done enough for the day. She had sent her to her room to rest, telling her they would meet again at dinner.

She eased off her slippers and wiggled her toes, remembering the summers when she ran barefoot in the yard, the cool blades of grass tickling the bottoms of her feet. If life could always remain so simple, she thought.

Lord Trent was already in the drawing room with a glass of amber liquid in his hand when she arrived just prior to dinner. He poured another glass and handed it to her.

"I shouldn't," she said.

"Just a sip or two," he urged. "It will relax you and Aunt Charity said you had been working hard."

Vanessa could not hold back her laugh. "What I do is scarcely hard labor," she replied.

"I do not know what you go through, but I can imagine that it is tiring at times."

"When I connect with a spirit, it does take a toll. Depending upon what I encounter it can drain me of energy," she admitted. "However, that was not the case today. Although it is too soon to say for certain, I don't feel there is anything here."

His brow furrowed as he took in her words. "I am disappointed."

"I thought finding nothing was exactly what you wanted in order for Lady Cornelia to feel comfortable in your home."

"Yes, of course I did," he replied quickly. "But Aunt Charity was counting on a ghost or two to enliven her conversations."

"I'm certain she won't mind if it means that Lady Cornelia will look favorably on your suit."

Lord Trent appeared distinctly uncomfortable. Perhaps it was because she had spoken so openly about his intentions toward Lady Cornelia.

"Ah, yes," he said, then drained his glass of sherry. "Lady Cornelia should be pleased when she hears you are here."

"You mean you have not told her?"

"I thought to surprise her."

"Then you had better tell her quickly for I have observed nothing remains private in the *ton.*"

"She will know soon for she is joining us for dinner this evening. My good friend, Viscount Huntly, will also be here."

"I did not know you were having guests, my lord. I will take dinner in my room or in the kitchen so I will not intrude."

"You will do nothing of the sort. You are my guest as much as the others," he said, taking a step toward her. He reached out and grasped her arms between elbow and shoulder and she thought he meant to shake her. However, as she gazed at him wide-eyed, his expression softened and his hands caressed her arms lightly.

"You will join us at the table tonight," he said.

They stood there for a moment longer before he

stepped away. Vanessa was rattled by his outburst and sipped more sherry than she intended.

"Do the ghosts hide from you often?" asked Lord Trent, pouring another glass of sherry for himself.

"Sometimes at first. They are accustomed to going unheard so it takes them a little time to become accustomed to a person who knows they are there."

"I'm curious. What do they say to you?"

Vanessa shrugged casually. "Surprisingly, their conversation is not that different from the living. They speak of people they have known and things that they have done, trips they have taken and if they have a family, their children. On occasion, I will find a soul that has been kept from going on even though it wishes to do so. It is usually an unsettled act of violence that has caught the person unawares and unprepared to leave the world."

"What happens then?" asked Ellery, interested despite his cynicism.

"Sometimes I can help them; sometimes I must leave them as they are. So you see, my gift is not one that is a blessing in many cases."

"You could refuse to acknowledge them," he suggested.

"I could," she agreed. "Over the years, I have strengthened my ability until I can block out the voices at will. At first, I felt guilty, then I realized that if I couldn't silence them, I would most probably lose my sanity."

"Then why do you continue?"

"It might be difficult for you to understand, but I feel a certain obligation. I have been given a talent—no matter how bothersome it is at times—and surely it was meant that I should not ignore it. Of course, since I have become an adult it has been more of a blessing, allowing me to earn enough to support my family."

At that moment, there was the sound of voices in the foyer and a moment later Lady Cornelia, accompanied by Lord Huntly, entered the room.

"I am so relieved you agreed to search Ellery's home for spirits," gushed Lady Cornelia. "I am frightened out of my wits just thinking of some wispy apparition floating around my head."

"They seldom take a form," said Vanessa, "and they probably would not harm you unless you had performed some heinous act against them while they were alive."

"So you see, you are safe," interjected Ellery. "I advised you previously that there was nothing to fear in my home. I don't believe many of my ancestors have turned into ghosts, disgruntled or otherwise, and they would certainly not have the poor taste to haunt such a lovely lady. But when Miss Grayson finishes you may lay all your fears to rest for she has already opined that she expects to find the house to be spirit-free."

"Have I missed anything?" asked Lady Venable as she sailed into the room.

"Sherry and good company," replied Ellery, handing her a glass.

"I apologize. I did not realize the lateness of the hour." She greeted the two guests, then turned her attention to Vanessa. "Did you have any luck this afternoon?" she asked eagerly.

"I was just advising Lord Trent that I have yet to find any indication of spirits in the house."

"And I, for one, am absolutely delighted," remarked Lady Cornelia.

"I am happy it has eased your mind," replied Lady Venable. "But I must admit I was hoping to have perhaps just one kindly spirit around for company."

"You would never know they were here," said Lord Huntly.

"Perhaps if they knew that I knew they would reveal themselves. Did I say what I meant?" she asked.

"I believe so, Aunt Charity," replied Ellery, with an amused expression on his face.

"If Miss Grayson cannot find one here, perhaps she will run across one later who would consider moving into the house for your entertainment. We could offer him one of the best chefs in London, a private room, and if he is unmarried, we could attempt to scare up a lady spirit for him."

Lady Venable laughed along with the others and then tapped Ellery on the arm with her fan. "You may make fun of me, but a good spirit enlivens a family to no end."

"I will take your word for it," he replied. "Now, shall we go in to dinner?" He offered his arm to his aunt and Max followed with Cornelia and Vanessa.

The dinner was more elaborate than Vanessa had previously experienced. Dish after dish was brought from the kitchen—duck soup, poached fish with fruit, Cornish hens with rice stuffing, Beef Tremblant with two sauces, stuffed artichokes, asparagus in cream, quince pie, gooseberry tart, and almond cake were among the dishes served.

"Your chef is too good," complained Lord Huntly. "I don't believe I will be able to rise from the table."

"In an hour or two, you will be dancing the night away," predicted Ellery.

"More like nodding off behind a flower arrangement," replied Max.

"If you are going to the Danforth ball, then I will make certain that you dance at least once before dozing in the flowers like a contented bee," quipped Lady Cornelia. "And then you must promise to take me in to dinner."

Max grimaced. "How can you think of another dinner so soon?"

"I shall be dancing all evening and will be looking

forward to refreshments by then and so, I'll wager, will you."

The men decided to forgo brandy and cigars at the table and followed the ladies into the drawing room.

"Shall we all go to the Danforths' together?" asked Lady Cornelia.

"You and Max go ahead," said Ellery. "I have a few things to do and then I'll join you."

Lady Cornelia pouted a little but eventually left with Max, reminding Ellery that she expected to see him in time for a waltz. He agreed and ushered them to the door, watching them climb into the carriage in the sweltering London night.

He walked back into the drawing room to join Vanessa and his aunt. "I wish you would reconsider and come out with us this evening," he said to Vanessa.

"I have not been invited," she answered with a slight smile, wishing he would not broach the subject again. They had discussed it earlier and she had assured him she would be perfectly happy staying in.

"You do not need an invitation if you accompany us."

"He's right, my dear, you would be welcomed," agreed Lady Venable.

"I appreciate your concern, but there's no need to include me in any of your plans. I will use part of this evening to determine whether you have any spirits who are night creatures."

"You mean you might yet find a rogue who spent the time from dusk to dawn prowling the streets of London looking for excitement?" he teased.

"If Lady Venable desires a spirit, I will do my best to find one. Although I cannot guarantee success."

"I can ask for no more than your best," remarked Lady Venable, rising to her feet. "I will be ready to leave in just a few minutes, Ellery. I will wait for you in the foyer."

"I can see that it would be useless to appeal to you," he said.

"I have work to do, my lord. That is why I am here."

"There is nothing that says you cannot also enjoy yourself," he protested.

He was extremely handsome in his black evening clothes with a diamond sparkling in his perfectly tied cravat. Vanessa felt positively dowdy in her green gown, which was not meant for evening wear.

"I never thought to be asked to join in London's entertainments and I did not bring anything suitable to wear," she explained.

"No one will notice," he said, thinking that he had not given one thought to what she wore.

"Oh, yes, they will, my lord. Ladies always remark on what is being worn and I would not want to be an embarrassment to either you or Lady Venable."

"You could never be that," he asserted, "but if you would feel uncomfortable I will not press the issue. I will see you in the morning then."

"In the morning, my lord," she replied.

Vanessa remained where she was until she heard the front door close behind Lord Trent and Lady Venable. How she wished she could have agreed to accompany the earl this evening. But she would soon return to her own home, where her time would be taken up helping to raise her nephew. Balls and lilies in carriages would be a thing of the past, something to dream about on the long cold winter evenings in the country.

Vanessa stood and shook the wrinkles out of her skirt. It was still early yet according to London time and she decided to continue what she had begun earlier in the day. She would attempt to visit all the rooms again and see whether her initial determination was correct. She was nearly positive that there were no spirits in Lord Trent's house, but she owed it her best effort.

She went into the foyer, where Thomas was still on duty. "I shall be visiting most of the rooms again this evening," she told him. "You might want to warn the staff not to be alarmed if they see me or hear anything unusual."

"Thank you, Miss Grayson, I will advise them," he intoned in his solemn manner.

"Beware, ye spirits, if you are here," she murmured under her breath as she climbed the stairs, "for I am on my way."

Six

A maid tapped gently on Vanessa's door just before dawn was beginning to break. "There's a lad waiting for you in the kitchen, ma'am. He said it's important that he talk to you immediately. He said to tell you Annie sent him."

"Help me on with my gown," said Vanessa as she scrambled out of bed. Her imagination ran wild while she hurriedly dressed and dashed down the back stairs into the kitchen.

Once there she found Nate, the son of one of their neighbors at home. Nate often helped around their homes, performing tasks that were too arduous for the women.

"Nate, what are you doing here? What's happened? Has someone been injured?"

"Miss Annie told me to come straight here as fast as I could, Miss Vanessa. She said to give you this." He held out a crumpled piece of paper.

Vanessa jerked it out of his grasp and unfolded it with shaking hands. Annie wrote that Melanie had disappeared, leaving baby Jonathan. She begged Vanessa to come home at once.

Vanessa asked Cook to feed Nate while she packed and made ready to leave. She sent for a footman to take a message as soon as she wrote it. Penning a note to

Rudy, she asked for his traveling coach to arrive as soon as possible in the mews behind Lord Trent's town house. She handed it to the footman and told him to deliver it with as much haste as possible and to make certain it was delivered to Lord Corbin immediately, even if it meant waking him.

While the maid was packing her trunk and portmanteau, she wrote notes to the next two people whose houses she was to visit, advising them that a family emergency had called her home and that she would contact them when she returned to London.

She wrote messages to both Lord Trent and Lady Venable. Rising from the table, she took a tissue-wrapped item from her embroidery box and put it with Lady Venable's note. By the time her clothes were packed and she was ready to go, the eastern sky was beginning to show a pinkish hue.

A footman carried down her trunk and portmanteau while Vanessa went in search of Thomas. She found him in the kitchen with the rest of the staff, having breakfast.

"Thomas, would you see that these two messages are delivered this morning? And I would like Lady Venable and Lord Trent to have these as soon as they arise." She handed the notes and tissue-wrapped parcel over to him. "May I depend upon you?"

"You may, madam," he assured her gravely.

"Thank you, Thomas. I want you to know that I appreciate how well I have been received in this house. I have been in others where the staff has not been as agreeable."

"I would never allow that to happen here," he replied, unbending a little.

"I know you wouldn't and I would like you to pass along my thanks to the entire staff. I would do it myself, but I do not have the time."

"I will tell them, madam."

She nodded and turned to Nate, who had just finished a substantial breakfast. "Nate, come to the stable with me."

When they reached the stables they found Lord Corbin's large traveling coach already waiting, with Corbin pacing back and forth beside it.

"What the devil has happened?" he asked, without preamble.

She pulled him aside, away from the ears of the stable boys and coachman. "Melanie is missing," she said abruptly.

"What! How?"

"I don't know. Annie sent Nate with a note telling me she had disappeared. She didn't elaborate, so I don't know any more than that. I believe she was too upset to explain, but she begged me to come home immediately."

"I'm going with you," he said.

"There's no need," she said. "And we shouldn't be traveling so far with one another."

"Propriety be damned! You need someone with you."

"I don't know what has happened. Melanie might be home and well by the time I arrive," she said, although she no more believed her statement than he did.

"I do not like it," he growled.

"I will let you know what has happened as soon as I find out myself," she said. "There is one thing you can do."

"Name it," he said.

"Take Nate with you. Both he and his animal need to rest before starting back."

"That isn't much, but consider it done."

"Thank you," she said, her eyes misting slightly. She took a deep breath and blinked rapidly. She could not allow herself to show any signs of weakness. Annie, Melanie, and the baby were dependent upon her. She

called Nate over and explained that he would stay with
Lord Corbin until his horse rested enough to make the
return trip.

"Shouldn't be later than in the morning," he said.

"Here, take this." She removed some coins from her
reticule. "This should pay for food and lodging if you
need to stay overnight on the way home."

"Thank you, Miss Vanessa. I'll be back as soon as I
can." Nate went into the stables to bring out his horse.

Corbin pulled out a small pouch and thrust it into
Vanessa's hands. "You may need this," he said.

Vanessa knew what it was without looking. "I have
plenty of funds to see me through."

"You don't know how much you might need before
this is over. At least allow me to do this much," he said
gruffly.

She was becoming a regular watering pot, thought Vanessa as her eyes filled with tears. "I will take it only to
please you, but you will get it back," she promised.

He took a step closer and brushed away a tear which
had escaped and was trickling down her cheek. "If I do
not hear from you in a timely manner, I will come to
the country to find out the reason."

She nodded, unable to answer because of the lump
which had formed in her throat.

He helped her into the coach and watched as it rolled
out of the mews into the streets of London. Motioning
to Nate, he mounted his horse and the two rode away.

Ellery had awakened to the sound of wheels rolling
over the cobblestones in the mews. Looking out, he observed Miss Grayson and Lord Corbin in what appeared
to be an intense conversation. At one point, Corbin
moved closer and touched her cheek. Then, she climbed
into Lord Corbin's traveling coach and the coachman

shook the reins over the backs of the black horses that pulled it.

Ellery found his fists were clenched at his side and made an effort to release them. What had it meant? What was Corbin doing here at such an early hour and where was Miss Grayson going? Had they found out that he was watching them because of the Hell-Fire Club and decided to get away from him as quickly as possible?

He fought back the urge to have Corbin's coach followed. He had no one at hand who could perform the undertaking clandestinely and he did not want to show his hand if they did not already know about his surveillance.

Ellery could not go back to sleep and decided that a ride in the park at dawn might help calm the myriad feelings that churned inside of him. He called for his valet, who arrived with Vanessa's note in hand.

Ellery quickly tore it open, noting the graceful flow of her handwriting across the page. She advised him that she had been called home and had left immediately upon receiving word. She apologized for leaving so quickly, but assured him she had spent the last evening going through each room in his house and that she had not found any indication of spirits inhabiting them. Lady Cornelia could enter his home without fear. She thanked him for his hospitality and hoped she would see him in the future so that she could offer her apology in person.

He ran a fingertip across her signature. She had not explained why she had appealed to Corbin for help instead of coming to him, but he knew the answer. Corbin was a longtime friend and Ellery was just another person who doubted what she did. How close were Corbin and Miss Grayson, he wondered. He also questioned the feelings that rose in him when he had watched the two of them together.

It could not be jealousy, for he had not known her

long enough to even begin to consider her more than an acquaintance. He did admit to an attraction to her, though. She was an attractive woman who possessed a clever mind. The very mystery of whether the spirits were real or figments of her rich imagination was also compelling, daring a man to prove the right or wrong of it. Desire for a woman was a common enough experience for Ellery and he settled on it for an answer, mostly because it did not alarm him.

Comforted that he had found a suitable explanation for his emotions, he continued dressing for his ride.

A short time later he was in the park, urging his mount into a gallop along the deserted pathways. A figure appeared ahead of him and he nearly pulled his stallion to a halt to avoid an encounter. Realizing his foolishness, he slowed his pace and came up beside Lord Corbin.

"You're out early this morning," said Corbin, glancing sideways at him.

Ellery decided to be candid. "I was awakened when your coach arrived."

Corbin smiled faintly. "I'm sorry to have disturbed you. I hope it didn't awaken the rest of the household.

"Miss Grayson was with you," said Ellery, stating the obvious.

"There was a crisis at Vanessa's home and she needed to get there quickly," explained Corbin.

Ellery noticed his use of Miss Grayson's first name and did not like it at all. "She would have been welcome to my coach had she let me know."

"Vanessa has always been an independent person and does not accept help easily. If she had not been so concerned for her family, I am certain she would have hired a coach rather than asking for mine. In any event, she would have considered it too great an imposition to have called upon you."

"She would have been wrong," Ellery argued stubbornly. "I find her to be an agreeable young lady and my aunt is quite fond of her."

From the sound of Trent's voice, Corbin judged that he also found Vanessa agreeable and wondered what his intentions would have been if Vanessa had not left his house in such a rush. Corbin knew Trent to be an honorable man, but when a woman as attractive as Vanessa was involved, honor was sometimes forgotten.

"I have known her for many years and I would do whatever I could for her." It would not hurt to allow Trent to see that Vanessa was not alone in the world.

"She left me a message," revealed Ellery, too proud to admit she did not reveal the reason that had caused her to leave so abruptly. It galled him to ask anything of Corbin, but he did. "Do you know of anything I can do for her?"

"Nothing at the moment," replied Corbin. "I offered, but she knew so little about the problem that she could not decide on an action until she reached home."

"Will you get in touch with me if you hear from her?" asked Ellery.

Corbin felt a bit of sympathy for the man. "I will," he answered shortly.

"I must get back," said Ellery. "My aunt will be upset when she finds Miss Grayson is gone and I must be there to calm her."

Corbin nodded and Ellery turned his horse, retracing the path to the entrance to the park and out into the nearly deserted streets of London.

"She has gone," said Lady Venable when Ellery entered her small sitting room.

"I had hoped to be the one to tell you," he said, taking a seat next to her.

"My maid gave me this as soon as I awakened," she said, indicating a note and a small package in her lap.

"What does it say?" he asked.

"She apologized for leaving so quickly, but said she was needed at home at once. And she thanked me for being kinder to her than was necessary. What a sweet girl." She lapsed into silence, staring down at the letter she held.

"Is that all?"

"What? Yes, all of any import. She left a gift that she made particularly for me." Lady Venable folded back the tissue paper and revealed a fine lawn handkerchief of lavender, trimmed in lavender lace and a narrow purple ribbon. Lady Venable's initials were embroidered elaborately in one corner along with a small violet.

"She has been working on that for some time."

"Long before she came here, that's to be sure," agreed Lady Venable. "I felt an immediate bond with her and she must have felt the same for me or else she would not have spent her spare time embroidering this."

"I am not surprised she is fond of you," said Ellery, patting her hand. "I'm certain Miss Grayson will call on you when she returns to London."

"If she returns." Lady Venable sniffed. "Suppose whatever happened keeps her in the country."

"Then I shall take you to visit her. It is not so far away and I'm certain we could find an inn nearby where we could stay while you called on her."

Charity looked at him, her expression brightening considerably. "That would be wonderful," she said, clearly cheered by his suggestion.

"Miss Grayson also left a message for me," he disclosed. "She has declared the house free from spirits and says Cornelia may visit without fear."

Lady Venable did not respond immediately and when she did it was with a tepid "That's nice."

"You don't like Cornelia, do you?" he asked.

"There is something about her," his aunt replied slowly. "Outwardly, she seems to be the perfect lady. She is lovely and dresses to the nines, but when I look into her eyes there is something missing. I believe that she is a cold woman despite her pretensions toward affection for you."

"You mean you do not think she is capable of loving me?"

"Every woman in the *ton* would welcome the chance," she teased, finally smiling at him. "You are the object of Cornelia's interest, that is clear, but I question whether the emotions she attempts to shower on you are sincere."

"It would not be the first time a woman pursued a man without love being an issue."

"You cannot tell me anything about love and marriage that I don't already know. But I have always wished yours would be a marriage beginning with love between you and your bride. There is nothing to prevent you from choosing any woman for your wife. I hope you will choose with your heart."

Unlike many men, Ellery always took his aunt's advice seriously. She was right to think that his and Cornelia's would not be a love match if it occurred. He had initially been taken by her pale beauty; her blond hair, ice blue eyes, and tall slim figure were her best attributes. She had made no attempt to disguise that she was immediately attracted to him and he was flattered by her overt attention since the first time they had met.

Aunt Charity was right though. Other than admiration for her looks, his deeper feelings had not been touched by her. He had wondered whether he had become jaded after all the years of being pursued by the young ladies who came out each Season, searching for a husband. His doubts had been put to rest, however, once he met Miss Grayson.

How he could feel anything for a woman who professed to speak to spirits, he did not know. What he finally acknowledged was that he desired her. The truth had begun to dawn on him as he watched Corbin touch her cheek that morning. It had heightened when he realized that she had not turned to him for assistance.

As he had ridden home from Hyde Park, he admitted to himself that he had wanted to be the one touching her, helping her into the coach, climbing in after her, and shutting out the rest of the world while they traveled to her home. He wanted to be at her side, facing whatever had happened to disturb her so.

Ellery did not make the mistake of assuming it was love, but he had never wanted a woman as he wanted the Spirit Lady. Max would no doubt contend it was merely the chase for someone denied to him and he might be right, but Ellery was in no mood to be impartial in his feelings toward Miss Grayson at the moment.

"Ellery?" said Lady Venable. "Have you fallen asleep? I know you went out entirely too early this morning."

"I am wide awake and considering your words," he said, rising to his feet.

"As usual your observations are acute and I will take them into serious consideration. Now, if you will excuse me, I believe I will visit Gentleman Jack's establishment." Where I will take out my aggression on some poor soul, he added silently.

Vanessa's hands were clenched tightly in her lap as the large black traveling coach rolled through the parched countryside. The heat of the past weeks was extracting a toll even here in the country. Dust thickly coated each side of the road, deposited there by the passing of other vehicles, and Corbin's coach added another layer to the collection.

If Vanessa had noticed, she would have seen that the fields were browning and the animals had retreated into what shade they could find. Even the leaves of the largest trees were drooping under the continuous assault of the fiery orb that blazed down on them from the time it rose in the morning until its merciful dip below the horizon at twilight.

But she noticed nothing beyond the windows of the coach, thinking only of Melanie and her fate. Annie's note had been so brief that it told her nothing more, and no matter how she reassured herself, Vanessa imagined the worst that could happen.

The coachman changed horses twice during their journey since the pace they were setting in the heat was too much to ask of the animals for any length of time. No matter how fast they traveled, it was still far too slow for Vanessa.

Despite her belief that she would never reach home, the coach pulled up in front of her house before the day was gone. Annie ran from the house to meet her, sobbing in her arms.

"She's gone, Miss Vanessa. Our Melanie's gone."

"Collect yourself," ordered Vanessa, patting her on the back. "You must tell me what has happened 'else I can do nothing."

Remembering the coachman and horses, she turned back. "Can we give you food and drink?"

"No, thank ye, ma'am. I'm to stop at the inn for the night and travel back tomorrow on Lord Corbin's instructions."

"You have my thanks," she said to him. He touched his cap and turned the coach, allowing the horses to walk down the road toward the village inn.

"Now, Annie," she said to the woman, who was rubbing the tears from her eyes, "what happened?"

Annie spoke as she led the way back to the house. "It was about midmorning yesterday. Little Jonathan had kept Melanie up most of the night, so I brought him out into the yard so that she could sleep. I didn't mean to stay long, but the baby seemed to be comfortable so I just . . ." She began to cry again.

"You did nothing wrong, Annie," Vanessa said, attempting to console the woman.

"Well, it was time to feed him and I brought him back in. The house was still quiet so I tiptoed into Melanie's room to see whether she was awake. That's when I found she was gone. I searched the house and when I reached the sitting room—well, you had better see for yourself."

They had reached the hall while Annie was explaining. She preceded Vanessa into the sitting room and walked to a small desk set beneath a window. It was a pleasant place to sit while answering correspondence and gazing out over what was normally a verdant meadow.

There was a single piece of paper laying on the polished rosewood surface. Vanessa read the five words scrawled there and her body turned to ice despite the heat of the day. She had no doubt that Melanie had written the message for she had taught her sister to write. "Take care of the baby" was all that she had written, or perhaps been allowed to write, for there was a line of ink across the paper where the pen had been dropped and rolled to the floor.

"Have you done anything at all?" she asked, still staring at the note.

"Nate and I searched as well as we could, but I didn't know whether you wanted to alert the neighborhood or not, so I sent for you as fast as I could."

"You did the right thing, Annie. I don't think Melanie would willingly leave her baby. But why would anyone force her to leave?"

"Do you think it was the baby's father?" asked Annie. "She mentioned going to Gretna Green to be married."

"But, surely, she would take her child or let you know," reasoned Vanessa.

"The weather would be hard on the baby," replied Annie. "Maybe she didn't plan on being gone long and felt better leaving him behind."

"It's possible, I suppose," said Vanessa, attempting to order her jumbled thoughts into some coherence. "If she did go to get married, why make such a secret of it? There would have been no reason not to have told you what she was going to do and to discuss little Jonathan's care while she was gone."

"Perhaps she meant to surprise us," suggested Annie.

"Perhaps," murmured Vanessa, but in her heart she did not believe it.

"What are you going to do?" Annie asked.

"I am going to think about it before I decide on any action. We must approach this clear-headed and not allow ourselves to fall into a panic."

"You must be hungry after that trip," said Annie, falling back on her favorite remedy—a good meal.

Vanessa had not been able to swallow a bit of breakfast even though Lord Trent's cook had urged her to do so. Nor had she been able to eat at any of the stops the coach had made on her way home. Now her stomach was reminding her that it needed sustenance.

"Don't go to any trouble," she said, still preoccupied with Melanie's disappearance. "Whatever you have on hand will do."

Annie bustled out of the room, leaving Vanessa at the desk, staring at the note. While she could not completely accept Annie's version of an elopement, it was the only thing that came anywhere to near explaining Melanie's absence.

They were not rich enough to be targeted by kidnappers and Vanessa could think of no other reason Melanie would be forcibly taken from their home.

"Come and eat something," said Annie from the doorway.

Vanessa chose to eat in a small room off the kitchen. The women often ate there rather than in the larger dining room.

Vanessa took a slice of ham, some fresh asparagus and a stuffed egg. She forced herself to eat the food in its entirety because she knew she could not afford to become ill and also to appease Annie, who watched over her like a hen with its last chick.

There was only one thing that Vanessa truly enjoyed. "The muffins are perfection," she said, spreading fresh-churned butter over one before she took another bite. "I miss them terribly when I am away."

"You have liked them since you were a child," said Annie, smiling at the remembrance. "And so did Melanie. She said she couldn't wait until Jonathan was big enough to taste one." Tears gathered in her eyes again and she dabbed at them with the corner of her apron.

"Don't cry anymore," begged Vanessa. "As you say, Melanie has probably eloped and in her usual fashion she did not stop to think about how we would react."

"Oh, Miss Vanessa, I pray you are right."

"We will wait a week before doing anything more," said Vanessa. "I know that is a long time, but if Melanie has eloped I do not want to embarrass her by asking around the neighborhood about her. If she has not returned in a sennight, then I shall begin inquiries."

"Can't we do anything more?" asked Annie.

Vanessa closed her eyes and considered the problem. "Perhaps there is one thing," she said, opening her eyes and looking up at Annie. "Lord Corbin offered to do anything he could to help. He has contacts everywhere. I will write and ask him if he could inquire discreetly at Gretna Green whether anyone answering Melanie's description has been wed there."

"If you will write the letter tonight, I will take it to the

village in the morning and it will be in London by tomorrow night."

"I hope it will yield positive results for this will be the
longest week of my life," remarked Vanessa, rising from
the table and returning to the sitting room, where she
once again was forced to face Melanie's last words.

Time passed slowly for the two women even though
they had the baby to keep them occupied. When they
did hear from Lord Corbin it was not by letter, but came
in the form of his large black traveling coach carrying
Corbin with another man accompanying him.

"There was no need to come yourself," protested Vanessa. "A letter would have sufficed."

"Melanie is also a friend of mine, and I will do anything to see her safe. This is Mr. James Browning, who
is a business acquaintance."

Even though Vanessa thought it strange he should
bring a businessman along with him, she greeted him
and invited them both into the house. After they were
settled in the sitting room, Corbin leaned forward and
took her hands in his.

"I'm sorry to say that there was no news of Melanie
in Gretna Green."

Annie gave a cry from where she stood in the door,
holding Jonathan.

Corbin glanced over at her and his eyes narrowed
when he spied the baby, but he made no comment.

Vanessa swallowed several times, but still could not
speak. She had been counting on Corbin's being successful in his endeavors. She had wanted more than anything to find Melanie at Gretna Green. She would have
accepted her marriage to a stranger if only her sister
had been safe. Now her last hope had been shattered
and she did not know where to turn next.

"I don't want you to despair," said Corbin, squeezing her hands lightly. There is a reason Browning is here. He is a former Bow Street Runner and has worked for me many times in the past. He is excellent at what he does and I have hired him to search for Melanie."

"I don't know," she said, never feeling so uncertain in her life.

"Let me do this for you and for Melanie. Nothing is more important right now than finding her and bringing her home safe."

"What do you think could have happened to her?" she asked, glancing from Corbin to Browning.

"There's no way to tell right now," answered Browning. "I'll want to talk to you and to your maid to see if there's a clue. Then I'll widen the circle until I find someone who has seen her."

"Is it possible?" asked Vanessa, hope attempting to flicker to life in her heart.

"Most assuredly," he said confidently. "If we were in London it would be nearly impossible to find anyone who had seen a specific person on a particular day. However, here in the country the passage of a coach or strangers arriving in a neighborhood is uncommon enough to be noted and remembered. At least, for a short period of time."

"When will you begin?" she asked.

"Immediately if your maid feels up to talking with me."

"I'll do whatever it takes," said Annie. "If you come through to the kitchen, I'll see you have something to eat. You, too, Lord Corbin."

"You go ahead, Browning. We will join you in a few minutes."

Browning rose and followed Annie through the door into the hallway.

"You do not have any more bad news, do you?" inquired Vanessa.

Corbin finally released her hands and leaned back in his chair. "None whatsoever," he replied. "I wanted to ask you to return to London with me."

"What? I can't leave here with Melanie still missing."

"Vanessa, you will go into a decline if you have nothing to do but sit here day and night and worry about Melanie."

"I have never been in a decline in my life and I am not so poor-spirited to do so now," she shot back.

"You will not be able to help yourself," he insisted. "You cannot do anything here but worry."

"I can take care of little Jonathan," she said.

"Annie is more than able to take care of the baby. You'll recall she raised both you and Melanie without any help. And by the way, why is it that I must travel all this way to find you have a baby in the household?"

He sounded disgruntled and Vanessa sought to explain it to him.

"I only discovered Melanie was increasing shortly before she gave birth. We were attempting to keep it quiet for as long as possible. Melanie swore that the father was going to return and marry her. That is why I thought she might have eloped to Gretna Green," Vanessa explained. "In any event, I did not feel that I could reveal her situation without her permission. I would have told you if it had been at all possible. In fact, it was extremely difficult for me to carry the weight of that knowledge without sharing it with anyone."

Corbin's face softened. "I wish I could have made things easier for you."

"You have done more than I ever expected," she said. "I cannot thank you enough for bringing Mr. Browning. I will admit I did not know which way to turn next. You must tell me how much to pay him."

"I will take care of the matter," he said.

"I will not take charity," she replied proudly. "I can pay my own debts."

"I do not doubt you in the least, but at least allow me to deal with Browning and then I will tell you the cost when everything is over."

Vanessa grudgingly agreed, thinking that she might never know the full amount paid to the man; however, she was too grateful to Corbin for bringing Mr. Browning to argue.

"Now back to the issue at hand," he said. "I want you to take advantage of my coach and return to Town with me. Browning will report what he finds out directly to us and we will be close enough to make decisions without making the trip from Town. That is if you want me to stay involved."

"Of course, I do," she replied promptly. "I did not know where to turn until you arrived and while I am not a weak person, I am out of my depth here."

"Then come back with me," he said again. "We will pay Nate to stay here with Annie and the baby so you will know that they are safe. I do not think anything will happen to them or it would have occurred the same time Melanie went missing."

"Annie will feel safer if Nate is here," Vanessa agreed. "And if Melanie should happen to return, Nate could come as quickly as he did before."

"I could have some of my men sent down to guard the house if it would make you feel better."

"No. I agree that there is probably no threat to Annie or Jonathan. And while she is accustomed to Nate, I believe that she would not like having strangers watching her every move."

"Then you will come?" he asked.

"I must discuss it with Annie first," she said. "If she is comfortable with the arrangements then I will go back to Town. If I am to pay Mr. Browning, I will need every bit I can earn."

"I've told you not to worry about Browning until this is all over. As soon as he is finished with Annie, you must talk to her. If she agrees, I will spend the night at the inn and we can return to London in the morning."

"So soon?"

"There is no reason to stay," he replied gently. "Melanie is not here."

"You are right," she agreed. "But sometimes I think I can hear her singing to the baby."

"Then it's time for you to get away," he concluded. "Let's have a glass of sherry while we are waiting and recall better times."

Seven

"Where is my nephew?" demanded Lady Venable as soon as she entered the door of the town house.

"I am unsure of his exact whereabouts, my lady, but he is at home," said the butler.

"Find him, Thomas. It is of the utmost importance that I see him immediately. I shall wait in the drawing room." She sailed past him and through the double doors. Removing her hat and gloves, she tossed them on a conveniently located table, nearly knocking over an arrangement of pale pink roses. "Serves them right for not being purple," she mumbled, and began pacing restlessly around the room.

Just as she was ready to go search out Ellery herself, he strolled into the room. "What has you up in the boughs?" he asked curiously.

"It took you long enough," she complained. "I have news for you."

"You always do," he said, smiling.

"This is not my usual gossip," she replied, with a haughty expression.

"Well, do not keep me on pins and needles, tell me what it is," he urged.

"Vanessa—that is what she urged me to call her before she left Town," Lady Venable took the time to explain. "Vanessa is here."

"Here where?" asked Ellery, looking around the room in order to hide his own excitement.

"Do not tease me," she said. "You understand perfectly well what I mean. I have it on good authority that she is in London and is presently at Lord and Lady Bowden's home."

"Do you know when she returned?"

"Not that it matters, but I believe it was only yesterday afternoon."

"Corbin told me he would let me know if he heard from her."

"Perhaps they have not been in touch with one another," said Lady Venable.

"I cannot believe that he would not know she was in Town."

"Even if he was aware of it, you can't condemn the man for not running to you the moment she arrived. Perhaps he is taken with her and does not want another man around," she suggested, closely watching her nephew's face for his reaction.

"They have been friends since childhood," he said.

"All the more reason for him to care for her. He must know her well enough to realize that she would make an excellent wife."

"Why are you taking up for the man?"

"I am always on the side of true love," she said.

His aunt's words caused him to remember the scene he had observed in the mews on the morning of Miss Grayson's departure. He reminded himself that he only desired the woman. If Corbin wanted to marry the chit, then Ellery would leave him to it.

"I'm happy your friend is back," he said evenly.

"Is that all you have to say?" she asked incredulously.

"You know that I think she might know something about Phillip and I am anxious to make contact with her again. Perhaps you can help me arrange what will appear to be an accidental encounter repeated."

Lady Venable knew her nephew well enough to see that he was not as impervious to the news of Vanessa's return as he wanted her to believe. After being around her, Lady Venable was not convinced that Vanessa could have acted to harm Phillip. One thing she did know was that Vanessa was much more suited to Ellery than Cornelia and she meant to do what she could to switch her nephew's attention to the Spirit Lady.

"We shall do exactly what we did before. I will call on Lady Bowden and you will accompany me. You can be forthright this time. Tell Lady Bowden that Miss Grayson has declared your town house free from spirits and you would like to have her do the same for your country estate. You might even mention Lady Cornelia's concern. She should have no reason to begrudge a few minutes of her time spent with you arranging the details."

"Aunt, you should be working for the Home Office. Not only is your suggestion an excellent one, but I will truly offer an invitation to Miss Grayson to visit the country. I had previously mentioned to her that I was planning a house party and I will even invite her good friend Corbin to entice her even more."

"What is your objective, Ellery?" asked Lady Venable.

"As it always has been—to find Phillip. If Corbin and Miss Grayson are at my estate, I will find it much easier to watch them, and perhaps I can get to know both of them better. They may lower their guard in such a setting and say something that will help locate Phillip."

"I cannot believe that either of them is involved in this whole Hell-Fire Club thing," she fussed.

"Outward appearances can be deceptive," said Ellery.

"I suppose you expect me to cut short my stay in Town and chaperone at your house party."

"I could not do it without you. Besides the Little Season will be here before you know it and I will guarantee that you will have a new wardrobe of purples that will stun the eye."

"You know exactly what to say to persuade me," said Lady Venable.

"Then I will assure Miss Grayson that you will be there. You should invite anyone you choose, of course. I would like a sizable party for I will be able to move about more easily with a larger number of people."

"Perhaps I will invite the Halburtons. Vanessa and Susan got along quite well. When do you expect to travel to the country?"

"Soon," he said. "The heat is already driving some people from Town early. Shall we say Thursday next? That should give everyone time to make their plans."

"I will begin making a list immediately and send the invitations tomorrow."

"I'm going out to see whether I can accidentally run into Corbin. It will be interesting to hear why he didn't get in touch with me as promised."

"Now, Ellery, you must be nice if you expect him to come to your house party," warned Lady Venable, sounding as if he were a young boy asking another out to play.

"I would do nothing to turn Corbin away," he assured her. "Too much rests with him."

Ellery called for his phaeton. He heard it come to a stop in front of the house, accepted his hat and gloves from Thomas, and went out the front door. He was surprised to see that it was Corbin who had arrived and was ready to climb down from his curricle.

"I have come to bring you news of Miss Grayson," said Corbin, settling back into the curricle.

"She is back in Town," stated Ellery.

"How the devil did you know? She just got back yesterday afternoon."

"My aunt knows everything nearly the moment that

it happens. I understand that she is at the Bowdens' home."

"That's true," agreed Corbin. "This was the earliest I could get by to tell you."

"Thank you. Lady Venable and I are going to call on Lady Bowden and I hope to see her then. I'm planning a house party at my country estate and wanted to invite both Miss Grayson and you. I hope she will agree to search for spirits while we are there. We will travel down Thursday next or whenever is convenient for you."

Corbin gave the invitation some thought. He knew the location of Trent's country estate and it would fit in nicely with the activities he had committed himself to attending. It would also keep him close to Vanessa. He was confident she would accept Trent's request to search for spirits for she meant to earn as much as she could to be able to afford the search for Melanie.

"I have a good trout stream, which should keep us cool at this time of year," Ellery said.

"It sounds like just the thing," replied Corbin. "This heat is making life unbearable here in Town."

"It may not be cooler there, but we won't have the smoke and soot and perhaps it will rain soon."

"I will look forward to it," said Corbin, thinking that Trent's house party had come at an advantageous time.

"Good. I will send you directions. If you would like to drive down at the same time, we will arrange to meet. Otherwise, you should arrive whenever it is convenient for you," instructed Ellery, thinking everything was working out exactly as planned.

Late the next morning found Lady Venable and Ellery in Lady Bowden's drawing room.

"It is so good to see both of you," said Lady Bowden.

"There are not many men who would take the time to accompany their aunt on making rounds."

"Ellery is an exceptional nephew," said Lady Venable, both praising and embarrassing him simultaneously.

"I do have another reason for being here in addition to the pleasure of seeing you again," Ellery said to Lady Bowden.

"I should have known," she replied with a good-natured smile. "What favor can I do for you?"

"I would like to speak with Miss Grayson for a few minutes. I have been wanting her to search my country home for spirits and I have not been able to catch up with her to make my request."

"It's no wonder; she has been out of Town. Some kind of family crisis, I believe, although she has not mentioned it to me. But, of course, you are welcome to speak with her. She is somewhere in the house, but I am not certain where. She just wanders about listening, I think." Lady Bowden's brow furrowed. "Such an odd way to earn an living, but then she is all the rage."

"She certainly is," agreed Lady Venable. "And you are lucky to have gotten her this Season."

"Yes, I suppose I am," acknowledged Lady Bowden, nearly smirking with satisfaction. She looked up at Ellery, who was patiently waiting for her to remember him. "You must ask the butler where she is; I'm certain he will know."

"Thank you, my lady," said Ellery, turning back to the hall while the ladies began their endless exchange of gossip.

He found her in a small sitting room on the first floor of the house. She was sitting in a chair, her eyes closed. He stood at the door for a moment studying her. She appeared so innocent that he wondered why he thought she would be capable of being involved with either the Hell-Fire Club or Phillip's disappearance.

She seemed more frail than when he had last seen her. Her face was pale against the dark print of the chair and she looked as if she had lost weight in the days she had been gone. He wondered what had happened at home to have sent her running back to the country in such haste. He would not ask Corbin and he did not know whether to broach the subject with Miss Grayson. She might think it none of his business and take such umbrage that she would refuse to accept an engagement at his country estate.

"Would you like to come in, Lord Trent?" she asked, then opened her eyes.

"I suppose I shouldn't wonder that you knew I was here," he said, stepping into the room.

"It's nothing magical. You have a heavy tread."

Ellery smiled. "That is one thing that I've never been accused of before."

"There is no shame in it unless you are a thief and then you would be caught as soon as you attempted to sneak into a room."

"Then I am glad I am not forced to rob for a living."

"Did Lady Bowden tell you I was here?"

"No. My aunt heard that you had arrived back in town and she had a sudden urge to visit Lady Bowden."

Vanessa brightened a bit. "I wonder whether Lady Bowden would mind if I said hello to your aunt. I feel guilty leaving as abruptly as I did and would like to apologize to her—and to you, too, of course."

"An apology isn't necessary, but I'm certain Aunt Charity would be happy to see you. I hope your problem was settled satisfactorily," he added, wondering whether she would confide in him.

"I am working on it," she replied, ambiguously. "But I do thank you for asking."

He was disappointed, even though he did not expect her to pour out her troubles to him. "If there is anything

I can do to help, I hope you know I will be happy to assist in any way I can."

"You are too kind, but I'm afraid there is nothing more to be done," she replied, rising and moving to the window, staring down at the small back garden and mews behind.

He joined her, startling her as his shoulder brushed hers.

"Perhaps your tread is not as heavy as I thought."

"Are you saying I could be a successful thief, after all?"

"I would need more than this one instance to determine your ability for the life of a successful burglar."

He was encouraged that she was not so down-pinned that she could not respond to his bantering. He turned to her and she looked up, meeting his gaze. Her eyes were golden in the light coming through the window and he was mesmerized by them. All thought of what she might be disappeared from his mind and he found himself nearly whispering to her.

"I feel that something is gravely wrong and I don't want you to suffer." He leaned toward her and she closed her eyes. He pressed his lips against her temple. "Tell me what is bothering you," he murmured, nuzzling the wisps of hair that curled around her face. He traced a line with his lips to the delicate shell of her ear where he allowed himself a small taste of her.

Her breathing quickened and he knew he must kiss her, must test the softness of her lips, which were slightly parted, seeming to invite his own to match hers. He could feel the feather-soft touch of her breath on his cheek as his lips gently brushed hers.

She surprised him by leaning into his embrace and he took her gently into his arms, feeling the slightness of her figure through the thin muslin gown she wore.

The kiss became more insistent and she met his demand by giving herself more fully, sliding her arms around him, up under the back of his jacket, her fingers spreading over the hard muscles, which were rigid with suppressed tension.

Suddenly she pulled away, looking up as if surprised to see him there, to find herself standing compliantly in his arms. A blush rose to her face as she pulled away.

"You must find me too coming by half," she murmured, her gaze directed toward the floor.

He placed a finger under her chin and tilted her face until she was looking at him again. "I find you altogether delightful," he replied, his voice dropping a note.

"I don't do this . . ."

"I know you don't," he said, interrupting her. "There is no need to be embarrassed. This happens every day between men and women and the world continues on its course."

His gentle teasing caused her to smile. He was right; there must be numerous women all over Town who had shared a kiss with him. It was no doubt common among the *ton,* for unlike herself, he seemed entirely unmoved by it.

She gathered her composure and spoke as normally as she was able. "Perhaps we had best go find Lady Venable."

"I have not yet told you why I came to seek you out."

She raised a dainty arched brow at him.

"It is nothing outlandish," he promised. "I am holding a house party at my country estate and thought it would be an excellent time for you to travel down and search for spirits there."

She opened her mouth to refuse, but he stopped her before she could speak.

"Before you answer, let me tell you that Corbin is going to be there, as will Aunt Charity and the Halburtons. The guest list has not been drawn up but I'm certain there will be others with whom you are acquainted so you should not feel uncomfortable.

"Aunt Charity is greatly looking forward to it and sent me to invite you. She threatened all manner of horrible fates if I did not return with your consent."

"You are bamming me," said Vanessa, accusingly.

"Perhaps I am overstating the danger," he admitted, "but she will be exceedingly disappointed if you are not there. And as I told you, I will double your fee if you will search the house for me."

"You were too generous for what little I did at the town house," she replied.

"I always keep my word."

Vanessa thought of the fee she would owe Browning for searching for Melanie and knew that she could not afford to turn down Lord Trent's offer. It would not be so bad, spending some time in the country in the company of Lady Venable. And she would be much closer to home; perhaps she could take time to see little Jonathan and Annie while she was there.

"I must finish with Lady Bowden before I do anything else. When will your house party begin?"

"We will travel down to the country Thursday next. I'm certain that Aunt Charity will want you to travel in her coach. If you finish here before Thursday, then you must come and stay with us again."

"I cannot continue imposing upon you, my lord. There are rooms I can rent if need be. I have done it before and fared very well indeed."

"I won't have it," he said, a trace of anger in his voice.

"It is not for you to say," she replied stubbornly.

He nearly reached out for her, wanting to convince her with his kisses that she would be much better off beneath his roof. But he controlled his impulse and merely said, "If not for me, then for Aunt Charity. She would be hurt beyond all reason if you chose a rented room over keeping her company."

"You are a shameless schemer, but I cannot refuse your plea for Lady Venable's sake."

Relief flooded through Ellery. He had convinced her. "Shall we go tell Aunt Charity the good news?" he asked, holding out his arm to her.

She took his arm and they went down the hall and descended the stairs; all the while Vanessa was questioning whether she had done the right thing by accepting the invitation. It was true she would be working, but Lord Trent had made it clear he also expected her to take part in the house party as a guest.

She did not like the way she was beginning to feel each time she was near the earl. There was no future for the two of them even had he indicated he wanted one. He was merely amusing himself with her. She was certain that the kiss—which had shaken her to the core—had meant nothing to him.

She would go to the house party and search out his country spirits if he had any, she decided, but that would be the extent of their association. She could not preach to Melanie without following her own counsel.

"I was so looking forward to Vanessa's company on the trip to the country. Not that you are not company enough," Lady Venable added quickly.

"Miss Grayson would have been a good traveling companion for you," Ellery agreed, as he handed his aunt into the traveling coach. "But she said she wished to go home before she joined us in the country. There is some trouble of a personal nature which she will not confide, even though I offered assistance."

"Vanessa is a proud young woman," observed Lady

Venable. "I believe it would be difficult for her to admit she could not handle whatever arises in her life."

"A person can be too proud," muttered Ellery.

Lady Venable heard his comment. "You certainly are not one to be critical of that fault," she remarked. "Why I remember . . ."

"It isn't necessary to unearth my every youthful mistake and examine it," grumbled Ellery. Seating himself beside his aunt, he knocked on the ceiling of the coach with his silver-headed cane to alert the coachman they were ready to leave. The horses leaned into their harnesses and the coach rolled through London while many people were still abed.

"When is Cornelia going to arrive?" asked Lady Venable. "I'm surprised she didn't insist on coming with us."

"Tomorrow, I believe. She did not want to miss some event or another this evening. She will be traveling with Barbara Lambert and her parents."

"They are close to Cornelia, are they not?"

"They introduced her into society when she returned to England from France," said Ellery. "I believe Lady Barbara's father was acquainted with Cornelia's parents."

"I know little about Cornelia's background," commented his aunt.

"From what I understand, there is little to know. Her mother died when she was young and her father sent her to live with relatives in France. He died not long after that and she stayed in France until she came of age. When both the aunt and uncle who had raised her passed on, she took what she had inherited from them and from her father and returned to England. She had evidently corresponded with the Lamberts and they opened their home to her when she arrived."

"They are generous people," said Lady Venable. "But

I'll wager Lady Cornelia will not be with them long. If you do not offer for her, there are others who will be at the ready."

"Why everyone has determined that I am going to step into the parson's mousetrap with Cornelia, I do not know," he complained.

"Only because your actions have led them to believe it," she replied calmly. "You are seen with her everywhere and she certainly displays a proprietary air whenever she is around you."

"She has no reason to do so," he protested.

"She has every right to," argued Lady Venable. "And you do nothing to dispel her presumption. It has only been recently that you resent people assuming the two of you are smelling of April and May."

"We are doing nothing of the sort," said Ellery, defending himself.

"Then why did you invite her to the house party and why are you having Vanessa search for spirits in the country?" When he did not answer, she answered for him. "Because Cornelia vowed she would not stay under your roof until you did."

"I could not insult her by not issuing an invitation, but you should not presume any more than what it is."

A sulky expression appeared on his face—one that he often had as a boy when he did not get his way—so Lady Venable decided it would be prudent to allow the matter to drop for the moment.

"There will be quite a large party when they all arrive. Unless you have invited someone else, the last count I made was a total of twenty-eight."

"We could have twice that many and still have room in that pile of rocks we call home," he said, smiling fondly.

"I hope the staff was able to do a complete airing with such short notice," fussed Lady Venable. "It is so easy for such a large place to smell musty if not used for any length of time."

"Considering the size of our staff, it should always be ready for occupancy."

Ellery rapped on the top of the coach again, signaling the driver to stop. "I believe that I will ride for a while since we are out of the city." He opened the door and stepped down to take his horse from the groom that had followed behind them.

"Tell the coachman to drive as smoothly as he can," instructed Lady Venable. "I intend to catch up on my sleep before we arrive."

Ellery mounted his stallion and passed the coach, riding on ahead. He needed solitude in order to consider everything that was unsettled in his life.

Vanessa had taken advantage of the time between when she left Lord and Lady Bowden's and the beginning of Lord Trent's house party to make a quick trip home.

She was pleased to find little Jonathan thriving under Annie's excellent care. Nate was still staying at the house, watching over the two.

"Have you seen Mr. Browning?" she asked Annie.

"Not for some days. He hadn't discovered anything the last time he was here."

"I wonder whether I am wasting money keeping him on. Perhaps I should try something else."

"And what would that be?" inquired Annie.

"I don't know," she admitted dispiritedly.

"Lord Corbin believes in this man," Annie pointed out.

"I know, but I feel so helpless sitting here doing nothing."

"There's nothing else either of us can do. We must

trust that Mr. Browning knows his business well enough to help us."

"I can only stay until Thursday, Annie. I have been engaged to search Lord Trent's country home for spirits. I wouldn't go, but I think I will need every shilling I can earn to pay Browning"

"Don't fret, Miss Vanessa. I know you'd be here if you could, but there is nothing to be gained by it. Go while you can, for when Miss Melanie comes home I know you will want to be here."

"You have enough faith for both of us, Annie."

A wail broke the silence of the house and both women hurried into the next room, where little Jonathan stared up at them with the exact replica of his mother's eyes.

"I will leave early Thursday morning," said Vanessa, picking up the baby. "It is not as far to Lord Trent's estate as it is to London. I should arrive sometime that afternoon. I will leave directions should you need to get in touch with me."

"We'll be fine," said Annie to console her. "Nate is on watch night and day so we are well looked after."

"When all this is over, we must do something to thank him," said Vanessa.

"The money you're paying him is more than enough," said Annie. "With the dry summer, the crops are not what they should be and this will enable his family to make it through the winter in comfort."

"Nevertheless, I will think of something more. Is there talk in the neighborhood about Melanie?"

"I haven't been anywhere to find out. Mr. Browning has been as careful as he could be, but I would imagine there are some questions being asked."

"Well, we will face them when the time comes," said Vanessa, sitting in the rocking chair with little Jonathan and beginning the soothing back-and-forth motion.

"I believe I will go to the village while you are here," said Annie.

"Take yourself off," instructed Vanessa. "You have been confined too long. For the few days I am here, I will take care of Jonathan and you must get out as much as possible."

Annie nodded and left the room to don her bonnet before taking the pony cart to the village a short distance away.

Vanessa rocked and cooed to Jonathan, who seemed entirely content to be the focus of her attention.

Lord Corbin was seated around a table at a country inn along with a dozen other men. They had just finished a plain but satisfying meal and were now lighting up cigars to go along with the brandy that was being poured.

He had been led to this secret meeting by two recent acquaintances and was unsure whether he would end up dressed in a devil's outfit or tied up as a sacrifice for the secret ceremony made famous by the Hell-Fire Club.

Neither had yet proven true, however, and he found himself dining with men who, no doubt, were involved in normal activities most of their days. Secret organizations tempted men, though, and he recognized that the ones in this room were here looking for more excitement than their usual lives offered.

The man who sat at the head of the table was a tall, slim, impeccably dressed gentleman. He was of middle age, with a full head of hair distinguished by splashes of silver at each temple. Corbin had seen him around Town but had never met him before this evening. He was James Colburn, Lord Thornhill, a man who often raised eyebrows for his unorthodox ways.

There were always rumors flying about the *ton* concerning him, but then the upper ten thousand were continually searching for outrageous actions to enliven their gossip. Corbin paid them little heed until he found that Thornhill was involved in the resurgence of the Hell-Fire Club.

It would be an activity that would come naturally to the man if even half of what was said about him was true. Last Season prostitutes began disappearing from an area of London. Their friends swore that the women did not leave of their own free will, but had met a man who matched Thornhill's description and then never returned.

One of the women was found floating in the Thames, her hands tied behind her back with a gentleman's cravat and stabbed a dozen times or more. Other atrocities had been practiced on her body, but they were too horrible to be repeated except in the men's club where the ladies' delicate feelings would not be disturbed. Not a sign of the other missing women was ever seen.

Thornhill went about his usual business throughout all the whispers and innuendo that accompanied the scandal. Not once did he address the matter of his resemblance to the man who was last seen with the women. Since there was no proof, except for the word of some hysterical streetwalkers, nothing official was ever done about the accusations.

There were murmurs of other aberrant behavior on behalf of Thornhill, some including young boys and girls off the streets of London; however, if it was true, none had been officially reported missing, nor had a hue and cry been taken up for Thornhill's head.

The man had come through every scandal broth without so much as a scrape and continued in his usual manner as if nothing at all had occurred.

They had been introduced when Corbin had first arrived and had spent several minutes exchanging pleasantries. Then Thornhill had been called aside by another man and Corbin had met the others who were present.

They were all titled men of more than moderate means and Corbin wondered that they were risking their good names to be here. But perhaps that was part of the excitement they derived from the club and its rituals.

Then Thornhill had risen and was speaking, his voice cutting through the smoke that swirled about the room. He greeted the men, then took a swallow of brandy before continuing.

"Some of you here tonight have not yet passed through the initiation and been sworn into the club. I know that you are eager to take your place beside us as full-fledged members and I beg you to be patient for a little longer."

Murmurs of unrest were heard around the table.

"It will not be for long, I promise you. Our leader needs to make further preparations in order for the initiation to be something none of us will forget."

"You mean you aren't the leader?" said Corbin.

"I am only second in command. There is someone far more qualified than I am. Someone younger, with more foresight and who has a compelling purpose to want the club to be successful this time," replied Thornhill. "You will meet the leader once you have been initiated into the club."

"And when will that be?" Corbin inquired.

"As soon as preparations are made," Thornhill answered sharply. "This is to be a special ceremony. One that will be remembered for years to come and it cannot be rushed. However, I have it on good account that it will occur within a fortnight. Each of you will be advised before the ceremony as to the time and place. Special instructions will be issued to those of you who will be initiated that evening.

"If any of you have doubts about going through with the ceremony, now is the time to speak. You will not be able to turn back once you have entered the ceremonial hall," he warned.

Corbin had no doubt as to what price would be paid by any poor soul foolish enough to attempt to reject membership at the last moment. This new Hell-Fire Club seemed far more deadly than the ones that had come before.

"I will be attending a house party for the next fortnight," said Corbin.

"Give me your direction before you leave and I will contact you there," instructed Thornhill. "Gentlemen, there is more brandy along with several prime articles waiting upstairs. I suggest you take advantage of both."

The men cheered, lifting their glasses to salute Thornhill's expert planning.

Corbin squinted his eyes against the smoke and hoped he had not gotten in too deep.

Eight

The coach slowed to turn into the drive at Lord Trent's estate and Vanessa peered from the window, curious to see the home the earl spoke about with such affection.

Huge trees blocked the view from the main road and it was only as they followed the drive through the park that the house was slowly revealed. The grounds were in excellent condition despite the dry weather. The drive was level and free from ruts, leading them over two bridges which spanned the same rock-bottomed stream that wandered through the grounds.

In the distance, Vanessa observed a lake with a small island in the middle where a summer house was invitingly situated.

Near a copse of trees, three deer lifted their heads and stared at the vehicle invading their solitude. Sensing no danger, they returned to grazing.

Vanessa could not believe her eyes as the house came into full view. It was enormous. Appearing to have been built onto from generation to generation, it sprawled in a particularly pleasing design over the land as if it had been there from the beginning of time.

It was built of stone, probably cut from a spot on the estate itself. The front of the house, which they were approaching, had a shallow flight of steps leading to a massive double door. The long windows which were spaced across the front sparkled in the afternoon sun.

Vanessa speculated that there were at least three floors and an attic looming over her as she stepped out of the coach. The doors opened immediately and Thomas, followed by four footmen garbed in the earl's livery, marched out of the house to greet her. She was ushered inside, while her trunks were unloaded and carried into the house.

The foyer was a marble-floored room unto itself. The walls were paneled in oak and two large fireplaces with carved mantels were placed on the right and left walls of the room. Directly in front of Vanessa was a wide staircase which rose gracefully from the front hall to the upper floors.

A woman bustled from the hall leading to the back of the house. "You must be Miss Grayson. I am Mary Gregory, the housekeeper. Lord Trent told me to especially watch for you either today or tomorrow. He will be disappointed, for he wanted to be here when you arrived."

"I need no special treatment," said Vanessa, still awed by the sheer size of the establishment.

"You are not the first to arrive. However, the others are resting after their journey. I will show you to your room where you can refresh yourself. I don't believe anything is planned until dinner, but feel free to make use of whatever you like. I will give you a tour later so that you will know where the library, the music room, and other places are located."

"I don't know whether Lord Trent told you that I will be working while I am here."

"Oh, yes," replied Mrs. Gregory, preceding her up the stairs. "He said you were going to see whether this pile of rocks had any spirits lurking about—his exact words." She did not seem at all distressed about what Vanessa was going to do. "I've no doubt you'll find someone hanging

about from years ago. There are enough creaks and
groans in the house for a whole passel of ghosts."

Mrs. Gregory led her down a wide hall. "This will be
your room," she said, stopping in front of a door, opening it, and stepping inside. "I hope you will be comfortable here."

Vanessa stepped though the door and looked around
the suite of rooms. There was a small sitting room and
bedroom, with a dressing room beyond. The rooms were
furnished with Louis Sieze furniture. A short sofa with
oval back and two armchairs were positioned in front of
the fireplace. The wooden arms, legs, and other trim
were expertly carved and the upholstery was a delicate
floral design. Several small tables with the same carving
were included in the grouping, with a small lady's *secre-
taire* at the side of the room.

In the next room, the bed had a high headboard with
a carved cresting in the middle; the legs and bedposts
were also carved and capped with acanthus leaves. An
embroidered canopy hung above the bed.

The carpets were thick and soft and mirrored the col-
ors of the furniture upholstery. Vanessa had never stayed
in such luxurious rooms.

"If you need anything at all, you can ask Delcie," said
Mrs. Gregory.

The girl who was already unpacking Vanessa's trunk
paused and gave a quick bob to Vanessa.

"She'll be your maid while you are here," continued
Mrs. Gregory.

"A maid isn't necessary," said Vanessa.

"I'm only following Lord Trent's orders, Miss Grayson.
You must deal with him if you don't want Delcie. I must
say, though, it's a good chance for her to move up to a
better position."

Vanessa did not want to be responsible for ruining Delcie's chance for advancement, so she said, "Delcie will be fine."

"I will have tea and cakes brought up. If you would like to bathe or have any other needs, tell Delcie and she will see to it. Now, I will leave you to your rest. The guests will meet in the large drawing room before dinner. Delcie will show you the way."

"Thank you, Mrs. Gregory. I'm certain I will be comfortable," said Vanessa. She breathed a sigh of relief when the door closed behind the housekeeper, then remembered Delcie was still unpacking in the bedroom.

The girl appeared in the doorway just as a knock sounded at the door. Delcie ran to open it, took a tea tray from another maid, and set it carefully on the table in front of the sofa.

"Will there be anything else, ma'am?"

"Nothing at the moment, Delcie."

"You must ring if you want anything," said the maid. "I'll be back in time to help you dress for dinner."

"That's very kind of you, Delcie."

The maid bobbed again and left the room.

Vanessa stood in the middle of the floor for a moment, listening to the silence until the fragrant tea drew her to the table. She sat and poured a cup, then took a bite of saffron cake while waiting for the tea to cool.

She did not know whether she could accustom herself to being waited on by an abundance of maids and housekeepers, but such delicious teas would be welcomed every day.

She sipped her tea and considered that once again she was beneath Lord Trent's roof. It did not feel as strange as it had the first time; perhaps she was becoming accustomed to the earl's company. Her face became warm as she thought again of the kiss they had shared and her reaction to it.

She quickly finished her refreshments and readied herself for a nap in the cool dimness of the bedroom. She stretched out, studying the embroidered canopy above her, wondering whether Lord Trent was interested enough to kiss her again.

Max had arrived at the estate shortly after Ellery and Lady Venable, and had joined Ellery to look over the clearing of underbrush and small saplings in the woods which bordered the south meadow. They kept their horses to a walk in the heat of the day and were able to easily converse as they rode through the meadow.

"Did Corbin accept your invitation?" asked Max, allowing his reins to lay loose on his mount's neck.

"He did," stated Ellery, with a satisfied tone. "He will be here by tomorrow evening at the latest."

"And Miss Grayson? Will she be chasing spirits through the hallways?" inquired Max, lightheartedly.

Ellery smiled at the picture. "She will be searching," he affirmed, "however, I am not privy to the means she intends to employ. She took the opportunity to pay a visit to her home before traveling here, but I'm hoping that she will arrive today."

"Did you find out why she was at sixes and sevens?"

"No, and I doubt that she will tell me, so if I want to know, I must ferret it out myself."

"Think it has anything to do with the Hell-Fire Club?"

"Your guess is as good as mine. I am not well enough acquainted with Miss Grayson to predict anything about her, but I mean for that to change very quickly once she is in residence."

Max directed a sharp gaze at his friend. "You don't mean to do anything to compromise her, do you? She seems to be a decent person merely attempting to support her family."

"Don't fly into the boughs. I am not out to ruin her," replied Ellery.

Max was relieved until Ellery's next remark.

"Unless she deserves it," he added.

Max had observed Ellery's anger several times over the years, but he had never heard his friend's voice sound as inflexible as it did at that moment.

"The more I see of Miss Grayson, the more I think you might be mistaken about her link with the club. She appears much too gentle to take part in the ceremonies that are rumored to take place."

"It could be that she is skilled at convincing others that she is exactly that," said Ellery. "You may think what you wish, but I am going to consider her suspect until I prove otherwise. Even if she is innocent, she has served her purpose in drawing Corbin here. I don't believe he would have accepted my invitation unless I had advised him Miss Grayson meant to attend."

Although he did not speak his mind, Max did not approve of Ellery's using Miss Grayson as a cat's paw in the game he was playing. Circumstances could turn ugly and he did not like to think of the Spirit Lady being caught in the middle.

"Could you help me keep a close eye on Corbin while he is here?" asked Ellery. "I am hoping that there will be meetings or some such that he must attend in regard to the club. He may lead us to Phillip if we are able to successfully follow him."

"I made inquiries of Phillip's friends before I left and none of them had heard from him," revealed Max.

Ellery's face darkened. "It is my opinion that Phillip is in no condition to send us a message."

"You don't think . . . ?" asked Max. Unable to finish the thought, he allowed his words to trail off.

"I don't know whether he is being held or . . . worse.

But I know that he would not go this long without letting me know that he was unharmed."

"But if he was sworn to secrecy," said Max.

"He would find a way without compromising his mission," Ellery stubbornly insisted.

"Then I suppose we must hope that Miss Grayson or Corbin will give us some information that is useful."

"I have men searching for more, but at the moment they are our best chance of finding Phillip. I will begin concentrating on Miss Grayson this evening. The company will be small and I don't believe that Corbin will arrive today, so nothing should interfere with a few private moments with the Spirit Lady."

"And when Corbin does get here, I will watch him carefully."

"Be cautious," warned Ellery. "If he gets wind that we are on to him, he may bolt."

"He will never know," Max said, confidently.

"I wonder if it will ever rain again," commented Ellery, studying the dry pasture.

"If the sky is an indication, there is no need to hurry home," said Max, looking up at the cloudless expanse of blue.

"Nevertheless, we will return as quickly as we can. It's possible that Miss Grayson has arrived and I can begin my campaign sooner than I expected. When I think of Phillip, I feel that every moment counts if we are to bring him safely home."

When Ellery reached the house, he learned that indeed Miss Grayson had arrived, but was resting in her room. He fought back the urge to send a maid to request her company, since he did not want to appear overeager.

Vanessa felt a bit of trepidation as she dressed for dinner. She had not seen Lord Trent since the day he had

kissed her at Lady Bowden's home and was uncertain as
to how she would react to seeing him again. She hoped
that she could control any embarrassment that might
yet linger for she did not relish blushing like a green
girl in front of him.

She dismissed Delcie, telling the maid she would find
her own way to the drawing room. Vanessa needed a few
minutes alone to prepare herself for the evening ahead.
She had indulged herself and had brought some of her
better gowns and felt confident that she was looking her
best. She had gone so far as to pack the topaz set that
Lady Atterly had given her in case an evening called for
something special.

She wore a cream-colored gown this evening with a
trim of green leaves and blue and yellow flowers around
the neck and hem. Matching blue ribbon caught the
cap sleeve at the bottom, forming tiny bows on the outside of each arm. She had used the same-hued ribbon
to embellish the curls which had been drawn to the back
of her head. Altogether, Vanessa thought she would do
very well indeed.

She selected a fan with ivory ribs covered with silk,
which was hand-painted with a pastoral scene. Melanie
had given it to her for her last birthday, and Vanessa
cherished it even more so now that her sister was missing.

The thought of Melanie brought tears to her eyes and
she felt the urge to pack her trunk and return to her
home as quickly as possible. It would not do any good
to go into a decline, she told herself, blinking back tears
which threatened to overflow. Melanie would best be
served by Vanessa's staying and earning enough to employ Mr. Browning to continue his search.

She had left instructions that if he found anything,
he was to send a note to Lord Trent's home and arrange
a particular time and day to meet her at the village inn.

While it might ruin her reputation if she were seen, she was willing to take the risk to find Melanie.

Vanessa could delay no longer. She took a deep breath, straightened her shoulders, and stepped through her door into the hallway.

The company had gathered in the large drawing room; a chamber of magnificent proportions with a wealth of lovely furnishings. Sofas, chairs, and tables were skillfully placed in order to form conversation groups. There was a small desk if someone felt the urge to complete their correspondence in the room, and several glass-fronted cabinets contained books, even though the house included a library that was continually being updated with the most current works.

There were perhaps a dozen people in the room when Vanessa arrived. Lady Venable excused herself from the ladies with whom she was speaking and came forward to greet Vanessa.

"My dear, I am so happy to see you have arrived safely. I was afraid you might be needed at home and decide to stay."

Lady Venable did not know how close she had come to doing just that, thought Vanessa. "I had promised," she replied.

"I own, you are certainly in looks tonight," complimented Lady Venable. "You do not at all resemble a spirit lady."

"And what would that be?" asked Vanessa.

"Oh, a gown of black perhaps, with black lace gloves and a veil. Possibly some fringes dangling, too."

Vanessa laughed at Lady Venable's description. "I have nothing of that sort, but perhaps I should adopt the style. It might make me more believable."

"I cannot conceive that anyone who sees you work

would doubt your veracity," she replied, taking Vanessa by the arm. "Let me introduce you around. I expect you already know many of them from Town."

"I see a few faces that are strangers," said Vanessa, as they walked deeper into the room.

"Only about half of the guests have arrived," Lady Venable informed her. "We expect the others tomorrow. Are you comfortable in your room? I apologize for not asking earlier."

"I have never had such beautiful surroundings," Vanessa admitted.

"Good," said Lady Venable, a satisfied expression on her face. "I want you to enjoy your stay. Besides, Ellery insisted you be given that suite. I believe he particularly thought it would suit you."

Vanessa could not imagine Lord Trent taking the time to consider where she would stay while at his home. Did he hold her in higher regard than she thought? She would not allow her mind to even form such a ludicrous idea. She must remember that the only reason she was here was to search the house for spirits so that Lady Cornelia would be comfortable making it her home. No, Lord Trent was merely being kind to her and she should not make any more of it than it was.

"I will stay where I am for the moment, but you must tell me immediately if you need the suite. I would be entirely comfortable in a single room."

"You might be, my dear, but Ellery would be irritated beyond belief if you were stuck in some dull room in the attic."

"I cannot believe that any room in this house could be called dull," protested Vanessa.

"Well, you shall soon know, for I'm certain you will see all of them in your search for spirits."

"Did Lady Cornelia come despite the possibility of spirits being in the house?"

"She will be here tomorrow with the Lamberts," Lady Venable informed her. "And, just between the two of us, I am not so certain Cornelia has such a fright of spirits."

"But why would she say so if she did not?" asked Vanessa.

"She is determined to snare my nephew in the parson's mousetrap and will use any means available to her. It is my belief that she thought to gain attention from Ellery if she insisted she could not abide the thought of spirits in his houses. To my mind, she's being a bit too forward since Ellery has not offered for her yet."

"But it is only a matter of time, is it not?" asked Vanessa.

"If you listen to Cornelia it is, but Ellery's reticence tells another tale. I am hoping that this house party will cause him to see that she is the wrong woman for him."

Vanessa did not dare ask who she thought was right for her nephew. It was just as well, for she did not want to think of him with yet another woman. She attempted to put Ellery out of her mind while she was being introduced to the other guests.

Some of them she knew and some of them she didn't, but they were uniformly agreeable people who were not too high in the instep to greet her warmly. She was feeling decidedly more comfortable when a voice she would never fail to recognize spoke in her ear, nearly causing her to jump in surprise.

"Miss Grayson, I'm pleased that you were able to arrive today."

She turned and found him standing far too close. Taking a step back, she managed to speak. "I always keep my word."

"Ah. Is that all it is?" he asked, a teasing light in his eye. "Have you been made comfortable?"

"Oh, yes, but as I told Lady Venable, it isn't at all necessary."

"What isn't necessary?"

"Why, the wonderful room and the maid and being waited on. I am accustomed to doing for myself and do not expect to do less while I am here."

"It would be an insult to me if you refused my hospitality. Anyone who enters my home is treated equally and you will not be the exception."

Vanessa heard an edge of irritation in his voice and decided not to make an issue of it for the moment. "If you insist, my lord. Your home is lovely, but I had no idea it was so large."

"It started modest, but as each generation has added on to it, I'm afraid it has grown entirely out of hand."

"I believe I heard you have a brother. Does he live here also?"

Ellery studied her face but could detect not a hint of malice. Could she be as Max suspected—entirely innocent of involvement in the Hell-Fire Club and Phillip's disappearance? It was possible that Corbin had not drawn her into the scheme, but he could not accept it without proof.

"I have a younger brother whose name is Phillip, but he is not at home. It is just myself and Aunt Venable for the moment."

"She is a wonderful person," said Vanessa, "and is entirely dedicated to you."

"More than I deserve," he replied, wryly. "What of your family?"

"I have a younger sister," she revealed, hesitantly. "And then there is Annie who has been with us for our entire lives. I don't know what I would do without her. She holds the house together while I am away."

"You are fortunate to have her. Did you find them well when you visited?"

"I—I—" she stammered to a halt before continuing. "They were as well as could be expected."

"I'm sorry. I didn't mean to disturb you. Aunt Charity mentioned a family crisis and I should have known better than to pry. If there is anything I can do, you need only ask."

"Thank you, my lord, but it is nothing with which I cannot deal."

The call came for dinner and Ellery led his aunt in with the rest of the company following. Vanessa found herself sitting at Ellery's right hand with Max next to her.

The dining room was as impressive as the rest of the house. The table was long and made of mahogany with matching chairs surrounding it. It was set with gold-rimmed china and silver utensils, both carrying the family crest. Large crystal chandeliers hung from a ceiling painted as a blue sky with white fluffy clouds and rosy-cheeked cherubs cavorting on it.

The dinner had more dishes than she could count. There was a sweet melon soup to begin with, followed by braised fish from the estate's own stream, a hot and flavorsome chicken mousse, Beef à la Royale stuffed with bacon and oysters, browned, then cooked in a red wine sauce. Vegetables had been cooked with the beef and were crisp instead of being served overdone as many vegetables were. There was also a leg of mutton, Cornish hens, and many side dishes of fresh country vegetables. A variety of breads was served with the dishes, still hot enough to melt the sweet butter which accompanied them.

Vanessa did not think she could consume another bite until the desserts were brought to the table. There was apple pie with fresh whipped cream and the Duke's Custard, which consisted of the bottom of the dish being covered in brandied cherries, then custard poured over it, with macaroons garnishing the edge. Lastly, rose-colored whipped cream flavored with brandy topped the rich dessert. There was walnut pudding, cheesecake with raspberry sauce, and a spice cake that smelled heavenly.

"Never say that you have two wonderful chefs," said Vanessa, laying aside her fork.

"Claude traveled down with us. He usually does not like to leave Town, but could not resist when he heard how many people would be here to offer accolades to his talent."

"I believe Lady Venable is rising," said Vanessa.

"We will join you in the drawing room shortly," replied Ellery, also rising and reaching Vanessa before the footman could slide her chair back. "I will show you the gardens at that time." He lifted her hand and gave it a light brush of his lips.

Vanessa shivered in spite of the warmth of the room. She could not stop herself from reacting to Lord Trent's touch and felt helpless in his presence. She did not want to be drawn into a garden filled with fragrances of roses and other flowers, where she would be even more vulnerable to his charm.

She could not allow herself to forget that Lady Cornelia would be in residence tomorrow and would surely claim most of his time. If she could only avoid him until then perhaps she could get through the party without making a fool of herself.

She was being paid to be here to search for spirits and nothing more. No matter how well Lady Venable and Lord Trent treated her, no matter how grand her room, which included a maid all her own, she was still in the hire of the earl.

If he had any intentions toward her, there would be nothing serious involved. He was courting the lovely Lady Cornelia and Vanessa must accept it. She would put Lord Trent and his kisses from her mind and concentrate on why she was here and on getting Melanie back.

Vanessa followed the other ladies from the room, leaving the men clustered around the table, lighting cigars and accepting glasses of brandy from the footmen.

Ellery watched her leave, thinking she looked extremely fragile in her light-colored gown with blue ribbons. He would rather have gone directly into the drawing room and taken Miss Grayson for a walk in the gardens than to remain with the gentlemen, but he was the host and he was not left with a choice.

"Doing it up a bit brown, aren't you?" asked Max as he moved to the chair Vanessa had just vacated.

Ellery was annoyed at his question. "What do you mean?"

Max nodded toward the door. "Miss Grayson. It almost appears as if you are dangling after her."

"Don't be foolish. I am merely being courteous."

"If you were always this courteous, you would have been brought up to scratch long ago."

Before Ellery could answer, a footman brought Max a note which—with a murmur of apology—he opened immediately. "I will be back shortly," he said, once he had finished reading it. Pushing back his chair, he hurried from the room without a backward glance.

Ellery was puzzled about what would cause his friend to move so quickly. Taking a sip of brandy, he turned to Lord Halburton, who was on his other side, and struck up a conversation.

Just as the men were rising to join the women in the drawing room, Max reentered the dining room. He made his way straight to Ellery.

"Hold back," he said, raising his hand when Ellery began to follow the others. "I have something you need to hear. I don't know how useful it is, but it is telling."

"Is it something about Phillip," Ellery asked eagerly, as the dining room cleared.

"Not directly, but it may substantiate some of our suspicions."

Ellery waved the footmen out of the room and made certain the door was closed behind them. "Get on with it, man," he urged.

"Before I left London, I entrusted the surveillance of Corbin to two men who are expert in the art of following without being detected. I just met with one of them who thought we should know what happened last night."

Ellery stirred restlessly, but held his tongue, allowing Max to tell the story his way.

"It seems that Corbin left his town house after dark last night, departing from the stables in the mews rather than having the coach brought to the front of the house. They followed his coach to an inn outside of London called the Dove and the Bull.

"The inn has a reputation of being a discreet place to stop if you do not want everyone to know your business. The back of the tavern is kept in darkness so that a person can arrive and depart without being seen. They offer private rooms and, if need be, sturdy men who will guard the door for a price. The food and ale are good, and they have a private cellar which furnishes other liquors. All in all, it is an excellent place for gentlemen to meet and still remain comfortable."

"Were they able to discern whom he was meeting?"

"Not completely," said Max. "They were able to see that he entered a room with several other men he met outside and they could hear other people inside when the door was opened to allow Corbin and his friends in.

"They stayed until the early morning hours. From what my men heard and saw, it seems there was a dinner, followed by a meeting of sorts. After that, it degenerated into drinking, with some of the men joining lightskirts in the upstairs rooms."

"How did they find this out?"

"They spread around a little money. Every man has his price and with the kind that works at the Dove and the Bull, it doesn't come high."

"Do they know anything specific about Corbin's activities?"

"Only that he arrived late and left early. He didn't avail himself of the women and he was walking straight when he left."

"Dammit! I wish they had seen or heard more."

"They waited and watched as the coaches left the inn and they were able to make out some of the crests on the coach doors."

"Shame to go to all that expense to remain private and then drive crested coaches," remarked Ellery.

"Most of these men have never had to hide anything. They've felt safe from retribution no matter what the deed and have no reason to think otherwise now."

"Then whoever is leading them either does not care whether they are recognized or is as careless as they are. Anything more?"

"I have names of people they think were there."

"Or their coaches were," added Ellery.

"That's true," agreed Max. "But then there are several others who were followed directly to their doors, so there is no question about them."

"Can we assume this was a meeting of the Hell-Fire Club?" asked Ellery.

"I think we must," replied Max, belatedly sipping at a glass of brandy. "I have told my men to keep an eye on those they definitely identified from the meeting. If Phillip is being held against his will then perhaps they will lead us to him. One thing is certain, no one of Phillip's description attended the meeting last night."

"If the club follows in the footsteps of the past, they have a place to call their own. It is probably out of town in a fairly deserted part of the country and probably too far from London to travel to and fro for a single meeting. That is probably why they met at the Dove and the Bull."

"That sounds reasonable," acknowledged Max. "And if you are right, that is where we will most probably find Phillip." Max was silent for a moment. "Are you certain Phillip has been found out?"

"I know of nothing else that would keep him away for such a length of time. Even if he was still free, he would find some way to get word to me. We have never been out of touch for this long. Phillip is smart, but he is also inexperienced," Ellery continued. "I don't think he would be a match for whoever is resurrecting the Hell-Fire Club."

"What shall we do next?"

"Since your men are keeping an eye on several of the others who attended the meeting last night, we will concentrate on Corbin. One of us will keep him in sight at all times."

"And if he becomes suspicious?" asked Max.

"We are such a concentrated party, he should take no notice since we are in one another's pocket most of the time. And if we trade places often, it will serve to make it even more difficult to detect us."

"I suppose we should watch for contact from anyone but those in the party," said Max.

"Exactly," acquiesced Ellery. "But we cannot count out the idea that there is another member of the club in the company."

"The men here are all reputable gentlemen," protested Max.

"As far as we know," said Ellery. "But no one, even the closest of friends, can claim to know one another's innermost secrets. It is possible for any of these respectable gentlemen to be a member of the club without our knowing. In fact, it would be quite a coup for the group if they could convert them."

"What if Corbin leaves the estate?"

"Then we will need to follow him. It will be difficult, I know, but if we are right about the club being located in a desolate part of the country, it's possible he is closer to it here in the country than when he is in the city. We should be prepared to secretly follow him should a meeting be called while he is here."

"And we won't know if it is a meeting of the club or simply an assignation with a woman until we arrive," commented Max.

"Either way, it should be interesting," commented Ellery, with a smile.

"I suppose you will seek out Miss Grayson and attempt to find out whether she knew where Corbin was last night," said Max.

"Devil take me, Max! She could have been with him," exclaimed Ellery.

"What are you talking about?" asked Max, thinking his friend had flown off the hook.

"Don't you see? Miss Grayson did not arrive until late this afternoon. She had ample time to attend the meeting before traveling to the country."

"You cannot seriously think . . ." began Max.

"Why not? Women were involved in the past, so it is not unheard of and she has been friends with Corbin since they were children. What could be more ordinary than for her to follow him into the club? And these trips home to handle a family crisis. They could be nothing more than excuses to join the club in other activities."

"You cannot genuinely believe that Miss Grayson . . ."

"For God's sake, Max! She talks to spirits. What better proof do you need? She would be the crown jewel for such a club as the Hell-Fire. And for her to be a guest in my house while Phillip was missing would be the ultimate sport for them."

"How do you know?"

"I've told you. I'm something of an expert. Searching out and destroying the clubs has become a family tradition. My father and his father before worked for the Crown in doing so. I had thought it was all over when my father finished with them, but evidently I was wrong. Phillip spoke briefly to me once about it and, in thinking about it later, I'm certain he felt destined to carry on the legacy. If I had taken him seriously at the time, we would not be in this mess."

"I still am not convinced you are right about Miss Grayson."

"We cannot overlook the possibility," said Ellery. "It could mean the difference between life and death for Phillip."

Unless it was already too late. The unspoken words lay heavily between the two men.

"I will spend more time with Miss Grayson beginning tonight. She may slip and reveal something useful," said Ellery, rising and leading the way into the drawing room.

But Ellery's talk with Vanessa would need to wait for another day, for by the time he and Max arrived in the drawing room, she had already retired for the evening.

Nine

Vanessa rose early the next morning, but not earlier than Delcie. The young girl was waiting to help her dress, then started to bring her chocolate and muffins when Vanessa told her she would go down to breakfast.

"But, ma'am, all the ladies have breakfast in their rooms," she protested.

"Then perhaps I am not a genuine lady," teased Vanessa.

"Oh, do not say so, ma'am. You are every inch the lady that anyone in this house is."

"Thank you, Delcie. Now let us be off to the kitchen and take us by way of the back stairs."

Vanessa had breakfast in the kitchen with Mrs. Gregory, listening to tales about the house and questioning her about the age of various parts.

After she had finished her meal, she said, "I would like to begin in the oldest part of the house. Perhaps you could have Delcie show me the way."

"I will do it myself," said Mrs. Gregory. "Delcie is a good child, but she would not be able to answer the questions you might have."

Vanessa followed Mrs. Gregory up the stairs and down one long hall after another. "Here we are," said Mrs. Gregory, stopping in the middle of the hall and motioning around her. "The original house was small by comparison to what we now have, but it was a mansion for its day. The rooms from here to the end of the hall, both upstairs and down were the first built."

"Thank you, Mrs. Gregory," said Vanessa, inspecting the area.

"Should I leave you?"

"Of course," she insisted. "I will be perfectly all right."

"Can you find your way back or should I send someone after you for luncheon?"

"I believe I can find my way back without help. If not, the spirits will lead me."

Mrs. Gregory looked a little taken back, then smiled when she realized that Vanessa was teasing. "If they do, invite them to join us for lunch," she replied, proving that the housekeeper had a sense of humor, also.

After Mrs. Gregory had disappeared around the corner of the hall, Vanessa entered the first room and began casting about for the sense of spirits. She would visit all the rooms in the old part of the house before moving on to the newer additions. If she did not find anything this time, she would revisit it periodically. On occasion, it took time for the spirits to show themselves.

Some hours later, Ellery found her sitting in one of the rooms, her eyes closed and her head resting against the high back of a chair. She appeared completely at ease, perhaps even asleep, and he hated to disturb her.

"Come in, Lord Trent," she said, without opening her eyes.

He stepped into the room and looked around.

"There is no one here but me," she said, finally looking at him. "Lady Cornelia should be pleased for I'm afraid I've come up empty this morning."

"But you've only begun," he reminded her. "There are dozens more rooms for you to visit."

"Will I be able to see the rooms that are being occupied?" she asked.

"I see no reason why you cannot. I will ask the guests, but I don't believe anyone will object. It will be just one more thing they can talk about when they return to Town for the Little Season.

"The reason I have come," he said, moving toward her, "is to remind you that luncheon will be served soon."

"Is it that late?" asked Vanessa. "I always lose track of time when I am working."

"Can you leave now? You're not leaving anyone . . . er . . . hanging around?" he questioned, looking into the corners of the room.

Vanessa giggled at his nonsense. "As I told you before, I have had no luck in locating even one small spirit."

"Then this is a good time for you to stop. You must eat to fortify yourself for I am certain spirit hunting sharpens your appetite. Which makes me question when you arose this morning."

"I am always up early and I wanted to get a start on the search. I had breakfast with Mrs. Gregory and she told me about the history of the house."

"You could find no one better," said Ellery, as they left the room and walked down the hall toward the main part of the house. "She was born on the property and has been here ever since, working her way up to housekeeper when she was but a young woman. I imagine she's heard every tale that I have about the building of the house and our family.

"But what I wanted to say is that there is no need for you to arise so early. The spirits will be here at midmorning as well as they are before sunrise. I hope you will set aside time to take part in the house party as well as searching the house."

"You are generous, my lord. Perhaps I will be able to once I have finished with more of the rooms."

"Do you ride, Miss Grayson?"

"Yes, I do, my lord. It is something I enjoy a great deal."

"Then you must come riding with me in the morning. Since you are an early riser, you should enjoy the experience."

"I could not . . ." she began.

"Of course, you can. We can discuss my spirits or lack of, whichever pertains in the morning, if that will make you feel better."

Vanessa smiled at his foolishness. It was true she would greatly enjoy a ride, particularly over such a lovely estate. She would not allow herself to think that the company of Lord Trent was a great inducement.

"All right, my lord. You have persuaded me. I look forward to a morning ride. I saw a lake with an island and summer house in the middle when I first arrived. Above all else, I would like a closer look at it."

"It will be our first stop," he promised.

They had reached the top of the steps leading into the entrance hall when Thomas opened the door and Lady Cornelia sailed into the house, followed by Lord and Lady Lambert and their daughter Barbara.

"What a hot, dusty trip," she complained, removing her bonnet. "I am absolutely parched. Where is Lord Trent?"

The butler looked upward and she followed his gaze to where Ellery and Vanessa stood at the top of the stairs. Her eyes narrowed momentarily, then she recovered and smiled at both of them.

"Welcome," said Ellery, descending the steps and bringing Vanessa with him. When he reached the bottom, he greeted Lord and Lady Lambert, Lady Barbara and Lady Cornelia. "You have arrived just in time," he told them. "We are nearly ready to go in to luncheon. I'll have you shown to your rooms and you can refresh yourselves before the meal."

Mrs. Gregory had been standing nearby and now took command of the party. She led them upstairs and Ellery stood watching until they disappeared from view.

Vanessa had removed herself from the group and stood at the side of the room, looking on. Lord Trent did not appear happy and just as she was ready to slip away, he turned to her.

"I'm sorry we were interrupted," he said.

"It's to be expected since you are hosting a house party," she reminded him.

"I am," he agreed, "but it does not make me wish any less that we could finish a conversation without interference. Perhaps we will have more success on our ride in the morning," he suggested.

"Are you certain . . . ?"

"It merits no further discussion. Now, let us join the others in the drawing room. I must advise my aunt the Lamberts have arrived and that we need to hold back luncheon until they are ready."

Lady Cornelia replaced Vanessa at Lord Trent's right hand at luncheon without even inquiring where she should sit. Vanessa took a seat further down the table and Max moved to sit next to her. The earl said nothing, but Vanessa—who was beginning to know him better each hour she was around him—did not think he was pleased.

He looked around the table until his gaze met hers, a small frown furrowed his forehead, then disappeared before he nodded at her.

"I see your friend Corbin has not yet arrived," remarked Max to Vanessa.

"No, but he said he could not be here until some time this afternoon," she responded, taking a portion of cold spiced chicken.

"You have known one another since childhood, I have heard."

Vanessa was becoming tired of answering the same questions about Corbin and herself, but Max had been everything that was cordial to her and she could not fault him for attempting to carry on a conversation.

"Yes," she answered shortly. "And you and Lord Trent have grown up together?"

"Since we were in leading strings," he confirmed.

"It is reassuring to have such friendships," she remarked. "To have someone to turn to in times of need."

"It is," he agreed. "We have helped one another out of countless scrapes, but then I suppose you know how that is."

"I do and I am continually surprised that Lord Corbin sustains our friendship even though his title would justify his forgetting all about me."

"I doubt whether any man could do that," replied Max, gallantly.

"You need not empty the butter-boat," she said, with a smile.

"Have you begun your search yet?"

"Just this morning, but I have found nothing. I'm not surprised, though, since sometimes it takes several days for the spirits to show themselves. Then again, I may find that there are none at all."

"In this house?" asked Max. "Of course they are here. They are simply getting to know you."

"For Lady Cornelia's sake, I hope you are wrong. I heard her say she could not live in a house that held spirits."

"And how would she know if no one told her?"

"She probably never would," agreed Vanessa, "but I will leave it to Lord Trent to decide that issue. She is a lovely lady and I cannot see Lord Trent denying her anything."

"Never judge Ellery on what appears to be," said Max. "He is sometimes full of surprises."

Vanessa did not ask Max for clarification of his comment and they finished luncheon with less personal conversation.

As they were leaving the room, Cornelia appeared at Vanessa's side. "I understand you did not find anything this morning."

"That's true, but I have only been in a few rooms thus far," Vanessa informed her.

"Even so, I feel much better about being here," said Cornelia, sighing deeply and looking up at Ellery, who had come to stand by her side. "I will sleep so much better now that I know you will soon detect any ghosts who might walk the halls of this old house."

"I've never been bothered by them," said Ellery.

"Men are not as sensitive as women," she pronounced, wrapping her arm through his. "You could probably sleep no matter how many ghosts were gathered in your bedchamber."

"As long as they kept their peace, it would not bother me at all," he answered.

"I have been meaning to ask whether Phillip will be here," said Cornelia, as they strolled toward the door.

"He is traveling at the moment," replied Ellery. "There is a slight chance that he will return before the party disperses, but I would not count on it."

"I am looking forward to meeting him," said Cornelia.

"And you shall as soon as he returns," Ellery assured her.

"If you will excuse me, I must get back to work," said Vanessa, turning toward the stairs.

"Miss Grayson, you cannot search for spirits every hour of the day," protested Ellery. "Come into the drawing room with us or else Aunt Charity will be disappointed."

"Lady Venable knows that I am being well paid to be here. She will understand why I cannot pretend to be a guest."

"You are a guest," he insisted. "You are merely helping me with a small problem."

"A problem which I caused," said Cornelia. "Join us, please, or I will feel terribly guilty."

"Do not worry, Lady Cornelia, I have been doing this for some time now and I do not feel set upon at all. I enjoy my work for it sometimes allows me to bring peace to many people. I beg you to continue with your festivities without a thought for me."

She hurried up the stairs before Lord Trent could raise any additional arguments. She was thankful for the appearance of Lady Cornelia for it had brought her back to her senses. Sitting by Lord Trent at dinner the evening before, and enjoying their time together earlier today, had nearly led her to hope that he could be within her reach.

Lord Trent was a gentleman and was merely treating her courteously, as he would any other guest in his house. He no doubt would be appalled if he knew that her dreams had been filled with him the night before. He was all but betrothed to Lady Cornelia, who kept it no secret as to how she felt about the earl.

She would feel better once Corbin arrived. He could always be counted on to help keep her feet on the ground. She frowned as she hurried down the hall toward the original part of the house again. He should have been here by now, she thought, glancing out a window into the merciless glare of the afternoon sun.

Most probably something ordinary had delayed him. Perhaps a new horse at Tattersall's; he dearly loved a fine piece of horseflesh. Although she had to admit that Corbin had been acting more mysterious than usual lately—traveling to and from Town more often than usual.

He had told her that his country estate needed guidance in changes he was making, but Vanessa knew his steward had been with the family since Corbin's father's time and could handle everything perfectly well.

She did not press him, however, for she did not want to force him into further deception with her. Sooner or later, he would tell her about whatever was bothering him. Until then, she would simply have patience with his erratic behavior.

While Vanessa was worrying about Corbin, Ellery was wishing he was anywhere but in his drawing room with Cornelia hanging on his arm. He wondered what had made him think he might want to spend the rest of his life with her.

It was true that she was more than attractive, but she seldom ceased speaking and what she said had as much substance as the very air they breathed. He did not want to think about going to bed at night or getting up in the morning, listening to her endless chatter.

He thought of Miss Grayson's well-modulated voice and the times that they had spent in a comfortable silence without need for speech. Why she would want to get caught up in the Hell-Fire Club he could not hazard a guess.

And that brought his thoughts around to Corbin. Where the devil was the man? He should have been here by now. Ellery only hoped that Miss Grayson's presence would be a strong enough reason for him to make good on his promise to come to the party.

Cornelia claimed his attention again, and he put the thoughts of Miss Grayson and Corbin aside to be examined at a more private time.

Ellery did not see Miss Grayson again until dinner. She did not appear in the drawing room before dinner and slipped into a seat midway down the table from him just before the meal began. The party had grown larger as additional people arrived that day, and she was entirely too far away for him to hear even a sound of her voice. His only consolation was that he had her promise to ride with him in the morning.

"Do you think Max is nurturing a *tendre* for Miss Grayson?" asked Cornelia, looking down the table toward the two people in question.

Max had made a comment to Miss Grayson which had caused both of them to laugh, leaning toward one another in shared confidence.

"Of course not!" Ellery snapped. "He is merely attempting to keep her entertained."

"And it looks is if he is doing a good job of it," shot back Cornelia. "You may lose your good friend to the Spirit Lady."

Ellery cut a bite of beef, chewed, and swallowed it before he answered. "Trust me, Cornelia, there is nothing between Max and Miss Grayson. She is a pleasant person with whom to talk. It is no more than that."

"I suppose you should know your friend," she replied, a great deal of doubt in her voice.

"I understood she had a family crisis of some sort or another and has had to travel back and forth to her home. Do you know anything about it?"

"I have not asked her, but whatever has happened, it is her own business. If she wants us to know, I'm certain she will tell us."

"I hope it doesn't harm her ability to find any spirits in your home. I am depending upon her to force them out if they are here. I could never live with spirits." She shuddered. "Never."

"Cornelia, there is something we should discuss," he began.

"Certainly, Ellery, but Lady Venable is giving the signal for us to retire. We will talk later."

Both Cornelia and Miss Grayson were swallowed up in the group of ladies that filed from the room, while Ellery sat at the head of the table, looking nothing like the genial host. Max joined him, leery of his dark mood.

"You don't have the look of a happy man," he ventured.

"I'm far from it," admitted Ellery. "My ears are ringing from a constant barrage of chatter and Corbin has not yet arrived."

"The fair Cornelia does seem to talk nonstop," agreed Max. "I never noticed in Town, I suppose, because there were so many others around that she did not stand out."

"Well, it is certainly evident now," growled Ellery.

"As for Corbin, that is a puzzle. Do you think he changed his mind?"

"If he did, I would expect to have received a message from him. He could have gotten a late start or had an accident on the road."

"Should we send out someone to search for him?" asked Max.

Ellery thought about his suggestion. "Let's wait until tomorrow and see whether he arrives. There will be plenty of time then."

"Anyone ready for a game of billiards?" asked Lord Haskins, a jovial man whose inactivity showed in his stomach. He received a chorus of agreement from some of the gentlemen who did not want to spend the rest of the evening in the drawing room.

"How about you, Trent?"

"I must play the host and visit the ladies first. I will join you later, though," he added.

"So you are going to spend the evening with Lady Cornelia even though she has driven you close to the edge during dinner," said Max, more as a statement than a question.

"It would be too obvious if I did not show up in the drawing room at least for a short time," Ellery explained.

"Ever the gentleman," remarked Max, "even when it hurts."

"I am convinced that is what makes a gentleman," quipped Ellery, as they stepped into the hall.

"You do not need to accompany me," said Ellery. "I know you would appreciate a game of billiards or cards more than this."

"I found dinner to be quite enjoyable and I will not be at all bored if Miss Grayson is in the drawing room."

Ellery frowned, but said nothing to his friend. He had no right to warn Max away from Miss Grayson, but he did not like it at all.

"Will you keep Cornelia entertained while I speak to Miss Grayson a moment?" asked Ellery, once they reached the drawing room. "I want to see whether she knows anything about Corbin."

Max looked down the length of the room, where Cornelia was holding court with two of the younger gentlemen of the party. "It doesn't look as if she needs entertaining, but I will stay on the fringes of her group in case she is deserted."

Ellery nodded in satisfaction and turned his attention to Vanessa. She had been cornered by Lady Matthews, a widow who was far from penniless, yet was known outside her hearing as My Lady Parsimonious, due to her miserly manner with money.

Ellery joined the two women for a moment, then asked, "Lady Matthews, do you mind if I speak with Miss Grayson privately? We need to discuss her search for spirits."

"Of course not," she replied, giving way under the influence of Ellery's smile. "But you come back to me, girl. I am not through with you yet."

She playfully shook an admonishing finger at Vanessa as she spoke. Although by the look in her eye Vanessa was convinced that she was not joking at all.

"Thank you, my lord," murmured Vanessa, when they were a safe distance from Lady Matthews.

"Need I ask what she wanted from you?"

"She wants me to also see whether she has spirits; however, she does not wish to pay for it. I've been invited time and again to stay in her house without charge merely to look for ghosts."

"She begrudges every shilling that she is forced to spend," said Ellery. "Even if you did agree, you would be extremely uncomfortable for she employs few servants and a miserable excuse for a cook, or so I'm told."

"I'm glad I have the excuse of not having a spare moment so that I need not insult her."

"Do you intend to return to London after the house party?" he asked.

She hesitated so long that he thought she had not heard him. "I am not certain," she said slowly. "It depends on what is happening at home."

"Is there nothing I can do?"

"I wish that there were," she replied. "In this instance, I would not hesitate at all to turn to anyone who could help, but I am doing all that can be done."

"You are not alone in your troubles then?"

"No, I am not."

"I imagine Corbin is helping," he said, subtly probing.

"He always seems to be lingering close by when I am in need of assistance," she agreed. "But I am worried that he has not yet arrived. The last word I heard from him was that he would be here this afternoon at the latest."

"I was wondering myself whether he had decided to forgo the party."

"I believe he was very much looking forward to it," replied Vanessa. "He said he had business to attend to before he left Town. Perhaps it has delayed him."

"I will send out inquiries if he does not arrive tomorrow," said Ellery. "It's possible his coach could have broken down on the road or one of his horses could have gone lame. In either case, he should not be difficult to find. He probably stayed at an inn if he was close to one."

"I should be eternally grateful," she said, a relieved expression on her face.

"It's settled then. If he is not here by luncheon, I will send my men to see whether he has had an accident on the road."

Ellery led her to the French doors, where the night air that drifted in was a little cooler. "Should I remind you that you are promised to ride with me tomorrow morning?"

"I remember," she said, "but wouldn't you rather ride with Viscount Huntly or some of the other gentlemen?"

"Max and the rest of the men can arrange for their own rides. Besides, depending upon how many glasses they raise tonight, an early morning ride might be the last thing they would decide upon."

"I suppose there is a tendency to drink more than usual since they do not need to make their way home."

"It is my opinion that in many cases they do it because it is a sure way to avoid their wives."

"My lord," replied Vanessa, pretending amazement, "I cannot believe that a gentleman would ever resort to liquor for that purpose."

"I'm certain you would never have that trouble with your husband, but there are some ladies who are best taken in small measures." His thoughts went immediately to Cornelia and the time he had spent with her. His temper would have been much better had he cut that time in half.

The summer night became much warmer as her imagination leaped to a scene where she and Lord Trent were exchanging vows. She immediately cleared it from her head and said, "I do not have that problem."

"Perhaps not now, but one day soon you will meet a gentleman who appeals to you. But you are changing the subject," he said. "We were discussing our ride in the morning. I hope you won't disappoint me."

"I have agreed and will not break my word," she said. "But I give you leave to change your mind at any time."

"You need have no fear of that. Have you forgotten that I have promised to show you the ornamental lake?"

"I am looking forward to it," admitted Vanessa.

"Good. I don't mean to be impolite, but do you ride well? It does not matter and I only ask so that I will know what mount to choose for you."

"My father took me up in front of him before I could walk," she replied. "And I will be highly insulted if you offer me an animal that will not go beyond a trot."

"I do not have a horse as decrepit as that in my stables, but I do have one that, once you ride it, you will vow it was born with you in mind."

"Ellery, there you are," cried out Cornelia, as she approached them. "I did not see you until a short time ago, and then each time I attempted to join you, Lord Baylor and Viscount Dalton insisted I converse with them just a little longer. They are such charming gentlemen, I could not refuse them."

"If you will excuse me," said Vanessa, preparing to leave the two alone.

"Do not allow me to drive you away, Miss Grayson. I would like to hear more about your spirit searches."

"There is not much to tell, Lady Cornelia. I have found nothing in either Lord Trent's town house or here. Of course, I am far from being finished with the entire house. For your sake, I am hoping that no spirits inhabit it."

"You must advise me immediately upon finishing the search," Lady Cornelia instructed.

"My usual policy is to first reveal the results to the individual who engaged me and then allow that person to disseminate the information as he or she sees fit," Vanessa replied in as agreeable a voice as she could muster. She was beginning to realize that there was something about Lady Cornelia she did not like and it was not entirely her association with Lord Trent.

Lady Cornelia linked her arm through Ellery's and smiled up at him, a smug expression on her face. "I am certain Ellery will share the news with me as soon as he receives it. Come walk in the garden with me," she said to Ellery, completely ignoring Vanessa.

Ellery looked at Vanessa and opened his mouth to speak.

"I believe that I will retire," she said quickly to avoid any acrimony.

"You should stay and enjoy yourself," he replied.

"I have had a long day, my lord, and will have another tomorrow."

"Let her go, Ellery," said Cornelia. "She has work to do tomorrow."

The intention was clear to Vanessa. Lady Cornelia meant to put her in her place and she had done so nicely. No matter how dark Lord Trent's visage became, Lady Cornelia was right. She was here to perform a task for the earl and was in no way a legitimate part of the house party. She wondered why she had not remembered that when she had agreed to ride with him in the morning. But it was too late now. She had promised and she would keep her word.

Ten

Vanessa was glad she had brought her riding habit. She had been thinking more of meeting Mr. Browning when she had done so, but here she was getting ready to ride with Lord Trent.

The habit was brown, which sounded dull until she donned it. The color set off her hair and the gold trim on the habit caused her eyes to appear even more stunning than usual. She wore a small hat tipped forward, with a wisp of a veil, and a long golden feather curved down beside her ear to touch her cheek. Altogether, Vanessa thought she would do very well indeed.

She took the back stairs and exited the house at the rear, filled with the expectation of riding again. Thoughts of Melanie popped into her head and she felt guilty that she was ready to enjoy herself while her sister's fate was unknown. She was ready to return to the house when Lord Trent approached.

"Miss Grayson, you are exactly on time."

"My lord, would you excuse me?" she asked.

He came closer and looked down at her. She was more appealing than ever in her riding habit with a tiny veil that only drew attention to her golden eyes. Eyes that were presently filled with tears.

"What is wrong?" he demanded. "If anyone has said anything . . ."

"No, it is nothing like that, my lord. It is just that I was reminded of the problem I am facing at home and fear it has gotten the better of me. There are times that I . . . that I . . ." She stumbled to a stop, biting her lower lip to keep the tears at bay.

Lord Trent moved closer, then placing a finger beneath her chin he lifted it until her gaze met his. "Evidently, you are facing a very difficult time," he said gently. "I know you don't feel like sharing it with me now, but know that I am here if you need me."

"You are extremely kind," she replied, blinking rapidly. "If there were anything you could do, I would not be too proud to ask, but I fear there is nothing."

"Then come ride with me," he said softly. "Staying inside will not help whatever is wrong, will it?"

"No," she whispered.

"And you look far too lovely to let it go to waste by returning to the house." He gave her an encouraging smile and took her hand. "You have no excuse then." He gave a gentle tug and she followed after him, as docile as a lamb.

Vanessa felt ashamed of herself until she realized that there was really nothing more she could do about Melanie and that sitting in her room would certainly serve no purpose. She did not want to fall into a decline and if riding with Lord Trent would help prevent that then she would continue as they had planned.

Was she attempting to fool herself? she asked, as they came closer to the stable. If she were truthful, she would admit that there was nothing more she wanted than to ride with the earl that morning. It did not diminish her sorrow or worry about Melanie's disappearance; it was merely a desire she could not thwart.

"This is Happy Lady," said Lord Trent, stopping in front of a sorrel mare that was saddled and ready to be ridden. "I named her that because she does not have a temperamental disposition." He rubbed the mare between the eyes and she butted him playfully. He handed Vanessa a sugar cube. "She is also a fickle lady. If you feed her this, she will be your friend for life."

Vanessa placed the sugar in her palm and held it out to the mare. Happy Lady sniffed once, then daintily removed the sugar.

Vanessa was delighted with the mare and could not wait to try out her paces. The earl tossed her into the saddle and then mounted his own large chestnut stallion. He led the way out of the stable yard and across the east meadow.

After a few minutes of becoming acquainted with Happy Lady, Vanessa urged her forward, passing Lord Trent and galloping on ahead. But it was only a moment before they were side by side dashing across the browning turf.

They pulled up as they reached the edge of the ornamental lake that Vanessa had wished to see. Vanessa's eyes were sparkling and her cheeks were flushed. Ellery thought she looked altogether charming; nothing like any Hell-Fire Club member he could remember.

"What a lovely spot," she exclaimed, looking at the lake.

They began walking their horses around the edge. "It was something my mother wanted," Ellery said. "She watched over every bit of the work and the design of the summer house on the island."

"I suppose the only way to get there is to row," said Vanessa, thinking she would like to visit it one day.

"Actually, the back of the island is close enough to land that there is a bridge leading to it. My mother could not handle a rowboat and insisted it be built so that she could gain access without calling on someone for assistance."

Vanessa spotted ducks close to the shore and a peacock strutting along not far away. The scene was one of utter serenity, absolutely the opposite of the turmoil that swirled inside her. She knew that Lord Trent was not for her, that he was nearly betrothed to the lovely Lady Cornelia, but she could not hold back the feelings that were growing in her. It would be best for her to hurry through the rest of the house and depart as soon as possible.

"You are decidedly quiet all of a sudden. You are not going to have a fit of the dismals, are you?"

His comment brought her around and she laughed out loud. "No, my lord, I will not foist such a thing as that on you. I was just thinking . . ."

"Promise me you will do no more of it then," he requested. "We will enjoy the rest of the ride and forget any problems we might have. Agreed?"

"Agreed," she said.

Their ride was quite lengthy and when they returned, a coach was being brought around to the stables.

"It's Rudy, I mean Lord Corbin's coach," exclaimed Vanessa, as Ellery helped her down from the mare.

"I believe you're right," he said, studying the crest on the door and wondering why her excitement at seeing Corbin's coach irritated him almost as much as when she called the man Rudy.

"I hope he is still below stairs, I would like very much to see him before I begin my search."

"I am not such a severe taskmaster that you cannot take some time to greet your friend," said Ellery, insulted that she should think so.

"I know you are not, my lord, but I have my own standards."

He took hold of her wrist, stopping her from going to the house. "Your standards are higher than most," he said, running his finger slowly down the feather that curved along her cheek. When he reached the end, his finger traced a path to her lips and then lightly over their fullness.

His touch made Vanessa fidgety and she nervously wet her lips, touching the warm roughness of his finger with the tip of her tongue. Both of them appeared paralyzed by the unexpected caress.

"Vanessa," he said, uttering her name for the first time, his voice raspy. He grasped her shoulders and would have pulled her to him had she not stepped backward."

"My lord, we cannot . . ."

"What is to stop us?" he murmured, stepping toward her again.

"It is broad daylight, for one. Secondly, you have a fiancée who could well be watching from the house and, as for number three, while it might only enhance your reputation, it would ruin mine. That might not matter much to you, but it would mean the loss of my livelihood at a time when I need it most."

Good sense was returning to Ellery under the impact of her words. What was he thinking to accost her in broad open daylight where anyone might see them? He glanced back at the stables but saw no one. Looking over her shoulder toward the house told him that no one was outside watching; however, the light on the windows did not allow him to see whether anyone was standing inside looking out at them.

"My apologies, Miss Grayson. I have no excuse, but I hope you will not hold it against me."

How could she when she welcomed his touch? mused Vanessa. If they had been more private, she wondered whether she would have had the strength to have insisted he stop.

"Do not give it a second thought, my lord. No harm was done." She spoke quickly and when she had finished, she turned just as quickly and walked toward the house with great speed.

"What have I done?" Ellery muttered to himself.

"If you are asking me, I have no answer," said Max, strolling out from behind a row of bushes surrounding the herb garden.

"What the devil are you doing spying on me?" demanded Ellery, anger nearly causing him to strike out at his friend.

"Easy, easy," Max implored, holding up his hands. "You cannot blame me if you chose to carry on your business in public view. If you want to know, I stepped behind the bushes so as not to embarrass Miss Grayson. You should be praying that I am the only one who observed that tender scene."

"Cut line," growled Ellery, knowing Max was right in everything he said. "It wasn't what you think."

"Then what was it?" asked Max, watching him expectantly.

"It was a . . . a mistake. It shouldn't have happened and I will see to it that it doesn't happen again."

"I think your intentions are good," observed Max, "but I wonder if you will be able to achieve that end."

"Have you eaten?" Ellery asked, abruptly changing the subject.

"No. I just returned from shooting with some of the men."

"Then I suggest we go in to breakfast. It appears to be the safest move I can make at the moment."

The two men walked toward the house, Max regaling Ellery with the men's various successes and failures on the shoot.

When they approached the front hall, they observed Corbin and Miss Grayson with their heads together. They both spoke softly and urgently and at one point Corbin handed Miss Grayson a piece of paper which she quickly folded up in her hand.

"Corbin, good to see you finally made it," said Ellery, striding into the hall.

Corbin moved away from Vanessa. "Sorry I'm late," he said, walking forward to meet Ellery. I had more unfinished business in Town than I thought. I would have sent a note, but I realized I would probably arrive before it did."

"We were worried about you," said Vanessa, the color high in her cheeks.

He turned back toward her. "I would not knowingly cause you concern," he replied, a look passing between them that made Ellery feel unnecessary.

"I must change and then begin my search," she said, starting for the stairs.

The paper Corbin had passed to her had disappeared and Ellery wondered what it contained. Was he right in believing she and Corbin were both involved in the club? Was he passing her information concerning a meeting or instructions for some plan in which she was involved? Her touch this morning had caused him not to want to believe she was capable of any of it, but her actions indicated something entirely different.

"You have not had breakfast," protested Ellery.

"I will have Delcie bring me something," she answered, over her shoulder.

He did not realize he was staring after her until Corbin spoke.

"Well, I for one would welcome breakfast. I left late yesterday and spent the night at an inn. You may take my word for it, the food was the worst I have ever tasted."

"Come into the breakfast room," said Ellery. "I imagine most of the other men are there now and you can meet anyone with whom you are not acquainted."

Ellery motioned Max and Corbin to precede him,

then gave a last glance up the stairs. Vanessa had already disappeared from view and he wondered whether his irrational action had caused irreparable damage to the tenuous ties that had been forming between them; ties that might mean the difference between life and death for Phillip.

As soon as Vanessa reached her room, she sent Delcie to the kitchen to bring her a light breakfast. When the door closed behind the maid, she unfolded the paper Corbin had given her. It was creased, but she straightened it as best she could before beginning to read. It was a short note from Browning, who told her he might have had a sighting of Melanie. He had heard this secondhand and was pursuing the person who had mentioned it in conversation. He suggested a meeting date and time a few days hence so that he would have time to investigate further.

Vanessa was happier than she had been since before Melanie told her about the baby. If all went well, they might all be together again soon. She did not know how she would contain her excitement until she met with Browning. She twirled around in the middle of the room, clutching the note to her chest.

Delcie entered at that time and smiled widely. "You must have gotten good news," she said, placing the tray she carried on the table by the sofa.

"I have," Vanessa confirmed, wondering whether she could sit still long enough to eat whatever smelled so wonderful. Nevertheless, she quickly changed out of her riding habit and into a plain muslin gown. She finally settled down and began to eat her meal. "I'll be in the south wing today, Delcie, if anyone is looking for me."

"Yes, ma'am. Do you mind if I ask . . . I mean everyone knows you're looking for ghosts. Do you mind if I ask if you've found any?" The young girl's eyes were huge in her small face.

Vanessa did not know whether Delcie would rather hear that she had or hadn't found any spirits. The truth was always best, she decided. "I haven't found anything yet," she admitted. Delcie seemed disappointed. "But I'm far from finished," she added.

"Then you think you might?"

"Anything is possible," said Vanessa. From the way the girl's face lit up, Vanessa decided she should not worry about frightening the maid if spirits should appear in the house.

A short time later, Vanessa found her way back to the last room she had examined the day before. She made herself comfortable in a high-backed, carved wooden chair in a large chamber on the first floor. She was hardly seated until she felt a flutter in the air so light that she wondered whether she had imagined it. She waited, barely breathing. She had almost given up when a slight coolness touched her, as if a window had been opened, and she knew she wasn't alone anymore.

You are happy today. Thank goodness, I cannot abide someone who is constantly blue-deviled.

"I received good news this morning," said Vanessa. She chose her words carefully, for at this delicate time a bond could either be forged or broken.

Then I am glad for the both of us for as much as I have been longing for someone new to talk to, I did not want to become acquainted with anyone continually out of sorts.

"I assure you, I am usually of good cheer, but I have recently had problems. I think now though that they might be nearly over. But I do not want to talk about it. Instead, we will discuss whatever you would like."

There is so much, I don't know where to begin. Is that gown the fashion now?

Vanessa nearly laughed out loud at the question. She had expected something far more serious such as the state of the monarchy. "If you are asking whether any titled lady would wear it, they would not. The cut is similar to what they would wear, but the material and the trimming are far less expensive. And, of course, the evening gowns are much more elaborate. You should come to the newest part of the house and see for yourself."

A ghostly sigh came from directly in front of Vanessa. *I have stayed away on purpose. I so enjoyed a good party in my day and I find I become so envious that I am miserable for days on end.*

"Is there not someone you could bring with you who might enjoy it?"

Oh, there is George, of course, but all that he is concerned with is horses, horses, horses. He spends more time in the stables than with me. You would think that if a pair of high-bred cattle caused your life to be cut short, a person would never want to get near such beasts again. But not George. He says it wasn't the horses' fault, that it was his. Actually, he says it was mine and that is one bone of contention between us.

"Is George your husband?"

Well, not exactly. There was a ghostly titter, then, *But we are well acquainted if you understand my meaning.*

"I believe that I do," replied Vanessa

George and I met on our first visit to London and became fast friends. However, we married others and, although our paths crossed frequently, our spouses did not particularly care for one another so our friendship lapsed. After his wife and my husband passed on, we gradually began to see one another again.

Vanessa was charmed by the story of young lovers reuniting years later.

Neither of us wanted to marry again, but we were very close.

Things were going very well; in fact, too well, and that is what brought us here.

"You were visiting when you passed on?"

No. We were on the way to call on my daughter. George had insisted on driving since we weren't going far and it was a lovely day. There was a new pair of horses he wanted to try out, so we were traveling alone. George thinks he can drive to an inch, while I consider him absolutely cow-handed when it comes to handling the ribbons. If only I had insisted . . .

"You must not dwell on what might have been," said Vanessa. "It will only cause you to fall into a decline."

I'm certain you're right, but it is difficult not to think about the past when I miss it so. Now where was I? Telling you about our accident, wasn't I? As I said, George was tooling along and having a wonderful time. The problem started after he had taken a few sips of the liquor he had brought. When George drinks he becomes . . . well, I suppose amorous is as good a word as any. He insisted that I move over closer to him, then that I actually sit on his lap and continue with our . . . uh, caresses. He happened to jerk on the reins—unintentionally, of course—and his prime bits of blood took objection to it. He lost control of them and the carriage turned over on that sharp curve in front of this house. We were both thrown out of the carriage.

"How dreadful," exclaimed Vanessa.

We were brought here after the accident and here we have stayed.

"And you are unhappy here?"

Not all the time, and I suppose no more than I was before the accident. I do miss Town though. Can you tell me what happened to some of the people I knew?

"I would probably not have been acquainted with them, but I could ask around. I'm certain that someone here could answer my questions. Perhaps if you would join us one evening, I could ask them in your presence, and you could inquire about anything else you wish."

Do you think it possible?

"I see no reason why not. I will need to tell Lord Trent about you and let him decide, but I should think it would make his house party a complete success."

Lord Trent is a fine figure of a man. You should set your sights on him.

"He is nearly betrothed to another," replied Vanessa.

Until he is, there is still a chance and you would be a fool not to take it.

"He has not indicated such an interest in me," said Vanessa, wondering whether the kiss counted.

Men have no idea that they are interested until you make it plain to them. I must encourage you how to go on while you are here. Now that we are acquainted, I believe I would enjoy it if you took up residence here.

There was a sudden silence. "Are you still here?" asked Vanessa.

Someone is coming. I will talk with you further tomorrow.

"But, wait, what is your name?"

My name? How thoughtless of me. I am Juliana.

"Miss Grayson? Are you in here, ma'am," asked Delcie, sticking her head around the door.

"I am here," Vanessa answered.

"Mrs. Gregory said to come find you. Since you missed luncheon, she wanted to remind you that it's near time for dinner."

"Thank you for coming, Delcie. I had not realized it had gotten so late. I hope you can help make me presentable."

Delcie giggled and Vanessa realized she had developed a fondness for the girl in the short time she had known her.

"Delcie," said Vanessa, a short time later, "I am convinced by your performance this past half-hour that you could become a perfect lady's maid if that is what you wish."

"Oh, ma'am, do you really think so?" asked Delcie, her eyes wide at the idea.

"I'm certain of it and I intend to advise Mrs. Gregory of the fact."

"Thank you, ma'am. Your are too kind."

"It is only what you deserve. You work hard at what you do and you should be rewarded for it. Now, go along and have your dinner. I am going to wait a few minutes before I go down."

After Delcie had closed the door behind her, Vanessa stared at her reflection in the dressing table mirror. How many times had she stared at herself before without speculating how someone else saw her? At least once or twice every day of her adult life. Now as she watched herself in the mirror, she wondered what Lord Trent perceived when he looked at her.

She had been truthful with Delcie. The girl had done a credible job of pulling her hair back in a profusion of curls, then artfully twining green ribbon through them.

Vanessa stood and moved to the cheval mirror standing in the corner and surveyed her gown. It was striped in varying hues of green, with small cap sleeves and three deep flounces at the hem.

She was too accustomed to herself to judge how she looked. She felt confident, but then she always did once she had made contact with a spirit.

Staring into a mirror would not change a thing, she decided. Picking up her fan, she made her way downstairs.

Most of the company was in the drawing room when Vanessa arrived. She had not been standing there long before Corbin came to her side with a glass of sherry in each hand.

"I've been watching for you," he said, handing her a glass.

"I don't know whether I should drink this. I'm nearly delirious with joy as it is."

"Browning's message was as encouraging as I told you, wasn't it?"

"Just so," she answered, with a huge smile. "He believes he has found solid evidence as to the whereabouts of Melanie. He warned me not to get my hopes up in case it comes to nothing, but I cannot help but hope."

"Browning is a good man. If anyone can find Melanie, he can do it."

"I am meeting him tomorrow afternoon to hear the results."

"Miss Grayson, you are looking well this evening. I believe spirit hunting becomes you," commented Lord Trent as he approached them.

"Thank you, my lord. When you have a moment, I would like a private word with you."

"If it will not take long, we have time before dinner," he answered.

"Then I shall make myself scarce and allow the two of you some privacy," said Corbin.

"Shall we go into the library?" asked Lord Trent, indicating the doorway with a wave of his hand.

The two of them left the drawing room and walked down the hall until they came to the large double doors of the library. Vanessa had admired the room when Mrs. Gregory had shown her through the house, but she had not had time to peruse the shelves. She and Melanie both read a great deal and she was certain she would be content to spend days at a time in this room. However, she was not here for her enjoyment no matter how often Lord Trent insisted she was a guest.

He went to a table and refilled his glass from one of

the decanters before turning to her. "What is it you wish to discuss, Miss Grayson?"

His formality startled her into silence. His voice was stiff, his words were clipped, and his usual congenial facade was grim.

"Miss Grayson?"

"I'm sorry, my lord, I suppose I was wondering how to begin."

"If it is about today . . ." he began.

"Not at all," she said quickly. "It is about the spirits."

"The spirits?" he repeated.

"You have them," she revealed, then nearly laughed at the various expressions that passed over his face.

"You mean there are actual spirits inhabiting this house?" he finally asked.

"I have only spoken to one so far, but I know there is at least one other to whom I have not spoken. It is too early yet for me to determine whether there are more than the two."

Ellery rubbed his forehead. "Two are quite enough for the moment. You are certain?" he asked again as if he could not quite believe her.

"Quite certain," she confirmed firmly.

"What should I do now?" he asked.

"You need do nothing at all," she answered. "There has been no change either in your life or in this house."

"Except if I am to believe you, I am now the proud owner of several spirits."

"I don't believe you can own spirits," replied Vanessa. "In truth, it might be better to say they own you."

"Do not attempt to frighten me, Miss Grayson. I will not be chased from my house by spirits."

"They mean you no harm and certainly do not want you to surrender your home to them."

"Then what the devil do they want?"

"For you to continue as you have been. I do believe

that Juliana would like you to have more entertainments for she sorely misses the soirees she once attended."

"Juliana? So you have named them already?"

"I do not name them, my lord, that is what she said her name was."

"Just Juliana?"

"Delcie interrupted us before she could tell me the rest."

"Am I allowed to meet these spirits or are you the only one who can speak to them?"

"Usually I am the only one, but if you are particularly receptive you might be able to hear them."

"Then I want to talk to them now."

"They are not to be summoned like dogs, my lord. If you like, you may accompany me tomorrow and we will see whether she will appear with you there."

"Did she say anything of note today?" he asked.

Vanessa related what Juliana had told her. During her recitation, Lord Trent emptied his glass and poured another. At one point, he motioned her to a chair and took one facing her.

"Dear Lord," he said, "where did you hear about this? Has Mrs. Gregory been telling tales again?"

"What do you mean, my lord?" she asked, puzzled at his reaction. "I have heard nothing from Mrs. Gregory concerning anyone named Juliana."

"George Sanderson, Lord Canfield and Juliana, Lady Ransley were thrown from their carriage in front of our house and were carried inside just as you described, but that was during my grandfather's time."

"Time means nothing to the spirits," said Vanessa.

"I cannot believe this," he exclaimed.

Vanessa had grown hardened to people who paid for her services and then doubted what she had to say. "Believe what you will, my lord. I am merely reporting what

I have discovered thus far." She rose to her feet and started from the room.

"One moment," he said, his voice bringing her to a halt. "Do not mention this to anyone else for the time being. I will go to the south wing with you tomorrow."

"Would you rather go in the morning or the afternoon?" she asked.

"What would be best for the spirits?" he inquired, a touch of sarcasm in his voice.

She gritted her teeth and replied pleasantly, "I'm certain they will look forward to meeting such a congenial gentleman at any hour of the day."

"Go about your usual business," he directed, " and I will join you when I am able."

She nodded and was ready to leave again when he spoke.

"And, Miss Grayson?"

"Yes, my lord."

"To set the record straight, I do not have a fiancée."

"That is too bad for I believe that Juliana feels you should be married." She left before he could comment.

"What was so important that you had to speak privately to Trent?" asked Corbin, who was waiting just inside the drawing room door, watching for her return.

"You should not ask such personal questions," she said.

"You mean you are not going to confide in me? My heart is shattered."

"It would take far more to break your heart. Truth to tell, I am not even convinced that you are in possession of one."

He placed his hand over his heart and said, "I most certainly do have one and it is beating just for you."

There was a noise behind them and they turned to

find Lord Trent looking on. Without a word to them, he walked further into the room and began conversing with his guests.

"Caught," said Corbin. "It will be all over by the morning that I was proclaiming my affection for you."

"Do not be silly," she reprimanded him. She thought of Lord Trent's kiss and his actions earlier in the day. Would he have treated Lady Cornelia in the same manner? She did not know the answer to it and did not want to ask Corbin.

"What is bothering you, Vanessa?"

"I'm sorry to have been so short with you, but Melanie's disappearance has brought my feelings closer to the surface than usual."

"It is to be expected, but you must be brave. Browning will come through for us and you and Melanie will soon be reunited. Have you heard anything from Jonathan's father?"

"Not a word," she admitted, "and I don't believe we ever will. At first I was worried about facing society with a fatherless child. I never thought he might also end up motherless."

"Melanie will come home and perhaps the father will appear. If so, you will have worried for naught."

"Oh, Rudy, I would do anything to see her again." Tears sprang to her eyes and she blinked furiously to hold them back. One spilled over, and as he had done before in the mews behind Lord Trent's town house, Corbin reached out and brushed it from her cheek.

Ellery had been surreptitiously observing Corbin and Miss Grayson carry on an intense conversation at the deserted end of the room. He watched as Corbin reached out and touched her cheek just as he had done before.

Ellery was angry. He did not understand how a woman who pretended to speak with the spirits and who perhaps belonged to a club he was pledged to destroy could bring him to such a boiling point.

He sought out Lady Cornelia and made her think she was the only woman in the world for him.

Eleven

The evening seemed endless for Vanessa. Although she was once again seated between Viscount Huntly and Corbin during dinner, she was unable to ignore Lord Trent. He sat at the head of the table as usual, with Lady Cornelia at his side. The two acted as if they were the only people in the room, speaking to one another in low voices.

Their actions seemed rude to Vanessa, but she assumed their dinner partners on the other sides of them forgave them since they were in love and nearly betrothed. She had heard one guest murmur that there might even be an announcement before the house party was over.

Vanessa attempted to convince herself that it did not matter that Lord Trent thought no more of her than a servant. He had not said so, of course, but he was paying her, was he not? And she had only to look at his conduct toward her this morning and when he had kissed her at Lady Bowden's to see that he did not hold her in high regard.

Her face burned at the recollection of her reaction to his kiss. Instead of pulling away, she had behaved like a wanton hussy, pressing herself against him and putting her arms around him, holding him tight. It was no wonder he thought he could take further advantage of her.

She had nearly decided to retire to her room as soon

as dinner was over, but then her obstinacy reared its
unwise head and she followed the ladies into the drawing
room. She sat with Lady Venable until the men returned
to the room and Lord Baylor came to speak with them.

After a few minutes of conversation with Lady Venable,
Lord Baylor turned to Vanessa. "Miss Grayson, I have
seen you several times when you have revealed spirits at
my friends' homes and I must admit I find it fascinat-
ing."

Vanessa never knew what to say when comments such
as Lord Baylor's were made. Should she thank them for
their interest or feign modesty because of her talent.
Neither seemed appropriate and many times she merely
nodded. This time she chose to reply.

"It is like anything else, Lord Baylor. After a time it
becomes commonplace."

"I cannot believe that I would ever consider talking
to ghosts commonplace, but I admire your ability to do
so."

"Thank you, but I don't believe what I do deserves
admiration."

"Will you walk with me and we will discuss it further?"
he asked.

She glanced at Lady Venable to see if she would ex-
press disapproval of Lord Baylor's suggestion, but the
older woman merely smiled and turned to Lady Halburton to continue their tête-à-tête.

"I would be delighted," said Vanessa, cheered that
she need not stand about attempting to look absorbed
in a conversation that did not include her.

Lord Baylor led her down the long room, pointing
out several of the paintings on the wall. When they
reached the French doors, he asked, "Would you care
to go outside? I believe we will find the night air cooler
than inside."

"For a moment then," agreed Vanessa, stepping through the doors.

Several pairs of eyes watched the two walk out onto the terrace. Corbin wondered what Baylor wanted with Vanessa. He must keep a sharp eye on the young man so he would not take advantage of his friend. He made his way down the room, stopping to speak with various people along the way, until he could see the dim outline of the two through the French doors.

Ellery also knew that Baylor had a reputation with the ladies and did not like it at all when he and Vanessa disappeared into the night. He began to move in that direction when he noticed that Corbin had already beaten him to it. He would allow the man to handle it. After all, Miss Grayson was his close friend.

Even though he had made the decision, he did not draw an easy breath until Lord Baylor and Miss Grayson returned to the drawing room. Her face was flushed and Ellery wondered whether she had granted Baylor a kiss such as the one he had received. The thought of her in the other man's arms caused his fists to clench at his side. He was a fool, he thought, then turned back to Cornelia and attempted to give her his full attention.

Vanessa had enjoyed the time she had spent with Lord Baylor. His light conversation and teasing comments had allowed her to forget the troubles that lay heavy on her mind. When they entered the drawing room, Lord Baylor's friend, Viscount Dalton, joined them and they stood conversing for several minutes before Lord Dalton asked, "Do you play the pianoforte, Miss Grayson?"

Vanessa had played since she was a child and was a more than credible musician. She did not, however, intend to put herself before several dozen of the *ton's* finest, particularly since Lord Trent was scowling at her from the other end of the room.

"I do a little," she admitted, "but not well enough to embarrass myself before such an august assembly."

"I am certain you would do no such thing. Do play for us," persisted Lord Dalton.

"I have no doubt that Lady Barbara or Lady Cornelia play much better than I do," she replied. "You should encourage them."

"Yes, do go ask," Lord Baylor urged him.

"All right," grumbled Lord Dalton, unhappy at being sent off like an errand boy to beg a favor.

While there was a music room in the house, the drawing room also held a pianoforte in one corner of the room. It wasn't long after Lord Dalton's request that Lady Cornelia was ensconced in the seat, looking through the music. Lord Trent was standing beside her, ready to turn the pages as she played.

Vanessa could not help but notice what a handsome couple they made—both were tall; one blond; one dark. At the moment, Lord Trent looked merely bored, while Lady Cornelia was clearly exhilarated at being the center of attention.

Lady Cornelia played several tunes of the day. They were simple and she managed to get through them with few mistakes. She received polite applause and looked up at Lord Trent as if she had just proven herself worthy of being his countess.

"Give us a tune, Barbara," said Lord Lambert. "Cost enough for that fancy French fellow to teach you. Should get something for my money."

Lady Barbara blushed, while the rest of the company smiled in amusement. When she did play, her technique far outshone Lady Cornelia's. That Lady Cornelia was highly unhappy showed in her tepid reaction to her friend's talent. She merely clapped her hands together lightly twice, but did not go forward to commend Barbara, as Barbara had done with her.

"Now, do you find your money well spent?" asked Lady Lambert, eliciting even further laughter from the onlookers.

"I do, my dear, and I never doubted it in the least," he replied, patting his daughter on the cheek, causing her embarrassment to heighten.

Then something happened that was so unusual that it was only later that Vanessa figured it all out. Lady Cornelia called out to her.

"Miss Grayson, we have not yet heard from you this evening."

"Thank you, Lady Cornelia, but I cannot compete with you and Lady Barbara," replied Vanessa.

"Nonsense. With your sensibilities to the spirits, I am convinced that you play very well indeed. Perhaps even one of the masters came back to teach you," she said.

The rest of the company laughed at her jest, but her remark only raised anger in Vanessa. She glanced toward Lord Trent and, while he was not laughing at her, he said nothing in her defense. He was looking on as if this were a play and she were the player.

His demeanor merely caused her indignation to simmer. Perhaps if she was not worried to the bone by Melanie's disappearance, or if Lord Trent had not treated her as if she meant something to him before allowing his lady love to attempt to embarrass her, then her reaction might have been different. She might have protested that she did not play and excused herself.

But her feelings had been battered about and she would not be made to look like an unschooled country miss before everyone. If it was entertainment they wanted, then it was entertainment they would get.

"I really couldn't," she said, hoping that someone would urge her on, and she was not to be disappointed.

Not only did Lord Baylor and Lord Dalton offer to turn pages for her, but Lady Cornelia spoke again and she said exactly what Vanessa had prayed she would.

"Come, Miss Grayson. I know that you have not had the luxury of the tutors that Lady Barbara and I have had, so we will not judge you harshly, will we?" She looked around at the interested faces turned toward her and smiled superciliously.

" 'Course not," boomed Lord Lambert, good-naturedly. "Thought my Barbara would never learn to play. Took years, but she finally managed."

Lady Barbara blushed at his revelation and Lady Lambert shushed him. Vanessa realized that Lord Lambert was attempting to put her at ease and she offered him a smile.

She looked again at Lord Trent, but his demeanor remained as expressionless as it had a few minutes before.

"We will both turn pages and stand beside you to give you confidence," offered Lord Baylor.

"That is very kind of you, my lord," Vanessa replied meekly. "If you insist then."

"We do," replied Cornelia firmly.

Vanessa made her way to the pianoforte with Lord Dalton and Lord Baylor trailing along behind her. While she was being seated and choosing music other than what Lady Cornelia and Lady Barbara had played, conversation was resumed and backs were turned on the pianoforte.

Vanessa purposely selected a simple ballad to begin with and when the first tentative notes sounded in the large room, hardly anyone discontinued their discussion. By the time she finished the first tune, much of the conversation had ceased, Lady Cornelia was looking decidedly perturbed and Lord Trent appeared highly interested in the playing out of the scene unfolding before him.

"Lady Cornelia," Vanessa said, at the end of the applause following the song, "you were right when you mentioned the old masters coming back. I was fortunate to speak with a composer whose name you might recognize." Vanessa had regained the attention of the remainder of the people in the room.

"It was George Frederick Handel," she continued, and was amused at the buzz which greeted her words. She had never met Handel's spirit and probably never would, but she felt a small deception was acceptable at this point.

"Of course, Mr. Handel did not have a great deal of time to spend with me, but while he was here he did teach me a part of one of his compositions. It takes an orchestra to make it worthy of his genius, but I will do the best I can on the pianoforte."

She turned her attention to the keys as if to begin playing, then stopped again. "By the way, this is a selection from the *Water Music.*"

Vanessa began to play without observing the startled glances and murmured remarks of the audience. Once she began, any self-consciousness she might have felt was washed away by her love of the music. She played without sheet music, which only emphasized her familiarity with the piece.

When she finished, she allowed her hands to rest in her lap and closed her eyes for a moment. Total silence reigned in the large room and she wondered whether she had made a fool of herself. She opened her eyes to find everyone staring at her. Then Lord Trent raised his hands and began applauding. The rest of the company enthusiastically followed suit, the men rising to their feet in honor of her performance.

"Bravo, Miss Grayson," said Lord Trent, when the applause had died down.

He walked toward her and took her hand when he reached her side, pulling her to her feet and leading her out from behind the pianoforte. "I did not know that you were such a musical expert, and if it is Handel we have to thank, then I do so with fervor. I believe that I speak for all of us when I say your performance was a delight to the ears." Murmurs of agreement greeted his remarks.

Vanessa glanced out from under her lashes toward Lady Cornelia, but she was no longer there. Becoming more bold, Vanessa glanced around the room, but Lord Trent's nearly affianced was nowhere to be seen.

It was nearly two hours after midnight when a shadow slipped out of the back of the house. Another figure stepped away from the dark shadows of the bushes around the herb garden and stood waiting.

"This was a foolish mistake," hissed the first figure. "We could be caught at any moment."

"That holds true nearly every time we meet," replied the second, in the low, well-modulated voice of Lord Thornhill.

"But there is no reason for this."

"I believe that there is," argued Thornhill. "We must finish what we started and soon. The longer we continue the way we are, the more likely we are to be caught. Some of the others are becoming jittery."

"They are acting like hysterical women rather than Hell-Fire Club members," jeered the first person. "Tell them they must remain strong and that we are near the end of our quest."

"They have heard it all before and I agree with them.

If you do not give the word to end this within the next
few days, then I will no longer be a part of it."

"You can't desert me now."

"Then say the word," Thornhill demanded.

A silence fell between the two shadows, which lasted
too long for Thornhill.

"I am gone," he said, taking a step back.

"All right. We will do it within a few days' time, but
we must make plans."

The two stepped into the darker shadows of the
bushes and began a whispered conversation.

It was nearly three o'clock in the morning and Vanessa
was sitting on the window seat, staring out into the nearly
moonless night. She wondered where Melanie was and
whether she was unharmed. If she allowed herself to
dwell on it, her grief would soon cause her to become
incapable of carrying on her everyday life, and she could
not let that happen for Jonathan's sake alone.

She thought back on the hours following dinner, attempting to deflect her thoughts to something else. Perhaps she shouldn't feel so smug, but the evening had
given her a great deal of satisfaction. She would probably
reap the rewards of embarrassing Lady Cornelia by not
having as many engagements during the Little Season
if the woman had her way, but at the moment it was well
worth the possible diminished earnings.

From the time she finished playing until she retired
for the evening, she had been complimented countless
times over. Lord Dalton and Lord Baylor stayed by her
side as if they had personally discovered her, and she
had to admit she was altogether pleased to be recognized
for something other than talking to spirits.

Lord Trent had disappeared along with some of the
other gentlemen and had not returned by the time she

excused herself from the company. She did not know whether he had joined the others for cards or whether he had gone in search of Lady Cornelia. If it was the latter, Vanessa wondered what kind of a reception he had received from his nearly betrothed.

Perhaps he would tell her when they met the next day. Vanessa smiled in the dim light of the single candle which burned in the room. She could not imagine Lord Trent confiding in her the details of his confrontation with Lady Cornelia.

Vanessa was puzzled by Lady Cornelia's manner toward her. Up until tonight, the woman had begged Lord Trent to have her in his homes, but last evening Lady Cornelia had turned against her. Could she have seen the interchange between Vanessa and Lord Trent after their ride this morning? If so, that could certainly explain her being at daggers drawn toward Vanessa and her desire to make her a laughingstock in front of the guests.

Vanessa leaned closer to the window, peering out. For a moment, she thought she had seen someone riding away from the house, but she could detect no movement now. Vanessa shook her head in self-deprecation. She accepted her ability to talk to spirits, but when she began seeing specters it was time to retire.

Vanessa rose from the window seat and returned to her bed. Blowing out the candle, she stretched out, attempting to relax and forget her worries for a few hours before facing them once again.

Ellery awoke the next morning, wondering whether he should stay locked in his room for the remainder of the day, or play least in sight until dinnertime.

He had no idea what Cornelia's reaction to the debacle of last evening had been, for she had fled the room while he was congratulating Miss Grayson. It was Cornelia's habit not to appear until just before luncheon and he supposed he must wait until that time to find out whether she was in high dudgeon.

It was questionable whether the conditions between him and Cornelia were worse than the dilemma posed by Miss Grayson. He clearly recalled each moment of the kiss they had shared at Lady Bowden's and it was that memory that had nearly caused him to repeat the pleasant sensation yesterday morning. And he would have done so, in front of anyone who was looking their way, if she had not stopped him. He had still been halfway discomfited by his actions the night before when Cornelia began luring Miss Grayson into what was to have been a humiliating moment. Instead, the tables had been turned on Cornelia and she had ended up looking the fool.

Taking a deep breath, he called for his valet and began dressing for the day. He had no desire to face either Cornelia or Miss Grayson after yesterday, but face them he must.

Vanessa decided to have breakfast in her room and then go straight to work. She would continue with the other rooms and when Lord Trent joined her, they could return to where she had met Juliana.

As she stepped out into the hall, she wondered what his demeanor would be when they met. He would probably be angry that she had misled Lady Cornelia the night before, even though the woman had been bent on mortifying Vanessa in front of the entire roomful of people.

Vanessa squared her shoulders, lifted her chin, and marched down the hall toward the older part of the house. She did not care what Lord Trent thought of her.

She was nearly finished with her job here and she would welcome the chance to return home early. She yearned to be with little Jonathan and Annie, waiting for Melanie to return.

Vanessa was surprised and gratified that Lord Trent chose to appear early that morning, for this was the day she was to meet Mr. Browning. He had instructed her to ride by the inn this afternoon and he would follow her until they found a spot where they could talk in private. Earlier, she had sent Delcie to the stable with a message that she would be riding at two o'clock that afternoon and had asked that Happy Lady be made ready.

When Lord Trent made his appearance, they exchanged greetings, but neither made mention of what had occurred between them the day before.

"Is Juliana here?" he asked, looking around the room.

"Not at the moment," she replied. "I met her in the room next door so perhaps we would have better luck there."

He stood aside while she stepped back out into the hall and led the way to the next doorway.

"I wonder whether this is where she died?" he murmured. Before Miss Grayson could answer, Ellery was startled to see her skirt swirl as if caught in a strong draft.

A rush of air surrounded Vanessa and she knew that Juliana was with them. She listened for a moment, then said, "She died when she was thrown from the carriage and was brought here afterward."

"She told you that?" he asked.

"Just now," said Vanessa.

Ellery looked around the room.

"Don't expect to see anything," warned Vanessa. "She is happy you decided to visit today because there is something you should know."

"And that is?" asked Ellery, uneasy that he was supposedly talking to a spirit through Miss Grayson. He did not like to appear a fool and he felt that was exactly what she was making of him.

"Juliana wanted to warn you that there is evil in your house."

Ellery's lip curled. "Am I to go scurrying back to London?"

"Not at all. She said you have no choice but to face it. She won't explain it to me in detail, but she says it involves Phillip. He is your brother, is he not?" asked Vanessa.

Ellery's heart plummeted when he heard his brother's name. "He is," stated Ellery, "but I do not see what Phillip has to do with a spirit."

"She has evidently overheard something that pertains to him. She tells you to look under your own roof for the answer."

"You expect me to believe this nonsense?" he scoffed.

A statue flew across the room and hovered for a moment before his face before crashing to the floor. Ellery's startled gaze met hers.

"She can do worse," warned Vanessa, " however, she doesn't want to destroy anything else."

"Can she not tell me who it is?" he asked.

"She could if she had been the one who had heard it. It seems that George was the one who actually came upon the conversation and George paid no heed to who it was. She has tried again and again to make him remember, but he cannot."

"I don't know how you arranged all this," he said, nudging the pieces of the broken statue with the toe of his highly polished Hessian boot, "but you will not make a dupe of me."

"I am not trying to, my lord, I am merely passing along what Juliana has said."

Ellery suddenly staggered and the door to the room slammed violently.

"What happened?" he asked, rubbing the spot on his chest where he was sure he had felt two hands push him.

"I'm afraid Juliana has a low tolerance for people who do not believe her. As you can guess, she has left the room. I pity poor George once she finds him."

"Miss Grayson, how . . ."

Vanessa held up her hand. "Don't ask me again how I did this," she cautioned him. "I have come here at your request, or perhaps better at Lady Cornelia's request, leaving my home when I would have been better served to have stayed there.

"Last night Lady Cornelia attempted to . . . you were there, you know what happened. And I can only assume that you must think little of me since you gave no thought to ruining my reputation yesterday morning. Now, when I tell you what you have paid me for, you question what I have to say despite proof. I do not know why you wanted me here in the first place, my lord. If it was to entertain you and your lady friend, then you have made a dreadful mistake for neither do I take kindly to being made to look the fool. I can be gone as soon as I am packed."

Even through his anger, Ellery could see the logic of Miss Grayson's argument. But he had invited her to the house party in hopes that she would lead him to Phillip, and it seems he had been right for she had just mentioned his brother no matter how vaguely. Was this merely to tease him? Did she plan on feeding him more information a little at a time until she had him where she wanted him? Perhaps she was insulted by his and Cornelia's behavior, but if what he suspected was true, she was involved in his brother's disappearance and a member of the Hell-Fire Club as well.

Ellery did not wish to frighten her off. "I am sorry

that you feel I have taken advantage of you, Miss Grayson, for it was not my intention. I'd like for you to stay for the duration of the party. Not merely to continue with this spirit hunting," he said, "but to enjoy the festivities."

Vanessa stared at him, attempting to gauge his sincerity. "I'm afraid I might cast a damper over your party in my present state."

"You have not done so thus far and if it would make you rest easier, you could make a short trip home. I understand that it is not far from here. Once your fears are abated, you could return for the rest of the house party."

"I do not know."

"Why not think on it?" he suggested. "We have a picnic planned for tomorrow and I would like for you to attend. We can discuss it further then."

"I don't know whether it would be appropriate or whether I would be entirely comfortable attending a picnic after all that has happened."

"Let me assure you that whatever happened last night has already been forgotten by the guests and, as far as I know, no one observed us after our ride yesterday morning."

The chime of a clock caused Vanessa to realize it was one o'clock. They were both missing luncheon and she had only an hour to change and be in the village to meet Mr. Browning.

"You must excuse me, my lord; there is something I must attend to." She brushed by him and rushed from the room, leaving him staring after her.

"I wonder what that was all about?" he murmured, following Vanessa at a more sedate pace.

He waited in an alcove down the hall from Miss Grayson's room. He heard the door open and shut and looked out into the hall to see her disappearing down the back steps. She was wearing her riding habit and Ellery wondered where she was off to. There was only one way to find out and that was to follow her.

Ellery stayed in the fields that bordered the road leading into the village while keeping his eye on Vanessa as she cut a direct path to the inn. She glanced sideways and nearly hesitated as she passed the building, but then kept her mare on the road leading out of the village.

Ellery paused, watching the large man who had been sitting on the bench in front of the inn. As soon as Miss Grayson had passed, he casually rose and stretched before climbing onto a horse tethered nearby and turning the animal in the same direction the woman had taken.

Ellery allowed enough space between them until he felt safe in putting his stallion in motion again. Once outside the village, the two guided their horses into a copse of trees to a small clearing. Neither dismounted, but sat their horses, speaking quietly and earnestly. Miss Grayson covered her face with her hands at one point and then reached out to the man, who clasped her hand in his. More words were spoken, none of which Ellery could hear, then Miss Grayson turned the mare and guided her back onto the road. The man waited a few minutes then rode in the opposite direction.

Ellery berated himself for not bringing Max with him. He could have sent his friend to follow the stranger since he could not be absent long enough from the house party to do so himself. What did it mean? he wondered. Did her mention of Phillip and her meeting with the man signal that the club was ready to make a move? He must be more vigilant than ever over the next few days.

Vanessa was jubilant. Mr. Browning had advised her that he might have a lead on someone who had seen Melanie the day she disappeared.

Alana Clayton

The information was sketchy—only that a traveling coach had stopped by the side of the road and a young woman with a man following close behind was walking nearby. The person who had seen them had been ready to stop to inquire whether they had experienced trouble, when he looked at the driver. He was certain he saw the man reach under the seat and come up with a pistol. Needless to say, the Good Samaritan kept on his course without stopping.

The news was secondhand and he hoped to speak to the person who had seen Melanie, perhaps as early as the next day. He would contact her as soon as he was certain.

Vanessa left the stable yard and hurried back into the house. She wanted to write Annie immediately and tell her the good news. With any luck, Melanie would soon be home and her small family would be one again.

Just before dinner, Ellery went into the library to sign several letters. The outgoing post was on a tray on the corner of the desk and he casually glanced at it. To his surprise there was a letter on top addressed to Annie Stewart. Ellery did not know her last name, but the only Annie he knew of was Miss Grayson's maid. Perhaps it wasn't ethical, but Ellery was dealing with his brother's life. He made a note of the direction on the letter in case it should come in handy one day.

The evening proved uneventful. Lady Cornelia was once again at Lord Trent's side, but did not look down the table toward Vanessa. Once in the drawing room though, Lady Cornelia approached Vanessa. She did not know what to expect, but she stood her ground, watching calmly as the blond-haired woman came to a halt directly in front of her.

"Miss Grayson, I want to apologize for any embarrassment I may have caused you last evening. I was merely teasing, but I understand from Ellery you may have misunderstood my little joke."

So, Lord Trent had spoken to his fiancée, or near-fiancée, as he insisted, about the incident the night before. She wondered about the reason behind his action. Perhaps he thought she might agree to stay if Lady Cornelia apologized. But why did he care so much whether she left before the end of the house party?

"Perhaps for a moment, but I soon realized it was merely a jest," said Vanessa.

"Then you do not hold it against me?"

"Of course not. Give it no further thought."

"I'm so relieved," said Lady Cornelia. "I would not like to have any hard feelings between us. After all, you are doing us such a favor by coming here."

Lady Cornelia sounded as if she were only awaiting the vows to move into Lord Trent's home, while the earl objected each time Vanessa referred to Lady Cornelia as his betrothed.

"Have you found any spirits yet?" Lady Cornelia asked.

"You must ask Lord Trent that question," said Vanessa.

Lady Cornelia managed to pout quite prettily. When Vanessa added nothing else, she said, "Then I suppose I must search out Ellery to hear what you have discovered."

"That would be best," agreed Vanessa, and watched while Lady Cornelia moved down the room to where Lord Trent was in conversation with several other gentlemen.

Lady Cornelia spoke in his ear and he turned to look

at Vanessa. At that time, she determined that an early night would be wise, for she did not want any further conflict to tarnish the good news she had received about Melanie.

Twelve

Vanessa had enjoyed a good night's sleep for once and arose looking forward to the picnic and a day out of the confines of the house. The day was not as hot as the previous ones had been and Lady Venable announced that it was a sign that their picnic was to be a success. Vanessa rode in the carriage with Lady Venable and Lady Halburton, greatly relieved not to be included in the one immediately in front of them, which contained Lady Cornelia.

"You are extremely quiet, my dear," said Lady Venable.

"I am enjoying the scenery," she replied. "The landscape is lovely."

"You should see it when it is not so dry," Lady Venable replied, "although I do believe it is surviving better than most. I suppose because of the streams we are so fortunate to have. We are going to picnic beside my favorite one."

When they reached the picnic spot, the staff had already arrived and were arranging tables and chairs in the shade of the large trees. There were also spreads placed on the ground piled high with pillows for the younger set.

The stream was all that Lady Venable had claimed—wide and shallow, with the clear water running over a smooth rock bottom. Vanessa was immediately drawn to it and leaned over, looking into the water to see whether she could spy any minnows swimming there.

Before she knew it, the locket that she always wore around her neck broke free and splashed into the stream. She gave a cry of alarm and was ready to drop to her knees and attempt to retrieve it.

"Allow me, Miss Grayson," said Lord Trent, from close beside her. He quickly stripped off his jacket and rolled up one of his shirtsleeves. Kneeling down, he reached into the water and in a trice, he rose with the locket in hand.

He reached out to her, the golden chain looping through his fingers, which were dripping with water droplets. When she took it from him, her eyes could not avoid the dark hairs which swirled wet and masculine on his forearm. It was then that her breath caught in her throat and a stricken expression appeared on her face.

"What is it, Miss Grayson?" he asked, concerned about her reaction.

Vanessa recovered quickly. "It is nothing, my lord, merely relief at getting my locket back safely. It was my mother's and I would have been deeply saddened had I lost it."

"I'm happy to have been of assistance," he replied, rolling down his sleeve and picking up his coat. "If you will excuse me, I must see to my other guests."

"Of course," she murmured, still clutching the locket to her breast.

When he left, she released a long breath that she did not realize she had been holding. It had not been the near loss of the locket that had caused her alarm, it was what she had seen when Lord Trent had handed her the locket. On his forearm was a mark that appeared to be a four-leaf clover. The exact mark that was on the arm of little Jonathan.

It could not be, she thought frantically. Her sister had never been to London to meet Lord Trent, but then it was not all that far from his country home to Vanessa's home. He could have been traveling nearby and observed Melanie on one of her many walks. It would be child's play for a man of Lord Trent's experience to meet her sister and flatter her into believing every word that he said.

Rage flew through Vanessa, filling every corner of her being. She squeezed the locket in her hand until it cut into her palm. She realized she was unable to return to the group and pretend that nothing had happened, so she followed the stream around a bend until she was out of sight of the company.

She found a fallen tree and took a seat on its rough bark, attempting to face the realization that Lord Trent might very well be the father of little Jonathan. Everything fit with what Melanie had said. The earl was certainly from a good family and he was considered a gentleman by everyone who knew him. He would probably promise anything Melanie wanted to hear to have his way with her. And when a child entered the picture, he had disappeared without a backward glance.

Vanessa would have thought that a man of his caliber would have at the very least settled an amount of money on Melanie. Perhaps he did not want to admit the child was his in order to avoid further demands.

If he thought he was going to get away with ruining her sister, he had a great deal to learn about the Grayson temperament. Was he aware that she was Melanie's sister or had he completely forgotten about the young girl he had seduced in the country? She could see no reason for him to invite her into his home if he knew of her connection with Melanie, except that Lady Cornelia had insisted and he certainly could not reveal the reason he did not want Vanessa around his nearly betrothed.

Vanessa almost felt sorry for Lady Cornelia. The woman was planning the rest of her life around Lord Trent and he would be unavailable. For Vanessa was determined about one thing, and that was that as soon as Melanie came home, Lord Trent would marry her sister despite the difference in their social standing.

Then a thought struck Vanessa that was colder than the water in the stream. What if Lord Trent was responsible for Melanie's disappearance? He could have thought that she and the baby were too much of a threat to his life. After all, Melanie also came from a good family, if from one not so well off. It might be more than a nine days' wonder if it became known that he had taken advantage of such a young, innocent country miss. If he considered at all that he might be forced into marriage, he could have decided to make Melanie disappear. Then it would make sense that he would ask Vanessa to visit his homes. Where else could he keep such a close eye on her and discover what she was doing to find her sister?

All those offers of assistance. It was merely a ploy to learn more. Her stomach turned and she was glad she had eaten such a light breakfast, for Lord Trent's depraved indifference made her sick to the core. Which begged the question of where Melanie was and had Lord Trent harmed her? She buried her face in her hands as if that could erase from her imagination the possible fate of her sister.

After a few minutes, Vanessa gathered her composure; she could not allow Lord Trent to see that she was upset. It was important to keep her knowledge secret until Melanie was safe at home again, and she would not even consider again that she would never return. Once she was back, however, Vanessa would allow the full force of her wrath to fall on the earl.

She rose from the log and made her way back along the stream until she reached the picnic area again. She must get away from Lord Trent for a short time. A trip home would be the very thing. Seeing little Jonathan and Annie would revive her so that she could play out Lord Trent's game to the end.

She found Corbin and drew him aside. "I must travel home first thing in the morning," she said.

"Have you had news of Melanie?" he asked.

"No more than I told you yesterday," she answered. "However, I must have some relief from pretending that nothing is wrong. I wonder if I may use your coach if you do not need it? I will be gone only overnight."

"You are more than welcome to it," he said. "Tell me when you wish to leave and I will make the arrangements."

"I would like to leave now," she said with a sad smile, "but I know that would be far too impolite, so I suppose I must wait until tomorrow. If I could depart at sunrise, I could spend a great part of the day at home, then I could leave in just enough time to return before dark the day after. Your driver is welcome to stay if he wishes or he could stop at the inn and I will pay for his room and for the animals' care."

"Nonsense. You will do nothing of the sort. My driver is well able to take care of himself and at no expense to you."

"I will not argue for I do not have the strength," she replied.

"You are not ill, are you?" he asked, concern intensifying his gaze.

"No," she assured him. "Merely tired and worried more than ever about Melanie."

"Perhaps she will be home by the time you reach there," he suggested, gently.

"I will not count on it," she said.

Ellery watched Miss Grayson and Corbin standing closely together and speaking intently to one another.

He wondered what they were up to now. Were they plotting another spirit trick, or perhaps exchanging information on the ceremonies of the next club meeting? Whatever it was, with Max's assistance he meant to keep a close eye on them both.

The day seemed endless to Vanessa as she forced herself to respond politely to conversation during the picnic. It appeared to her that Lord Trent was watching her far more closely than usual, but perhaps it was because she now knew the truth about him.

The picnic finally came to an end with the majority of the guests proclaiming it the perfect day. They returned to the house, each going his own way to meet again at dinner. Vanessa decided that it was best to approach Lord Trent in private and advise him of her decision to visit her home.

She made certain that she was the first down to the drawing room before dinner and waited by the door until the earl entered.

"My lord," she said, stepping in front of him, "may I have a word with you in private?"

He appeared curious, but did not question her at that time. "Perhaps we should go to the library," he said, moving aside so she could precede him.

When the heavy oak door closed behind them, it was as if no one else existed in the world. The silence wrapped itself around the two people who stood facing one another.

"Would you like to sit?" Ellery asked.

"No, thank you. What I have to say will not take long," she answered, looking everywhere but at him.

He wondered why she could not meet his gaze, since she had never had a problem before.

"Yesterday, you mentioned that perhaps I would like

to make a short trip home. I've thought about it and I believe that your suggestion is an excellent one."

"When would you like to leave?" he asked, accepting her revelation without any indication of surprise.

"I plan on leaving at sunrise tomorrow and will stay overnight, returning late the next day."

"There will be no problem with that. I will have my traveling coach ready at first light."

"You have my thanks, but I have already accepted Lord Corbin's offer of his coach."

So that was what they were discussing at the picnic, thought Ellery. And what else was Miss Grayson expecting to accomplish during her visit home? In reality, did her journey have something to do with the Hell-Fire Club and Phillip? It seemed a great coincidence that she chose this particular time to travel home. Just the day before she had met secretly with a man who left as quickly as he arrived and then today had spent even more time conferring with Corbin.

Maintaining his calm demeanor, he said, "It seems I can do no more than wish you a good trip. I hope you won't change your mind about returning once you are at home."

"That is one thing you need not worry about, my lord. After such a delightful time today, I find I am quite looking forward to the rest of the house party." And finding out what you have done with Melanie, she finished silently.

Ellery did not know what to think about the reversal in her thinking. Not a day ago, she was threatening to leave at a moment's notice and now she was assuring him how much she anticipated rejoining the party. Evidently after speaking with the stranger and Corbin, her plans had changed. What this meant for Phillip, he did not know, but he could do nothing else but play out the game.

"Another thing, my lord, I would prefer you say nothing to the rest of the guests. I will be gone and back before any of them know the difference."

"I doubt that will be true of Baylor and Dalton."

"They have been kind enough to keep me entertained," she replied, turning toward the door. "Your guests will probably be missing you."

He held open the door as she passed through. Her nearness caused unexplained feelings to rise in him. "You will return?"

She turned and looked directly at him. "I will, my lord," she confirmed.

"I must sign some letters, but I will be in shortly."

He watched her turn and walk down the hall toward the drawing room before stepping back into the library and closing the door. He poured himself a drink, then chose a high-backed chair and dropped into it, stretching his legs out before him.

He detested not knowing what was going on around him and he did not know what Miss Grayson, Corbin, and the stranger were up to. He could only imagine that it involved the club and perhaps Phillip. He had heard nothing from his other contacts who were searching for his brother. It was as if he had fallen off the edge of the world.

Phillip had been missing too many weeks now and Ellery could not help but think the worst. If anyone had harmed Phillip, they would pay and pay dearly. In the meantime, he would keep his eye on Miss Grayson. If she was going to rendezvous with anyone, he meant to be on hand to observe.

Ellery made a quick trip to the stables and ordered that his horse be ready to leave before dawn the next morning. He warned his staff that they were not to say a word to anyone about his early departure. Since he knew the directions to Miss Grayson's home from seeing the envelope on the desk, he would travel ahead of her and wait for her to catch up. He did not expect anything to happen before she reached the first village on the trip home. If she did not meet anyone here, he would continue following and watching her every move thereafter.

It would be necessary to explain to Aunt Charity that he would be gone on business concerning Phillip and she must act in his stead during his absence. She would also need to explain to the guests that a crisis on another estate had demanded his attention, but that he would return the next day.

Satisfied that he had handled everything as best he could, he joined his guests and went in to dinner.

Vanessa was surprised to find Corbin at the stables the next morning when she arrived to begin her journey. "It wasn't necessary for you to see me off."

"I thought I'd offer one last time to go with you."

"You know it would not be at all proper and what would you do while I was at home?"

"Drink, gamble, and chase the barmaids at the village inn. What else would a man in my position do to pass the time?"

"You are teasing, but I am certain you have done all of those at one time or another."

"That may be so, but it is all behind me for now."

"Is that where you are gone so often? Are you courting a young lady without my knowledge?"

"If I do, you will be the first to know," he replied, helping her into the coach. "The driver knows the way and will stop in order for you to refresh yourself. You should be home in time for luncheon, and having sampled Annie's cooking I know it will be a delicious one."

"I don't know whether I thanked you for all this," she said.

"All the thanks that I need is for you to come back with a smile on your face."

Vanessa had not revealed her discovery of the birthmark on Lord Trent's arm to Corbin. She had not yet taken in all the implications of the earl being Jonathan's father and could not face discussing it until she did.

"I will see you tomorrow evening," she promised, as the coach rolled out of the stable yard.

Ellery was well ahead of the coach, leaving home while the stars were still visible in the sky. If anyone had told him he would be departing before sunrise to chase a spirit lady, he would never have believed them. But here he was, suffering a little from a few short hours of sleep, with the stubble barely scraped from his chin.

He consumed a second breakfast at the inn while waiting for Corbin's coach. When it came to a halt in front of the door, he slipped out the back and chose a place to watch what happened.

The stop was not a lengthy one and they were soon back on the road again. This time Ellery rode behind the coach, staying in a position where he could see if anyone approached it. The results were the same from the first stop to the last. Miss Grayson did not meet anyone on her way home.

Ellery could not help but allow his spirits to lift. Perhaps he was wrong about her. The stranger she had met could have been a relative who had news about her problem at home, and Corbin could merely be doing what anyone would do—helping out a friend in need.

And the Hell-Fire Club and Phillip? inquired a skeptical part of his mind. Perhaps she is innocent of any involvement, he answered, unwilling to consider her guilt for the time being.

Vanessa arrived home to surprise a grateful Annie, who immediately burst into tears.

"Annie, what is wrong? Is Jonathan ill?"

"No. He's healthy as can be, but I've been so worried hearing nothing from anyone."

"I sent you a letter, but I will probably be gone again before you receive it. I met with Mr. Browning yesterday and he believes he might have found out something about Melanie." She went on to repeat what the former Bow Street Runner had told her.

"He said he would let me know as soon as he finds the person and I will pass the information along to you. Now all I want to do is wash away the dust and then play with Jonathan before dinner. Lord Trent has a fine chef, but I have been longing for one of your home cooked meals," she said.

"While you are with Jonathan, I'll fix your favorites," promised Annie.

Ellery sat his stallion in a small copse of trees where he had an unrestricted view of Miss Grayson's home. She had arrived a short time before and that had been the last he had seen of her. If he meant this to be successful, he should have brought someone reliable with him so they could have taken turns watching the house. However, since he was beginning to feel ridiculous imagining her in some nefarious activity, his anxiety was low. He was attempting to decide what to do next when the front door opened.

Miss Grayson emerged looking cool in a white dress with her hair pulled up to reveal the graceful line of her neck. She was carrying something which Ellery could not identify until a wail reached him. It took him several minutes to absorb what he was seeing. It was a baby! He could not believe what his eyes were telling him. Miss Grayson had a baby!

He continued staring at the woman now sitting on a bench before the house, his senses swirling with disbelief. He thought of her comments concerning problems at home and her frequent trips there. It all made sense now—she was coming to see her baby.

While some women might welcome being relieved of the duties of a child, others wanted to be with them every minute, and Miss Grayson must be one of the latter. No doubt, she would have stayed at home to be with her baby if she had not needed to earn what she could.

But what of the father? He should be providing for his child instead of leaving the mother to make her own way. Could the father be the mysterious man Miss Grayson had met near the village? He did not look to be someone she would be taken with. Then the truth struck Ellery with such an impact that he was forced to dismount to consider the implications.

Corbin must be the child's father. That explained why the man was continually hanging around Miss Grayson and why he had first introduced her to the *ton*. It was not a matter of money. Corbin wanted her near him and what better way without setting tongues wagging. No wonder she chose Corbin's coach over his for her travels.

There was no doubt then that if Corbin was involved with the Hell-Fire Club that Miss Grayson was also embroiled in its activities. The proof was before him, yet he was hesitant about accepting it. There had been a part of him that did not want to believe the worst of the woman and that still fought against it no matter how strong the evidence.

As he watched her and thought about what she had done, his anger built. There was no longer any need to stay, and he decided he would return home and wait for her to follow. What would happen when they next met, he could not predict.

Vanessa strolled around the yard speaking to Jonathan as if he could understand every word she uttered. Finally she sat on the bench in front of the house and, taking a deep breath, pushed back the tiny sleeve of his gown. She closed her eyes and breathed a prayer, then looked down. It had not disappeared. Jonathan's small arm bore the same mark that was on Lord Trent's forearm.

The proof was indisputable yet she found herself staring at the birthmark, willing it to vanish. It did not, of course, and she was left to face the undeniable truth—that Lord Trent was Jonathan's father. She could not imagine her sister and the earl together. She would have thought that Melanie would have been in awe of Lord Trent, unable to speak a word in his presence.

Perhaps he had played the part of seducer well, speaking softly and piling compliment upon compliment until her resistance melted away. Yes, she could picture it now, for she had been the object of his attention several times and had been hard-pressed to escape from his charm.

She wondered why—if Melanie and the baby were such a threat to his way of life—he had left Jonathan behind? Perhaps he was not hard-hearted enough to harm his own child and knew that with Melanie gone Jonathan would pose no threat to him. Vanessa felt nothing but contempt for Lord Trent and swore revenge on him. However, she must find Melanie before she attacked the earl; that is, if she was still alive.

Vanessa could not stop the tears that gathered in her eyes and poured down her cheeks. She held Jonathan all the tighter and mourned for her sister, praying that she could find her in time.

* * *

Ellery arrived home long after dinner had been served. He entered at the rear of the house and took the back stairs to reach his rooms. Jackson, Ellery's valet, insisted he have a bath to wash away the grime, and he had to admit a soak in the large tub helped him to relax from the long ride.

When he was dry, he found that a hearty dinner had been brought to his room, and despite the upset of his recent discovery, he realized his appetite had not been at all affected. While he ate, he reviewed what he had discovered about Miss Grayson and wondered how he could have even considered her to be an innocent.

He had finished dinner and was relaxing with a glass of brandy in his hand when a knock sounded on the door. Jackson opened it to find Max on the other side. Motioning him in, Ellery had the valet pour a glass of brandy for his friend, and then asked him to clear away the dishes.

"Has anything happened since I have been gone?"

"No news of Phillip if that is what you mean. I heard from the men I have searching and they have found nothing at all. They are beginning to think it is useless to continue."

"You didn't give them leave to stop, did you?"

"No, no," said Max, holding up his hand. "I did nothing of the sort. I will not call them off until you give me the word."

"That will be when Phillip is safe at home," said Ellery. The two men sat in silence, wondering whether that would ever happen, but not speaking it out loud.

"You were sorely missed today," said Max, breaking the stillness that had fallen over them.

"I thought you were going to play host."

"I can only do so much when so many are gone missing."

"What do you mean?" asked Ellery, straightening in his chair.

"By dinnertime, in addition to you, Corbin, Dalton, and Baylor were all absent."

"Do you know where they went?"

"It seems they all more or less gave out the same story. Dalton and Baylor said they were going to see how the country barmaids compared to London's and Corbin said he had a lady friend in the neighborhood with whom he had promised to dine. Of course, only the gentlemen heard those stories. The ladies were told that they were visiting friends."

"Did you believe them?" questioned Ellery.

"Not in the least. I had only kept one man nearby in order to follow Corbin. He said the man returned to the same inn where he had been before. He also said he thought he saw Dalton and Baylor enter, but he was not as familiar with them and the light was too poor for him to swear to their identity.

"My man left them there to come back and report to me since he was certain they would follow the same course of action that they had before. None of them has returned yet."

"So, Dalton and Baylor, too?"

"I would not be surprised," commented Max. "They are both young men who are looking for excitement and what better than the Hell-Fire Club?"

"They would be spitting in the face of convention to be sure," agreed Ellery, "and if the ceremonies follow the same line as the old ones, the two would thoroughly enjoy them." He also remembered the attention that the men paid to Miss Grayson and thought it likely that they knew her from the club.

"Corbin does not appear to be especially close to them," said Max.

"He's too crafty to make such a mistake," replied Ellery, his grip tightening on the brandy glass. "He's hiding quite a bit from us."

"What do you mean?" asked Max.

Ellery was not yet ready to share the news of Miss Grayson's baby with anyone, even with his old friend. He needed time to adjust so that he could discuss it calmly.

"Only that I'm certain once we reveal his secret life, we will find more than we bargained for," replied Ellery.

"What do you want to do now?"

"I intend to have a good night's sleep and I suggest you do the same. The next few days may prove to be demanding."

The next evening, the ladies had withdrawn and the gentlemen were gathered around the long mahogany table, enjoying their cigars and liquor when Thomas slipped into the room. He leaned over Lord Trent and spoke in low tones. Ellery nodded and lifted his glass again.

"She has just returned," he said, in answer to Max's inquiring gaze.

"Miss Grayson, I presume," replied Max.

"No other. I was beginning to wonder whether she would return at all even though she promised to do so."

"You doubt the lady's word?" asked Max, smiling faintly.

"Every one that falls from her lovely lips."

"You still think she's involved with Corbin and the club?"

"More than ever," confirmed Ellery. "She will not be down this evening, so I must wait until tomorrow to talk with her." He poured another drink from the bottle that was in front of him. "I am becoming extremely impatient going on as we are. We are not moving any closer to finding Phillip or revealing the Hell-Fire Club members so that they can be dealt with appropriately."

"Do you want to confront Corbin? Or perhaps Dalton or Baylor?" Max inquired, also replenishing his own glass.

"I don't think it would profit us to take on Dalton or Baylor. I doubt whether whoever is leading the club would trust anything useful to those green cubs. However, Corbin is another matter altogether. He is charming and good at covering his tracks. I believe he might be privy to what plans the club has, or he might even be the leader of the group."

"Corbin? I can't believe he would do that. I can see him becoming bored and taking part in the club simply for entertainment, but to be the instigator of the resurgence? That's difficult to accept."

Ellery wondered how Max would feel if he knew about Miss Grayson's baby. He opened his mouth to tell him, then closed it again. He still was not quite ready to reveal what he had learned the day before.

"Let us join the ladies," he said, tipping his head back and emptying his glass. "I must tell Aunt Charity that Miss Grayson has returned. She worries about her so."

Ellery had just finished relaying the information about Miss Grayson to his aunt when Cornelia appeared at his elbow. "I am so glad you are here. The company has been sadly flat without you," she complained.

"You are missing Dalton and Baylor," teased Ellery.

"It is true they are entertaining," she admitted. "I cannot believe they decided not to come down to dinner."

"I understand they did not return until late," said Ellery. "They probably require the rest."

"I saw them arrive and they certainly looked the worse for wear," she agreed. "I, for one, do not believe their story of visiting friends. Instead, I believe they were out with women of ill repute."

"Cornelia," said Ellery, feigning shock, "ladies do not think, let alone say such things."

"I am weary of being a lady," she replied, crossly. "We have no fun at all. Looking forward to spending my life making calls and embroidering causes me to shiver."

"I'm certain you will not allow your life to be boring."

She gave him an arch look before speaking. "I have not even seen Corbin yet."

"I am told he also visited friends," said Ellery, laughing at her expression of disbelief. "Do not ask me, I am only passing along what I have heard."

"You would never know this is a house party with everyone dashing in and out at all hours. It has put me so out of sorts that I have decided to take a small trip myself."

"Should I ask where?"

"It is no secret, nor is it exciting to anyone but me. Susan Leferre lives not too far away. We knew one another in France and she has written several times asking me to visit. Since I am so close, I thought I would take tomorrow and call on her."

"That sounds like an agreeable day for you."

"Oh, it will be. I am thoroughly looking forward to speaking a civilized language again. I probably should not have said that," she remarked, looking around to see whether she had been overheard.

"I don't think anyone would hold it against you merely because you would like to speak the language you grew up with. Would you like to use the traveling coach for your trip?"

"I would like nothing better," she said. "Lord Lambert offered his, of course, but yours is much more splendid and far more comfortable."

"Then I will arrange for it to be ready. What time would you like to depart?"

"No earlier than ten o'clock."

"Will that give you time to get there and back?"

"If not, there will be no problem if I should need to stay overnight."

"Consider it done," he said, wondering whether he and Cornelia were better suited than he had previously thought.

Thirteen

Ellery was at breakfast the next morning when Thomas entered. "I found this on the front doorstep this morning, my lord." He held out a silver tray upon which rested a letter. It was of buff-colored paper and when Ellery opened it, the writing stood out bold and black on the page.

"There was nothing else?" he asked the butler, who hovered nearby.

"Nothing, my lord. I looked around to be certain."

"Thank you," murmured Ellery, as Thomas bowed and left the room.

Max looked at him curiously, but did not ask any questions since they were not alone in the room.

"Later," said Ellery, returning to his ham and buttered eggs.

"Was it news of Phillip?" Max asked, as soon as they were private.

"It seems there is going to be a meeting of the Hell-Fire Club tomorrow night. It also gives the time and location."

"What! Who would send you such a thing?"

"Someone who wants to help, but does not have the courage to make himself known, I suppose," said Ellery. "It does not matter though, if it contains the truth. It could be that I will find Phillip there."

"There's no question that I'm going with you," said Max.

"I want you to call in your men. I'll tell you where and when to have them meet us and we'll all go there together. If the entire club is present, we will certainly need assistance. How many do you have?"

"Eight, possibly ten," replied Max.

"Good, I have several men here whom I can depend upon to stand by us. We should have enough to at least protect ourselves and rescue Phillip if necessary."

"I should alert the men as soon as possible," said Max.

"Let us lock ourselves in the library and make plans," suggested Ellery.

While Ellery and Max were closeted in the library, Vanessa was hastily pulling on her riding habit. Mr. Browning had sent one of the village lads with a message asking her to meet him in the same place as soon as possible. She was certain he had found news of Melanie and her hands shook with excitement.

"Here, ma'am, let me do that for you," said Delcie, fastening the buttons with nimble fingers.

"You are not to breathe a word of this to anyone," she warned the young girl.

"I won't, ma'am. If anyone asks, I do not know where you are."

"Thank you, Delcie, I won't forget this," she said, finally finishing dressing and hurrying out the door and down the back steps to the stables. Once again, she mounted Happy Lady and turned the mare toward the village.

Mr. Browning was waiting in the same clearing in which they had previously met. He helped her dismount and then tethered the mare to a tree.

"I believe I have good news for you," he said.

"Tell me quickly," begged Vanessa, her hands clasped tightly in front of her.

"I followed the lead I told you about several days ago and was able to locate the person who observed the carriage. From his description, I am as certain as I can be that the woman he saw was Melanie."

"Thank you," Vanessa whispered, as a surge of relief swept over her.

Browning saw her face pale and led her to a rock where she was able to be seated. "I did not want to shock you, but there was no other way to tell you."

"It is all right," she assured him. "Do you know where she is now?"

"I know where I think she may be," he said. "The gentleman to whom I spoke told me the coach turned down a lane that led to the remains of an old abbey. He said he believed that the members of the family who owned it had all died and he had no knowledge if it was being used by anyone else."

"Go on," urged Vanessa.

"I rode through the fields so that there would be less chance of being sighted and approached the abbey. A part of it is still standing and I noticed that there was evidence where a coach and perhaps horses had beaten down the grass from the lane to the building. There was a faint smell of smoke and cooking, so I am convinced that someone is staying there, but I did not see who it was."

"How can we find out if Melanie is there?" asked Vanessa.

"I am going to return tomorrow night. The moon will be full then and it will be much easier to see. I will get as close to the abbey as possible and see what I can find. With part of it in ruin, I might even be able to get inside without being found out."

"I am going with you," said Vanessa.

"It is far too dangerous, Miss Grayson."

Her chin lifted to a stubborn angle. "It does not matter. Melanie is my sister and she is in danger. I could not rest knowing that I would not be there when she needed me most."

"We do not know for certain that she is there," he pointed out.

"You must be nearly positive if you are willing to take such a chance," she argued. "If you do not take me with you, I will find some way to follow."

"That could ruin my chances of approaching them without being seen and also put your sister in danger," he said.

"Then take me with you," she repeated.

He was silent for a moment, watching her. Her gaze was steady as it met his and he realized she was a woman of her word.

"All right," he said, giving in. "You can come with me, but you must do exactly as I say."

"I promise," she said, an expression of relief spreading over her face.

"You will need to make excuses for not going down to dinner. Then as soon as it is dark, walk down the road until you come to the first group of trees. I will be waiting there for you."

"I will need a horse?"

"I will have one for you. It will be a long ride, Miss Grayson. I hope you have the stamina to complete it."

"When it comes to my sister, Mr. Browning, I am capable of doing whatever it takes."

Browning had to admit that if it depended on determination, then Miss Grayson would do very well indeed.

Vanessa did not know what to do with herself when she returned to the house. She was too excited to mix with the rest of the guests, so she wandered into the music room and sat down at the pianoforte. She thought of Melanie and how they had relied upon one another as they grew up motherless. Her fingers touched the keys, lightly playing the tunes of their childhood.

"You seem pensive, Miss Grayson."

She stiffened on hearing the voice. Of all the people she wanted to meet least, it was Lord Trent. "Music sometimes affects people in that manner," she replied, attempting to keep her tone even.

"I did not see you either last night or this morning and was wondering whether you were avoiding me."

Visions of Lord Trent and Melanie together made Vanessa want to avoid him forever. However, she could not allow him to know what she had discovered until her sister was safe.

"I was fatigued from my travel and slept late this morning," she explained.

"And how did you find your family?" he asked, as if he were truly interested.

She swallowed the bitterness that rose in her throat to choke her. "They were quite well, my lord."

"Then . . ."

She would never know what he meant to say for at that time a wind swept into the room, slamming the door leading into the hall. Vanessa raised her head and looked around.

"Juliana?" she inquired.

I am here, although it is not of my choosing. However, I find myself liking you and I would not be doing my duty if I did not warn you."

"What is it?" asked Lord Trent. He remembered the wind that had swirled around them before when Miss Grayson had claimed to be talking to Juliana. "Is she here?"

"Yes," replied Vanessa. "And she is highly agitated."

"What can upset a spirit?" he asked, skeptically.

"I believe she is upset for one of us." She closed her

eyes a moment, then turned to him. "She has made a great sacrifice coming to the newer part of the house for she is very set in her ways. Nonetheless, she said she came to warn us."

"Of what?"

"She is warning you again that there is evil in the house."

"She has told me that before and nothing has come of it."

"It is growing stronger and is now ready to assert itself," responded Vanessa. "She says you must defeat it not only for yourself, but for others around you."

Ellery stared at her, thinking of Phillip.

Vanessa's eyes closed again. "Your suspicions lie in the wrong direction. Now is the time to trust your heart over your mind," she instructed him, in a voice that sounded nothing like her own.

"You are saying this for your own benefit," he snarled, jerking her out of her reverie.

"I am passing along what Juliana is saying," she retorted.

Ellery could not believe her boldness. Somehow she had determined that he suspected she and Corbin were involved in the Hell-Fire Club and perhaps in Phillip's disappearance. Now she thought to distract him by telling him his conjectures were wrong. No doubt if she realized that he knew about her baby, she would have a reliable explanation for that, too.

"You are passing along whatever will serve you best," he said accusingly.

"I don't know what you are talking about," she replied quickly. "I have no reason to tell you anything but the truth."

"The devil you don't! Tell me there is nothing between you and Corbin then!" He took her by the shoulders and pulled her to her feet.

"What are you talking about?" she demanded. "You know that he is my friend and has been for years."

"Friends." Ellery sneered. "If only I had friends such as you."

"You are insulting, my lord."

"Not nearly as insulting as I am going to be," he warned, gripping her all the tighter and pulling her toward him.

Later, Ellery would question what had come over him. He had never been as impassioned about any woman in his entire lifetime. He would also later rationalize that it was his worry over Phillip that brought about his illogical behavior. But at the moment all he could think about was Vanessa in his arms, her golden eyes blazing, her lips parted as if expecting the touch of his.

He was still angry when his lips met hers. She struggled, but he held her tightly as his lips gentled and the kiss turned into something more than an angry punishment. He lifted her arms and placed them around his neck, leaving his hands free to explore the softness of her body beneath the thin summer gown along the curve of her waist leading to the gentle swell of her hips.

She no longer fought him, but gave herself fully to their embrace. He lifted her slightly, fitting her soft curves to his hard muscle, pulling her even closer than he thought possible. There was no thought in his mind of revenge, no worry about her harming his brother or being a member of the Hell-Fire Club. There was only desire for her the likes of which he had never felt for another woman before.

Someone tugged insistently at his jacket, and when he could no longer ignore it he raised his head, but no one else was in the room.

His movement allowed Vanessa to regain some of her good sense, for when he would have returned to the kiss, she shook her head and pulled away as far as she could.

"My—my lord, you must not; we must not. Someone could come in at any moment," she objected breathlessly.

"Then let them," he murmured, taking her chin in his hand, attempting to re-create the mood that had been broken.

"It is no good," she said. "Juliana will not allow it; at least, not for now, she says."

"Can't you forget your spirits for the moment?" he groaned, resting his forehead against hers.

Vanessa could not hold back a giggle. "She will not allow either of us to forget her. Who do you think was pulling on your coat?"

"Not . . . ?"

"Juliana," she confirmed, with a shake of her head.

"Show yourself immediately," he insisted loudly. "I demand satisfaction. Name your seconds and we will meet on the south meadow at daybreak."

"You cannot duel with a woman, particularly when she is already a spirit," Vanessa reminded him, forgetting for the moment of nonsense that they were enemies.

"I will duel with anyone who contrives to make my life miserable."

"Is it?" she asked.

"Not as long as I am kissing you," he admitted, causing her to blush with his bluntness.

"Juliana says she would be pleased to leave you in peace if you would only listen to her. She begs you to heed her warning."

They stared at one another and each remembered what it was that had set them up against one another. Awkwardly, they disentangled themselves and stepped apart.

For Vanessa, the hot summer day had turned too cool

to endure and she wrapped her arms around herself. She had almost given herself to the very man who was the father of Melanie's child and who, no doubt, was responsible for her disappearance. She abruptly turned away, unable to face him or to think about what had nearly happened with the brute who had dishonored her sister.

If she could only get through until tomorrow night when Melanie would be safe, then she would not need to conceal her distaste for Lord Trent. She did not know what she was going to do, but knew only that when she was finished, she wanted him completely ruined.

"I must go," she said without turning, her voice thick with emotion.

"Stay a moment," he said, wondering why he would want to extend his time with such a woman. It wasn't that she was not appealing to him, for he could not argue that. If he could put what she was out of his mind, then he knew their passion would be stronger than any he had experienced.

His conduct had just proven to him that he could forget her insidious manner for the length of their lovemaking. However, it seemed that Miss Grayson was unable to put aside their differences for the moment. He could not see that her dislike could be so strong merely because he did not completely believe in her spirits or that he had questioned her friendship with Corbin. He had not even mentioned her child, so it was not that knowledge that had turned her against him at the wrong moment. He could only believe that she was not as overwhelmed by desire as he was, which brought him back to her and Corbin.

"It would not be good for either of us if I stayed, my lord. I have given you Juliana's message and I hope that you will give it considerable thought, for spirits are sensitive to such things." She walked toward the door, which opened by unseen hands in front of her.

Ellery's mouth gaped upon viewing the incident; however, Vanessa simply walked through it as though it were an everyday occurrence. The sound of her footsteps faded, leaving him alone with his thoughts, and they were disturbing ones at best.

The next day, Vanessa kept to her rooms until just before luncheon, hoping to rest for the evening's adventure. After spending some time with Lady Venable, she returned to her room for an afternoon nap. Although she had thought she could not sleep, she drifted off and awoke anxious for the time when she would meet Mr. Browning.

She had felt Lord Trent watching her at luncheon. Each time she glanced at the head of the table his dark, brooding gaze was fixed on her.

She wondered whether he was thinking about the spirits or their encounter in the music room the day before. Or perhaps he was merely missing Lady Cornelia, who had set off to visit an old friend that morning.

After luncheon, Vanessa drew Lady Venable aside. "I believe I will have dinner in my room and retire early tonight," she said to the older woman.

"Are you certain you are all right, my dear? You have been in your rooms most of the day."

"I am still a bit fatigued from my trip home. The heat was so intense it took more out of me than I thought. I will be fine in the morning," she assured Lady Venable. "I have Delcie to look after me should I need anything."

"If you are certain," said Lady Venable, "then I shall make your excuses."

"Thank you, my lady," she said, turning to climb the

stairs as Lady Venable joined the other ladies in the drawing room.

That evening, she swore Delcie to secrecy concerning her absence. As she was changing into her riding habit, she told the girl to stay in the room until she returned. If anyone knocked, she was to say that Vanessa was sleeping.

It was finally time to go. Vanessa tiptoed along the hall and crept down the back stairs, holding her breath each step of the way. She kept in the shadows of the house for as long as she could then hurried down the lane until Mr. Browning called out to her in a subdued voice.

"Are you certain you want to do this?" he asked.

"There is nothing you can say to stop me," she answered, still breathless from her dash to meet him.

"Once we begin, we cannot turn back for any reason or we will miss our best chance at seeing whether your sister is in the abbey," he warned.

"I do not intend to stop until I discover the truth," she answered.

He helped her into the saddle, then mounted his own horse. "We will ride around the village and then pick up the pace once we are clear of it."

They were soon lost in the shadows.

Ellery had seen Cornelia off before luncheon and then spent the rest of the day watching Miss Grayson for the short time she was below stairs. His head was filled with conflicting images—Miss Grayson with her skirts swirling while she talked to the spirit, her eyes closed and her lashes laying thick and dark against her flawless skin after he had kissed her, and what disturbed him most, the manner in which she held her baby close as she sat on the stone bench in front of her home.

He could not settle on one feeling for the woman, he

thought, disgusted with himself; particularly when he considered the Hell-Fire Club and Phillip. If she was involved in Phillip's disappearance, he would be unable to ever think of forgiving her. On the other hand, if she had nothing to do with either his brother or the club, would he be able to put everything else aside?

And what would he do if that were the case? Even if they cared for one another enough to consider something more permanent, they were worlds apart. There was also Cornelia left to deal with. She considered, and he had to admit rightly so, that he would be offering for her. His head began to ache and he wondered whether he could follow the ladies' lead, claim a case of megrims, and retire to his rooms.

His role of host would not allow him to do so and he took his place at dinner, mired in a brown study. He attempted to keep his attention on his dinner partners, but his gaze continually drifted down the table to where Miss Grayson usually sat.

He remembered her appearance the night before, thinking that she looked more lovely than he had ever seen her. She had worn a dull gold gown, trimmed with lighter ribbon and a necklace and earrings of topaz which caused her eyes to glow like a cat's eyes. He had wondered where she had acquired the jewelry. Was it from the father of her child? The idea aroused another surge of an emotion he refused to acknowledge as jealousy within him.

If he thought he would have a word with her after dinner, he was to be disappointed, for Lady Venable advised him that Miss Grayson had retired early. It was just as well, he thought, for he must not chance being drawn back into her web.

Ellery cleared his head of Miss Grayson and confirmed that Corbin, Dalton, and Baylor were also absent from the dinner table. They had informed him that they had other plans and would be back late, leaving him to believe they each had assignations with a woman of one sort or another.

It was later and most of the guests had retired to their rooms. The gentlemen who hadn't were locked in a card game in another part of the house and would not hear anything through the thick walls.

Max and Ellery were in the library, going over their plan for the final time. Ellery unlocked a cabinet and withdrew two pistols. "Were you able to reach your men?" he asked.

"They will be at the meeting place at the appointed time," replied Max, taking one of the pistols.

"Good. We should be able to travel safely until we reach them. With such a large group, we will need to take care so as not to announce ourselves."

"All the men are experienced," said Max. "I foresee no problem."

"We will need to decide what to do once we reach the abbey since neither of us is familiar with it."

Max reached for his gloves and hat. "We'll hope that the club members are so involved in their ceremony—if that is what is going on—that they will not notice until we are upon them."

"You are optimistic, my friend," replied Ellery, leading the way toward the back of the house to the stables.

Mr. Browning pulled his horse to a halt in a thicket of trees and bushes not far from the abbey. "This is as close as we dare take the horses," he whispered.

Dismounting, he turned to Vanessa and helped her from the saddle.

"What should we do next?" she asked, following his lead and speaking in a low tone.

"We will watch for a short while and see if there is any activity. I can smell smoke," he commented.

"And food cooking," added Vanessa.

"There is an old stable on the other side of the abbey. Will you be afraid to remain here while I slip around and see whether there are horses there?"

"I will stay, but hurry back," urged Vanessa.

He disappeared with hardly a rustle of leaves to indicate where he had vanished into the thicket. Vanessa's heart leaped when he appeared a short time later.

"What did you find out?" she asked, urgently.

"Something is going on, that's for certain," he said. "And it bodes no good for our task."

"What do you mean?"

"There are both horses and coaches at the stable," he related. "I couldn't get close enough to tell anything more, but that many people at the abbey will make it extremely difficult for us find Melanie—if she is here— without being caught."

"We cannot turn back," said Vanessa.

"We will not," he confirmed. "I have been in tighter places than this and have emerged successful. The situation being what it is, though, I must ask you to stay here while I enter the abbey."

"No! I want to go with you."

"You are not experienced," he explained, "and might do more to endanger your sister than to help her."

Vanessa worried her bottom lip between her teeth, considering what he had said. "All right. I will do as you say, but you must promise me you will not return without Melanie."

"If she is there, I will find her and bring her out," he vowed, then once more melted into the shadows.

Mr. Browning had not been gone long when Vanessa

heard what sounded like several horses approaching. They came to a halt not far away, and despite Mr. Browning's warnings, she attempted to get near enough to see what they were up to.

Her limbs would not move when she recognized Lord Trent's voice. It only proved what she had surmised—he was Jonathan's father and he was responsible for Melanie's disappearance. But why was he being so secretive in approaching the abbey? She did not have time to consider an answer before two arms came around her, clamping her in a viselike grip against a muscular chest.

She struggled, but to no avail. The man simply lifted her off her feet so that she was helpless no matter how she attempted to kick him.

"Calm down, you termagant," he ordered, his lips close to her ear.

Lord Trent! Of all the people to have caught her it had to be him. "I will calm down if you will release me," she hissed.

"Promise that you will not try anything."

"I promise."

His arms loosened around her slowly and when she did not attempt to attack him, he motioned for her to join the others in the small clearing ahead.

"What are you doing here?" he demanded, still speaking in a low tone.

"It is none of your business," she replied.

"It is. You could have ruined everything we have been planning for months."

"And you expect me to be sorry about that?"

"No, considering your affiliation with the people in the abbey, I suppose I don't. But I don't understand what you are doing lurking about in the bushes."

"What affiliation? And I am not lurking in the bushes. I am waiting for Mr. Browning."

"Who the devil is Mr. Browning," asked Ellery.

"No one you need concern yourself with," she fired back.

"What I am concerned with is keeping you out of trouble until this is all over and I can deal with you. I can't spare a man to stay with you," he murmured to himself. "Don't take offense, but I must tie you to a tree."

"What!" she yelped, as he slapped his hand over her mouth.

"Do that again and I will gag you," he warned, before loosening his hold.

"You cannot tie and gag me or leave me behind. I have a right to see my sister even though you may think otherwise."

"What the deuce does your sister have to do with this?"

He sounded so completely confused that if Vanessa had not known better he would have convinced her of his innocence in the matter.

"I would think that she has everything to do with it. If it were not for Melanie none of us would be here."

"It sounds as if the two of you are talking at cross purposes," chimed in Max.

"And I don't have time to straighten it out at the moment," growled Ellery. "Promise you will remain here and I will not restrain you."

"I'll do nothing of the sort," she said, then quickly rethought her decision as Ellery asked for something with which to tie her up. Because she promised did not mean she must stick to her word with a man as dishonorable as Lord Trent. "All right. I'll stay behind."

Ellery glared at her suspiciously. She had agreed almost too easily. "Vanessa, if you do not do as you say . . ."

"I promised, did I not? And I have not given you leave to call me anything but Miss Grayson."

Ellery could hear muffled laughter from the men behind him but he did not look around. "We have no more time to waste." He turned toward his horse, then swung around again. "How did you get here?" It was something he should have asked her earlier.

"I rode," she answered smartly.

"With whom?

"By myself."

"I do not believe you rode two horses at one time. Now, tell me the truth or I will carry out my threat."

"I came with Mr. Browning," she admitted, her voice surly.

"Dear Lord, how many more are wandering around the abbey?" asked Max.

"Surely, you have more knowledge of that than I do."

"We have never been here before so there is no reason why we should," answered Max.

"Perhaps you haven't, but I'm certain Lord Trent knows the lay of the land and the inhabitants of the abbey very well indeed."

"What the devil makes you think that?"

"Because we have traced Melanie to this location. And you are the only one with good reason to bring her here."

"You are all about in the head," he said. "I do not know anyone named Melanie, nor have I taken her anywhere."

He sounded convincing, but he had that ability, thought Vanessa. Besides, she had proof that he was the father of Jonathan, so he must have taken her away. "Lord Huntly, I have great confidence in you despite your affiliation with Lord Trent," said Vanessa.

Ellery threw up his hands and walked a few steps away so that he was not close enough to get his hands around her lovely neck.

Vanessa continued to look up at Max, who still sat his

horse. "Do you know whether he had anything to do with Melanie's disappearance?"

Max dismounted and came to stand in front of her. "Miss Grayson, Ellery and I have been together nearly constantly the past two months, working on a personal matter. If he had known a Melanie, much less brought her to this abbey, I would have known it. Believe me when I tell you that tonight could be a matter of life and death and allow us to continue with our mission."

"I agree with you, for it is my sister who is in danger," she replied. "That is why I must go to the abbey with you."

"Unthinkable," said Ellery, returning to her side. The more she spoke, the more he was convinced that she had nothing to do with the club or she would have surely been inside by now. If he was wrong about that, then it stood to reason that she had nothing to do with Phillip's disappearance. "You must stay here where you will be safe."

Vanessa decided to make one last appeal. "My lord, there is a child at my home who has a birthmark that resembles a four-leaf clover on his forearm. It is for that reason that I must go with you."

Ellery felt the blood drain from his face and his heart seemed to turn to lead. His senses were numb with what she had just revealed—Phillip was her baby's father! He put out his hand and grasped the stirrup strap on his stallion's saddle to steady himself. If this was true—and it would be too easy to disprove—it was no wonder she insisted on going into the abbey with them. The father of her child was there and she meant to help save him.

He straightened and collected his thoughts. "You should have told me this earlier, Miss Grayson, and I would not have stood in your way. I will caution you to stay behind us for we might be forced to use our pistols."

Alana Clayton

"Pistols? What in heaven's name are you planning on doing?"

"We are acting for the Home Office and are going to break up a group that calls itself the Hell-Fire Club," he revealed. "As you also know, we believe they are also holding a hostage."

"But . . ." she began, intending to inquire what the Hell-Fire Club had to do with Melanie.

"We've talked too much already. What does Browning look like so we do not shoot him by mistake?"

"He is a tall man, with light brown hair and . . ."

"The one you met near the village a few days ago?" he asked.

"How did you know?"

"You heard her," he said to the assembled men. "Watch for the man, but do not jeopardize yourself for his sake. Let's move." The men followed him out of the woods, moving from cover to cover as they made their way toward the abbey.

Vanessa followed close behind, still confused about the conversation that had just occurred. There was a great deal that did not make sense to her, but she would deal with it once Melanie was safe.

Fourteen

Ellery had nearly reached the entrance to the abbey when he caught a slight movement in the shadow near the wall. He took a chance. "Browning," he called out softly.

"Who is it?" came the guarded reply.

"Lord Trent. I have Miss Grayson with me."

"Thank God," said the man in a fervent voice. He moved forward and joined the others.

"Did you see anything?" asked Vanessa.

"That I did," he replied. "There's a room full of men gathered around a table and plates piled high with all manner of food being served. Some of the men are wearing robes and hoods, while other costumes are hanging on the wall ready to be put on.

"One at the head of the table looked like the devil himself. All dressed in black with horns and an evil face painted on the hood. There were too many for me to face alone. I'm sorry, Miss Grayson."

"You have no reason to apologize," she said, while at the same time agonizing over the fate of her sister.

"We must hurry," said Ellery, reasoning that if Phillip was being held by the men, his life could end at any time. There were rumors of sacrifices at some of the old Hell-Fire Club ceremonies and for all he knew this group could be following their practices.

Ellery led the group forward again, all with pistols drawn. They advanced as quietly as possible down the hall of the abbey toward the room that Browning indicated. There was only one door leading into the room from the hall. Another was at the far end of the room and Ellery suspected it led to the kitchen. They would enter the room and spread out as quickly as possible, hoping to catch the gathering unawares. Ellery appointed two men to go immediately to the kitchen door and secure it.

Vanessa prayed that nothing would go wrong and that none of the pistols would need to be used.

Ellery nodded at Max and they stepped quickly through the door, training their pistols on the two robed figures at the head of the table. The other men surged in behind them, surrounding the table and bringing their pistols to bear on the remaining members of the group.

After all the tension, the reality of the capture was relatively simple. It seemed that while the Hell-Fire Club members relished secret ceremonies, they had no stomach for pistols.

Vanessa peered into the room once it seemed safe. The men were still seated around the table, many of them appearing shocked and frightened by the mess in which they found themselves.

Ellery turned, saw her in the door, and backed up until he reached her, his pistol still trained on the leader.

"I know some of them. They are peers of the realm." Her gaze continued moving around the table until an astonished expression appeared on her face. "Rudy!" she gasped. "And Lords Colby and Dalton! What are you doing here?"

Incredulity of such magnitude could not be fabricated and Ellery began to believe that she might be exactly what she had said. "Looking for excitement, I'll wager," he replied, a grim expression on his face.

"Hardly," replied Corbin, languidly reaching for his glass of wine despite the pistols trained on him. "If I could speak with you in private?"

Ellery hesitated to give an inch to the man.

"Please, my lord, give him a chance to explain," pleaded Vanessa.

"All right, out here." He motioned toward the door. "What is it?" he asked roughly as soon as they reached the hall.

Corbin looked at Vanessa, who had followed them. "Thank you for your faith in me," he said.

"Save the compliments for some time when they will do good. Tell me what you have to say and speak quickly for my patience is wearing thin."

"I am working with the Home Office," Corbin admitted. "I have been working my way into the club attempting to find out the identity of the leader. I also recruited Dalton and Baylor to assist me."

"You expect me to believe you?"

"I was the one who sent you the note about this meeting. I knew of no other way to get you here without exposing what I was doing to the others. You see, this was meant to heighten the interest of the men so that when the real ceremony occurred they would not back down no matter what was demanded of them."

"And what was that to be?" asked Ellery.

"From what I have been able to ferret out, I believe you and your brother were both targets of the leader. I believe you and he were meant to be killed as early as next week."

Vanessa was too horrified to utter a word. She leaned against the wall, thinking that she had fallen into a nightmare and would awaken any moment safe in her bed. However, it was not to be.

"Is Phillip here?" asked Ellery in a strained voice.

"I do not know for certain," replied Corbin, "but it's possible."

Although Ellery wanted to immediately begin the search for his brother, he realized that he must deal with the others first. He returned to the room and spoke to the men who were being held there. "Gentlemen, I know many of you and if you answer me honestly it may go a long way to helping your cause. Since you have been involved in the club have you committed any crimes in its name?"

A chorus of fervent denials rose from the men.

"Is there anyone being held hostage here at the abbey?"

The men looked at one another and the various answers were that none of them were aware of a hostage.

"And what say you?" he asked, looking directly at the two hooded figures at the head of the table.

"I say this is not worth my life," replied one of the figures, pulling off his hood.

"Thornhill! What the devil are you doing mixed up in a thing like this?"

"You might say I was lured into it," he replied, glancing sideways at the figure who remained hidden under a hood.

"Show yourself," ordered Ellery, "or I will do it for you."

"That might be extremely interesting," said the figure, the voice muffled by the hood.

"Oh, go ahead and do it," said Thornhill, reaching over and pulling off the hood.

Ellery was speechless, while Vanessa groped for a chair and fell into it.

Corbin laughed out loud at the revelation. "Lady Cornelia," he said, "how absolutely charming."

"Go to the devil, Corbin."

"I believe that is what you've been doing all these months, my lady."

"What is the reason behind this, Cornelia?" asked Ellery, finally regaining his voice.

"You and your brother are, you imbecile. My father was the leader of the last Hell-Fire Club and your family sought him out and destroyed him for it. I was sent to France and never saw him again. He died alone; a broken man. As young as I was, I swore revenge and it was finally within my grasp," she raged.

"The Lamberts were kin to my mother and I counted on them to introduce me to society so that I could meet you. Then I made the mistake of insisting you have your houses cleared of spirits. I thought it would be a good excuse to cling to you, but instead your Spirit Lady came between us. Even with that, another sennight and you would have been dead. Then she could have spoken to your spirit as well," she spat.

The shocks were nearly coming too rapidly for Ellery to absorb. He forced himself to concentrate on what was most important first. "Do you have Phillip?"

"Of course, I have him," she scoffed. "He's been locked up whining about his ladylove for weeks. I am sick to death of hearing it."

Cornelia had not said a word about Melanie, and Vanessa was distraught because this trip had all been for naught. Melanie had nothing to do with the Hell-Fire Club, so there would be no reason for her to be held prisoner here. She had come to a dead end and did not know where to turn next, for if Lord Trent was responsible for Melanie's disappearance, he was covering it up well.

Ellery glanced at Vanessa to see how she was taking the news. He was glad to see that she had remained calm. "Where is he?"

"Find him yourself," Cornelia sneered.

"Watch them," he ordered the men. "Shoot anyone who attempts to leave this room." The men around the table paled even further and sat as motionless as they could manage.

"Max, Browning, come with me."

"I'm coming, too," said Vanessa.

"As am I," remarked Corbin, taking Vanessa's arm.

"Do what you will," said Ellery over his shoulder as he rapidly strode from the room.

"Browning, did you have time to look over any more of the abbey?"

"I didn't, but I don't believe the upper floors are in good enough shape to hold a determined man prisoner."

"The upper floors?" inquired Ellery.

"The man who told me about the abbey said there were monks' cells below. Said it seemed more like a dungeon than a place of faith."

"That is what we must have now," he said. "Faith. Do you know where the steps are?"

"Follow me. I saw them on my way in."

The men each grabbed a torch from the wall sconces and hurried along the corridor and down the worn stone steps as quickly as they could.

When they reached the bottom of the steps, Ellery began removing the heavy bars that kept the cells locked. A curse came from the third one that he opened. "Phillip?"

"Ellery? Dear God, is that really you?"

The reunion between the two brothers brought tears to Vanessa's eyes. It was plain that there was a strong bond between them.

"Where is she? Where is my darling girl?" asked Phillip. "I know she is here."

Ellery should have known that Phillip would have

wanted to see the mother of his child. He stepped aside
so that Vanessa was revealed to his brother.

Phillip appeared puzzled, then spoke to Vanessa. "Do
you know where she is?"

"Isn't this . . . ?" began Ellery, when he was interrupted by Browning's voice.

"I believe this is the young lady you're looking for,"
he said, helping a disheveled Melanie into the cell.

Phillip took her in his arms and she buried her face
against his chest as Vanessa looked on in shock.

"Melanie," she whispered. "Oh, Melanie, I thought I
had lost you."

Her sister turned and saw her standing there. She
pulled away from Phillip and threw her arms around her
sister.

"Do you have any idea as to what is going on?" asked
Max.

"Not a clue," replied Ellery, appearing as bewildered
as his friend.

It was four days later and all the misunderstandings
had been straightened out. At least nearly all of them,
thought Vanessa, as she strolled toward the lake. There
were still the feelings toward Lord Trent that she was
unable to reconcile.

He had apologized to her for thinking she was a member of the Hell-Fire Club and for believing her to be first
Corbin's mistress and then the mother of Phillip's child.
He had even attempted to convince her that he believed
in her spirits, but she did not credit his claim at all.

Melanie and Phillip were recovering from their ordeal
of being held captive. They had explained that Melanie
had been taken in order to make Phillip's suffering
worse. The kidnappers had not known of the baby or
they would have no doubt taken him also.

The two were being wed in three days' time. They were waiting only for Annie to arrive with little Jonathan. They were inseparable and Vanessa envied them their happiness, wondering whether she would ever find a love to equal theirs.

Lady Venable was thrilled with the thought of a baby in the family and had already begun making a gown for him—in royal purple, of course.

Since no real crimes had been committed, the gentlemen at the abbey were released with a warning that their names were on file with the Home Office and that any repeat of their activities would bring severe punishment.

Thornhill merely walked away with a smile and Vanessa believed that he would be involved in something else before a fortnight was over. But he was a charming man and his charm had kept him safe for many years. Vanessa did not think that his charm would fail him anytime soon.

As for Lady Cornelia, she was on her way back to France, most probably considering how to reorganize Napoleon's army. Her punishment—never to set foot on English soil again.

Lord Trent remained quiet, his brow furrowed in thought much of the time. He did not smile often and when he did it was usually at something Phillip said. He had welcomed Melanie into the family without so much as a hint of censure about little Jonathan. However, he said only what was necessary to Vanessa, which was very little indeed. She wondered whether he was mourning the loss of Lady Cornelia.

Vanessa was slowly accepting what had happened and marveled that life could become so confused. She yearned to have the wedding behind them and to be able to return home with Annie. She had not yet decided whether she would travel to London for the Little Season. Without a child to raise, she and Annie could exist very well on what she had accumulated. She thought about Delcie. She had become attached to the girl, but could not offer her near what she had with Lord Trent, so that would be another sad good-bye to add to her list.

She was walking around the lake toward the arched bridge that led to the summerhouse on the small island, determined to spend at least a few minutes there. The grass was dry and brittle beneath her feet and she was sad that she would never see the meadow at its most beautiful, verdant and full of wildflowers. She was ready to step onto the bridge when she heard the sound of hooves. Looking over her shoulder, she observed Lord Trent astride his stallion pull to a halt a short distance away. He dismounted and strode toward her.

"I had not forgotten that I had promised to show you the summerhouse," he said. "Other things seemed to keep getting in the way."

"I understand," she replied. "I have had a pleasant walk, so no harm has been done."

"Aunt Charity said you were coming here, so I decided to follow. I hope I am not imposing."

"Not at all. It is, after all, your summerhouse."

"It was mostly my mother's. I believe I told you that she had it built and that it was her favorite place."

"I can see why," replied Vanessa, looking at the small house covered with pink climbing roses and blue morning glories, blooming profusely despite the hot weather.

"I have a confession to make," he said, looking everywhere but at her.

She waited, wondering whether he was going to say any more.

"I did not decide to follow you on my own. Aunt Charity called me a fool if I let you go."

"To the summerhouse?" she asked in bewilderment.

"I am making a mull of this," he murmured.

"Just say what it is you have to say," she urged him.

"I love you and want to marry you," he replied bluntly.

She stared at him a moment. "That is certainly plain speaking," she commented.

"I am only doing what you asked," he said. "And I would like to continue doing it for the rest of our lives."

"Lord Trent . . ."

"Ellery. I believe it might be proper for you to call me Ellery since I have offered for you. And I, of course, will finally be able to address you as Vanessa."

"I do not believe we are having this conversation. What about your love for Cornelia? I had assumed you were moping about after her all this time."

"I was not moping; I was merely thinking," he pointed out peevishly. "About you and whether you could ever forgive me enough to marry me. Then Aunt Charity brought it to my attention that if I waited much longer you would be gone and I would probably be forgotten."

"Lady Venable was wrong," said Vanessa. "I could never forget."

Ellery had received the first sign of encouragement from Vanessa and he took advantage of it. He took her hand and raised it to his lips, pressing a kiss on her soft skin. "Tell me you will accept my proposal. My love for you is so strong that you may have spirits in every room and I will not complain."

She stepped closer to him and gazed up into his eyes. "I think I have loved you for some time now, but I would not admit it. And when I thought that you were Jonathan's father, there was no hope at all that there could be anything between us. I had never envied my sister before until then."

He drew her into his arms and between their kisses and words of love, they did not notice the darkening sky until thunder broke over them. Before they realized what had happened, rain began pouring from the heavens, soaking both of them.

"It's a blessing on our betrothal," she said, laughing as water dripped off the end of her nose. "Come along." She raised her soaked skirts and ran across the bridge to the summerhouse, Ellery following close behind.

"Then you accept?" he asked, as they stood breathless within the structure.

"Did you doubt that I would?" she asked, pushing wet strands of hair behind her ears.

"There was always a slight possibility," he replied.

"Perhaps up until you said my spirits would be welcome," she revealed. "Then I knew I could not refuse."

He took her in his arms again and there was only the sound of the rain drumming on the roof of the summerhouse for a time.

Ellery finally lifted his head, but kept her in his arms. They both watched the rain splashing into the lake and soaking into the parched earth.

"It is the end of a long, hot summer," she said, thankful it was over.

"But just the beginning of a wonderful life together," he promised.

More Zebra Regency Romances